MW00617604

A VERY IRISH CHRISTMAS

DEBBIE JOHNSON

Storm
PUBLISHING

Ebook ISBN: 978-1-80508-779-3
Paperback ISBN: 978-1-80508-781-6

Cover design: Rose Cooper
Cover images: Shutterstock

Published by Storm Publishing.
For further information, visit:
www.stormpublishing.co

ALSO BY DEBBIE JOHNSON

For Paddy Shennan and the Cork gang

FIVE WEEKS UNTIL CHRISTMAS

'May you have the hindsight to know where you've been, the foresight to know where you are going, and the insight to know when you have gone too far'
Irish proverb

ONE

NEW YORK

Things I Love About Christmas

1. The lights and decorations – in gardens, on the streets, through people's windows. Classy or corny, I love them all. They make me feel like a kid again.
2. The music – little bit of Bublé, little bit of Bing Crosby – I'm not fussy. Listening to Christmas music while you wrap your gifts? Best thing ever.
3. The food – especially the cakes and the cookies, the smells of sugar and spice and gingerbread and cinnamon. Yum.
4. Seeing my nephews on Christmas Eve, when they're so excited it feels like they might actually explode.
5. Watching my wedding video, which was taken on a sensational snowy day in winter wonderland New York.

Things I Hate About Christmas

1. Shopping – it makes me feel like I'm a character in *The Hunger Games*. Not Katniss, just one of those really scared ones who die early because they couldn't use a crossbow.
2. Being cooped up with my family and feeling like a failure compared to everyone else. Depressing but true.
3. Feeling even sadder than usual about all God's creatures who might be lonely or neglected – stray dogs, the elderly, people without homes or loved ones. It all feels worse at Christmas, doesn't it? Then I feel horribly guilty about even having a family, and not appreciating what I've got.
4. Eggnog. Just no.
5. Watching my wedding video, which was taken on a sensational snowy day in winter wonderland New York.

TWO

I am in Macy's, hiding beneath a rack of taffeta cocktail dresses. My head is covered in a hot pink puffball skirt, and I'm struggling to breathe. My feet are still sticking out, and I mutter a little 'ouch' every time someone steps on them.

The Christmas music is jingling away in the background, and I'm formulating an escape plan. I can't stay here forever – the store will close, and I'll be alone with all the creepy mannequins. If I can make it to the restroom, I can barricade myself in and buy myself some time. All I have to do is survive the next few minutes.

I suck in air, tell myself I can do this, and clamber out. As I emerge, a woman with a toddler looks shocked, grabs her child and pulls her away.

I throw myself into the flood of bodies, caught in the human current. I ricochet between shoppers and rails of clothes and a display of cashmere scarfs, pinging around like a human pinball. I mutter apologies, make myself as small as I can, and finally make it to the restrooms.

I splash water on my face, staring myself down in the mirror. *Stop being so pathetic, Cassie O'Hara – this is supposed to be fun.* My skin is white and clammy, and my red hair hasn't coped well with the puffball skirt. I don't look like a woman having fun. My heart is racing, and my lungs aren't getting enough air. It's beginning to feel a lot like Christmas.

I grab my bags, and make the last crazy sprint to freedom, rewarded with a blast of icy rain. I lean against the wall, and try not to hyperventilate. People give me a wide berth, automatically swerving away from me as though I'm contagious. After a few moments, a woman wearing maybe twenty layers of mismatched clothing approaches me. She looks like she sleeps rough, a wild look in her eyes and a Santa hat perched on her head. Her feet are encased in sneakers coated in plastic sheeting, which is practical if not chic.

I root around in my pockets, find that I have no loose change. I mean, who does? Homeless people need card machines these days.

'Sorry,' I say, feeling like a louse. 'I don't have anything to give you.'

'That's okay. I just wanted to check you were all right. You need some help?'

Huh. Right. I must be looking even worse than I thought.

'Thank you, that's very kind. I just... well, I get a bit weirded out by Christmas shopping.'

Even as I say it, I realise how lame I sound. I'm guessing this woman's life holds a few more challenges that mine.

I dive into one of my bags, the one that contains the expensive suede gloves I bought for my sister, Suzie. Suzie hates everything I buy for her, every single year. She's one of those women who has everything – apart from manners. I once saw a purse I'd given her in the window display of her local thrift store, which was just plain rude – she could at least have donated it to one a few miles away.

'Here,' I say to the wild-eyed woman. 'Take these. Keep yourself warm, okay?'

She takes off the cut-down socks she's currently wearing, carefully stashes them in a pocket, and puts the gloves on. She smiles and waves her hands around like she's conducting an orchestra.

'I'm going now,' I say, pleased that the gloves will be getting some use. 'Stay safe, and... um, merry Christmas?'

There are actually five weeks to go, but I don't think anyone cares anymore. The stores have told us it's Christmas, so it must be.

I scurry home on a crowded subway and through rainy streets, relieved to finally make it back to my apartment. I put on my favourite green-and-red check pyjamas and my fluffy socks. I grab the cookies I'd baked earlier, and sink down onto my couch.

It's been a horrible day, and I vow never to repeat it. Next year, I won't be buying my mother and Suzie gifts at all, I decide. Next year, I'll be donating to a good cause on their behalf instead. I could get a pair of goats named after them – or even some toilets. I saw an ad for a water charity where you could do that. The Suzie and The Audrey. And even though they might secretly be annoyed, they'd have to pretend to be pleased, because it's for charity.

That makes me laugh, at least, as I settle down for one of my own Christmas traditions – watching my wedding video. I do it every year, and it's become part of my festive ritual – a bit like gingerbread or mistletoe or those cute Hallmark movies that make you smile. It wouldn't be Christmas without it.

I sip my milk, and press play.

It starts with me, up in my room, getting ready with Suzie and my mom. I'm sitting in front of a mirror, the make-up lady behind me. I wave at the camera, looking delighted and freaked out all at the same time.

Having Suzie around wasn't helping on the 'freaked out' front. I'd wanted my best friend June with me, but they hate each other. Mixing them on a day like this would have resulted in death by stiletto heel. Plus if you've got a sister, there's pretty much some unwritten rule that she has to be your bridesmaid, right? Even if she's the kind of sister who says things like 'It's a shame you didn't lose those last five pounds!' on your actual wedding day. Suzie hasn't eaten a carb since 2015, and what she's lost in body fat she's gained in meanness.

The video cuts to outside, and the guests gathering at the Plaza Hotel. They pull up in taxis and limos, some walking from the subway on 5th Avenue. It had snowed the night before, and New York couldn't possibly have looked any prettier. It was like Manhattan itself had dressed up for the wedding.

I smile when I see June arrive. She stops near the grand entrance to the hotel, then hops around on one foot in the snow as she changes her shoes from sneakers to high-heels.

I see my dad arrive, Mom running over to straighten his tie the same way she's done a million times before. My grandmother Nora, my favourite ever human, giving a saucy wink to the video guy. My sister's perfect husband, Stu, with their two almost-perfect sons. My friends from work, from high school and college – everyone I'd ever known.

Next, they're in the foyer, making small talk and getting to know each other. The video was taken from a position halfway up the stairs, and I am waiting for my favourite part.

My fiancé Ted works at an investment bank, and his friends all look like clones created in a lab – expensive suits, bland hair-cuts, shiny shoes. En masse at the wedding they kind of resemble a Mafia clan.

Nanna Nora is lurking behind one of them. He's maybe three times her size, and doesn't even know she's there. Her wrinkled little face creases into a mischievous grin beneath her silver helmet of curls, and she gives him a smack on the ass. He whirls around, but she's already gone – and who would suspect a tiny Irish woman in her nineties, right?

It's classic Nora. She really was awesome.

The video takes in clusters of guests, June gulping down Champagne, my nephew Michael – the naughty one – sticking out his tongue and getting scolded for it by Stu.

Soon everyone is ushered into the wedding room to the sound of Vivaldi, and I sigh at how beautiful it is. The rows of chairs are dressed in white linens and swooping red velvet bows, and the flowers are lush with white roses, calla lilies and sprigs of holly and mistletoe.

It wasn't Ted's deal, the whole wedding prep thing, and he was happy to leave me to it. It made sense – I was an event planner, and this was my very own dream wedding. The culmination of a lifetime of imaginings.

The video shows Ted, breathtakingly handsome in his black Tom Ford suit. He stands at the front looking like a male model posing for a wedding spread in a magazine. His best man, Ethan, is beside him, the two of them looking awkward as they wait for the bride to arrive.

The bride herself – that would be me – is standing outside the glass-paned doors. My dress is a Vera Wang, elegant and simple with a strapless top and a skirt covered in exquisite lace. It was so beautiful I almost cried when I tried it on.

The wedding was only three years ago, but I look much younger on the screen. My face is buried beneath a million layers of make-up and fake eyelashes I will forever regret, but I look like an excited teenager. More like someone going to her prom than a thirty-four-year-old woman about to get married.

I'd had an anxiety dream the night before about the aisle filling with quicksand. As I waded towards Ted, every squelching step sucked me deeper, until I was trapped. I think I was worried about being the centre of attention, but that all fell away on the day and I was blissfully happy.

My arm is linked with my dad's, and he leans towards me, uttering a few inaudible words. In a heartwarming rom com, he'd whisper something like: 'Are you sure, pumpkin? It's not too late to change your mind!'

In reality, what he actually says is: 'Cassie, I hope this is quick. I drank a glass of Champagne when I got here, and it needs to come back out. Urgently.'

That's my dad for you – he never met a tone he couldn't lower. Video-me laughs at his comment, and Suzie makes a last-minute adjustment to my veil as the Vivaldi segues into the Bridal Chorus.

On the day I was too dazed to take much in as I walked up the aisle, but on the video I see the smiling faces, the oohs and aahs at the dress, my nephew Michael picking his nose in bore-dom. I see June's little hand-wave as I sail serenely past, my mother looking proud. Nanna Nora with tears in her twinkling blue eyes. And right at the front, waiting for me – Ted. My handsome, clever, super-supportive Ted. The dream groom to go with the dream wedding.

As my eyes locked on him, I was flooded with an ocean of love for the man who had been my partner in life since we met in college. We'd made all our mistakes together, taken all of our firsts together, built our worlds around each other since we were teenagers.

He'd caught me in mosh pits at concerts, and given me piggy-back rides home when I was tipsy. He'd serenaded me on karaoke, singing 'I Will Always Love You' so badly he was booed. Once, walking home from a club, I got upset because there were snails on the path, worried they might get crushed. For the entire journey back, he moved every single one to safety, just to please me.

I'd been there for him when his dad died, and when he struggled to keep up with his schoolwork afterwards. We lived on my earnings when he was doing his internships, sharing a dilapidated walk-up in Brooklyn and finding a million and one ways to cook ramen. We had shared so much, and it had all led us here.

All the rest – the swish apartment we moved into when his career took off, the Vera Wang, the fancy venue – was just window dressing. It was nice, but it meant nothing. What really mattered was the man in front of me, and what we were about to do – stand before our friends and family and vow to be together, for better or for worse, for the rest of our lives.

Even now, if I close my eyes, I can almost physically feel that sense of joy – it's still so real to me even after all this time. It really was the perfect day.

Right up until the point where Ted holds my hands in his, gazes into my eyes, and mutters the immortal words: 'Cassie, I'm so sorry. I love you, but I just can't go through with this.'

THREE

By the time June buzzes at my apartment, I am a snotty, teary mess. I don't bother trying to make myself look better while she jogs up the steps – she's seen it all before – but I do at least blow my nose. A girl's got to have standards.

She knocks on my door, using the rat-a-tat-tat code we'd established when we were kids and had contraband to hide. The contraband started as candy Nanna Nora had snuck me, and changed over the years – make-up, padded bras, the romance novels we stole from my mom's bookcase and read out loud to each other. We couldn't resist the cover pictures of muscular Regency earls who owned half of England but could never afford a shirt.

Worse than Mom finding us, it could have been Suzie. After I saw *The Exorcism of Emily Rose* when I was sixteen, I became convinced my sister was possessed by a demon. I still have my suspicions that if I slipped holy water into her wine, she might burst into flames.

When I hear the knock code tonight, it brings a huge sense of relief. June is the best friend ever, and I wouldn't have survived the aftermath of that day without her.

She comes bearing gifts – wine and a big bag of Thai food. She dumps it on the kitchen table, and gives me a hug.

June is tiny, barely scraping five foot, with crazy blonde curls. She dresses like she's at a music festival, all flowing skirts and battered Converse, and looks like the kind of woman who works in a crystal store. She actually runs her own successful accountancy firm.

She wipes away my tears, and says: 'You've got to stop, Cassie. This isn't good for you. I don't want to be one of those insensitive assholes who says you've got to move on – but, well, you've got to move on. You've got to stop torturing yourself like this. I'm almost tempted to sneak in here and erase that damn video.'

'I know, you're right,' I reply, as we decant our food and settle on the couch. 'I know how insane it is, poking and picking at everything, but I just don't seem able to stop. It's like tugging at a broken nail, or biting your lip when it's already bleeding... it's bad for me, but something makes me do it! Especially this year...'

This, frankly, has been the year from hell. My hours at work were cut due to the 'challenging economic environment', and that stings. I used to be ambitious and driven, essential to the company. Now I am competent but easily sidelined – more likely to want to hide in a closet than pitch my vision to a client.

I have less money coming in, and too much time on my hands. I'm thirty-seven, and most of my peers are married, have kids, high-flying careers and vacations to the Bahamas. I just seem to be in freefall, stuck in reverse. If I keep on like this I'll be back to eating illicit candy and wearing a padded bra in my childhood bedroom.

Even worse, my beloved Nanna Nora died six months ago, just before her 100th birthday. We'd planned a big party, complete with an Irish band and male strippers (she was that kind of girl), but she slipped away in her sleep a few nights before. It was a good way to go – peacefully, after a long, full life – but it's left a Nanna-shaped hole in my life that will never be filled. I miss her every single day.

The third highlight of the year from hell was Ted finally getting married. It was a September wedding in the Hamptons, because that's how he rolls these days. His wife works at his bank, and is the very picture of refined old money. They have an adorable Labrador called Humphrey, enjoy biking and skiing, and wear matching outfits on their vacations. Best not to ask how I know all that. It's definitely *not* because I've stalked them on social media with fake accounts or anything.

Even though I knew the wedding was coming, it still hurt. He wore a white suit to match her dress, and the stormy weather that had been sweeping down the Eastern Seaboard cleared up as if by magic, just for that weekend. Most importantly, he actually went through with it.

'I saw him the other day,' June mutters between spoonfuls of tom yum soup. There is no need to explain who 'he' is. 'I was on my way from a client meeting in Midtown, and he was coming out of a bar.'

'How did he look?'

'Fat, really fat. Bright red zit on the end of his nose. Losing his hair. Revolting. I almost threw up in my purse.'

I have to laugh at this, because Ted has great hair and is the kind of guy who can eat pizza every day and not gain a pound. I can hold out hope for the zit though.

'He looked like a proper eejit, so he did,' she adds, doing a good impression of the Irish twang that Nanna Nora never lost despite all her decades in the States. 'Eejit' was one of her favourite words, and it slipped into our vocabulary over the years, along with its stronger sibling 'fecking eejit', 'what's the craic?' and calling handsome men 'a ride'.

June used to agree that Ted was a ride, but now she rates

him somewhere below plankton on the food chain – she's never forgiven him for what he did. If he ever plummets off a balcony or accidentally falls in front of a subway train, she's my prime suspect.

I'd been more forgiving – or, frankly, more desperate. I wanted to believe it was a blip –something we could overcome. I told myself he'd been overwhelmed by the pressure, the wedding, the planning.

I'd cried and pleaded and promised to do it however he wanted. We could elope, or go to Vegas, or not even get married at all – as long as we stayed together. If we stayed together, we could work it all out, I was sure.

I was still sure when he moved out the next day, leaving me in our luxury apartment with tear-swollen eyes and the rent paid up for a month. I was still sure when he changed his number, and told his PA to stop putting my calls through. I was still sure when he took a trip to Aspen with his new girlfriend, and when the girlfriend turned into a fiancée. Now, the fiancée is a wife – and there is no coming back from that.

'I think,' I say to June, feeling a fresh round of crying sneak up on me, 'that I've finally accepted it's over.'

'Well, that's positive,' she replies, patting my knee in reassurance. 'And it's only taken you three years.'

She's right, and I am a ridiculous woman. How could I have been holding on to this for so long? How could I have let myself sink so low? It's as though when Ted rejected me, I started rejecting myself, and I've never figured out how to stop. In fact, I've been getting better and better at it. Ted might have broken my heart, but I'm the one who has stopped it healing.

'This sucks,' I say, placing the soup down. I have no appetite anyway. 'I miss Nanna Nora, and Ted is married to Wall Street Barbie, and work is awful. They've put me back on children's parties, June!'

I started at my company straight out of college, and my first job there was organising events for rich kids. After a year of explaining to parents that it wasn't good for ponies to be dyed pink and have plastic unicorn horns glued onto them, I progressed.

I worked hard, was passionate about what I did, and made my way up the ladder to the really big events. Corporate gatherings, product launches, flashy charity fundraisers – the kind with celebs and lobster bars. Now, after the decline of both the economy and my self-belief, I'm at the bottom again. My whole life is a game of Chutes and Ladders.

'Babe,' June replies, squeezing my hand, 'I know – and it does suck. It's been a bad year, and it's going to be Christmas soon and that always makes you feel worse. Let's look ahead. What are your plans?'

I bury my face in my palms, anxiety settling in my stomach.

'Suzie's invited us all for Christmas this year,' I say. I sound about as happy as if the creepy clown from *It* had asked me round to his underground sewer for a body-part buffet.

'And how do you feel about that?'

'Like I'd rather put my head in a blender.'

'Nice image. So – crazy idea – why don't you just... not go? She always makes you feel crappy about yourself. I say screw Suzie. Give yourself the Christmas gift of not seeing her.'

'You know I can't do that, June! You know what they're like. You know how important family is to them.'

'Is it though? Your dad, yeah. He's just like Nanna Nora with a Magnum P.I. moustache. But your mom, and your sister? When they're on a roll, they make Cruella de Vil look like a pushover. They'd give Cersei Lannister from *Game of Thrones* a self-worth problem. They'd eat Regina George whole, and have room left over for Nurse Ratched. They'd—'

'Okay, okay, I get it!' I say, holding my hands up in surrender. 'They're mean girls. But they're mean girls I'm genetically related to, and it's just my fate. My Christmas destiny.'

'Well, screw destiny as well – make your own. Do something totally different. Something that's just for you.'

I tilt my head to one side as I consider this. I'm not totally sure what 'just for me' would even look like these days. I'd like to be more adventurous. I'd like to do something brave – but in reality, I suspect I might just sit here in my little apartment alone all Christmas, eating my way through a pile of take-out fortune cookies in the dark, in case Mom and Suzie did a drive-by.

'You used to want to travel,' she persists. 'You wanted to see the world.'

She's right, I did – but all of that was tied in with Ted. We'd made so many plans, but they all fell to pieces on our wedding day. When a guy jilts you at the altar with all of your friends and family there to witness it, it leaves a dent in your travel itinerary.

It also left a dent in me. It wasn't just the very public nature of the jilting, it was the fact that the man I'd loved, the man I'd trusted, the man I'd expected to spend the rest of my life with, decided that I wasn't enough. When the person who knows you best in the whole world rejects you, it leaves scars that nobody can see on the surface. It also made me doubt myself and my own judgement – how had I not seen it coming? How had I not known something was wrong?

I've felt constantly nervous ever since. Like nothing in life is solid, like nothing can be counted on. I'm always waiting for the rug to be pulled from beneath my feet. I even got freaked out by a trip to Macy's today, for goodness' sake – never mind anything further afield.

'Remember how much you wanted to go to England?' June continues, a determined look in her eyes.

'That was during my Hugh Grant phase. And I'm sure England isn't really like it is in the movies.'

'Probably not – but why don't you go and find out? Or see where Nanna Nora came from? I know you don't believe in yourself anymore – but I believe enough for both of us.'

'Well, that's really nice of you, June, but I don't think I can get a belief transfusion. England, Ireland... they're on the other side of the world!'

'Exactly. If you were in England – or Ireland, or France, or even Alaska – you'd have a really good excuse not to spend Christmas with your family.'

I have to admit that is tempting. It's always tough, but this year will be even harder because Nanna Nora won't be there as a buffer zone. She won't be sitting at the Christmas table in her leprechaun hat. She won't be leading a round of carols after the holiday ham, or drinking Guinness from her wine glass, or cackling away as my nephews make fart noises with their armpits. She won't be anywhere, and even the thought of it chokes me up.

'Nothing is quite the same without her, is it?' says June quietly, knowing exactly where my thoughts have gone.

'No, and her not being there will make Christmas even worse.'

'All the more reason to just say no.'

'But what about Dad?' I say, blatantly looking for excuses. 'What about work?'

'Your dad is a grown-ass man who can fend for himself – and as for work, didn't your boss send out that email, offering people unpaid leave?'

I mull it over, and reply: 'Yeah. Okay. But it'd be so expensive. I'm not sure I can afford it.'

June makes the kind of duh-duh buzzer noise you hear on TV quiz shows when the contestant doesn't know the capital of Venezuela, and says: 'I'm calling bullshit on that one. You can use the money Nanna Nora left you. I honestly can't imagine a better way for you to spend it. I'm worried about you, Cassie, and I know she was too. Ted's married. You've spent the last few years scared of your own shadow. Something needs to change. Use the money – she'd call you a *fecking eejit* if you didn't.'

She probably would – after all, I am acting like an idiot. After the whole wedding-that-wasn't, Nanna Nora was a rock. My mom and sister were devastated, but only part of that was for me. The rest was social embarrassment. They never vocalized it, but it was there, hidden beneath their subtle looks, the slightly judgemental tone, the way they'd go suddenly silent when I walked into a room. I'd made a mess, and they really don't like mess.

Nanna Nora, though? She didn't care how messy it all was. She told me she understood what it was like to have your heart broken, reassured me it was only a matter of time before it healed whole – and stronger than ever. I never quite believed her, but it was comforting. We'd always been close, but even more so after the wedding.

When she died, she left me a surprisingly large chunk of change in her will. We were all shocked, especially Suzie, who was gifted Nanna Nora's ceramic cat collection. One last joke from Nanna Nora, because Suzie is allergic to cats. To be fair to my sister, she has them on display in her otherwise minimalist house, but even looking at them makes her sneeze.

Some money was set aside for Suzie's boys, and she left small gifts for everyone, but the majority came to me. It's not enough to retire on, but it would be enough for a really nice trip. If she's up there watching me, she'll be laughing, I think. Maybe she'll raise a glass, and give one of her insane made-up toasts – something about the sun shining on my face and the plane staying in the sky and the runway rising up to meet me.

So far, I haven't touched the money she left me. I've learned to live within my reduced means rather than dip into my little nest egg. Somehow, spending it would make it too real – it would mean that she's really gone.

That's a hard concept to explain, so I just say: 'I was saving that for a rainy day.'

'Sweetie,' says June. 'It's already raining. It's time to buy yourself an umbrella.'

FOUR

After June leaves I sit at my little kitchen table with a glass of wine, browsing travel sites. Even though I am definitely, one hundred percent not going to do it, it will pass some time to look.

Predictably, I get sucked into the black hole of the internet, caught up in the logistics. I'm a details person – it's one of the reasons I like my job. I love the challenge of making all the small parts fit so the big part can happen. I love making lists, and planning a fantasy trip is diverting.

I base my research on perfectly logical reasons – movie and TV locations. I discover that Bridget Jones's family home was in a place called the Cotswolds, and that in *The Holiday*, Cameron Diaz relocated to the county of Surrey. *Bridgerton* was filmed in Bath, and London has *Notting Hill* and *Love, Actually*. Two of my favourites.

I give myself a good talking to at that point: I am not going to move to England and fall in love with Hugh Grant. He's, like, in his sixties and married, apart from anything else. I start to look at some places in Ireland instead, but soon realise that I barely know enough about Nanna Nora's background to choose somewhere accurately – all I know is she was born in the Cork area, so I check out places there.

As I sit there, finishing off the warmed-up soup, I realise something amazing. Since I sat down to do this, I haven't thought about Ted or my floundering career at all – not even once.

I've been so lost in the land of shires and villages that my whole mind has been laser-focused, no room left for sadness or grief. *Maybe*, I think, *June has a point.*

I scoot onto some rental sites, looking for somewhere cosy and pretty and safe. Somewhere I can be me, but a better version of me. Somewhere I can recreate myself, and not play the role of the girl-who-was-dumped.

I desperately need to not be her anymore, or I'm going to end up alone and surrounded by cats, watching my damn wedding video through my cataracts when I'm ninety. I'll be New York's answer to the doomed bride Miss Havisham from *Great Expectations*, covered in cobwebs while Ted ages gracefully and goes on a world cruise with his grandchildren.

My life in its current shape isn't working anymore; I have to accept that. And no matter how frightening I might find the thought of travelling alone, it could be a way to change that shape – to make a whole new one.

Plus, if I go, I will be tragically unavailable to spend Christmas with Suzie and my mom. I could avoid their questions about whether I've 'met anyone nice', their hints about dating apps, and their advice that I need to be less fussy at my age.

This all might be coming from a place of love, but if I keep seeing myself through their filter, as desperate and potentially unlovable, then I'm just one step closer to morphing into Miss Havisham.

I scroll through endless pages of perfect cottages that are

already booked, or available homes that come with a tennis court. I have about a million different screens open, hopping from one website to another, knowing I should be making notes but wanting to go with the flow. Cork, it seems, is a pretty popular place – the whole world must want to go there for Christmas.

I'm beginning to despair when I finally see it – and it is so perfect I drop my spoon in my soup. The cutest little cottage my eyes have ever seen has appeared on my screen.

The cottage is built from golden stone that looks like liquid sunlight, topped by a quaint thatched roof. The pictures were obviously taken in summer, and glorious boughs of wisteria drape the front door in a cloud of lilac. The small yard is a riot of colour – roses, hyacinths, a swathe of perfect pink peonies. I picture myself sitting out there with a coffee or a glass of wine, reading a book or maybe writing in a journal. Okay, so it's winter, and it won't look the same – but the image takes root.

There aren't many pictures of the inside, but the ones that are look gorgeous – all kitsch charm and low ceilings with beams, the kind of place you'd imagine Beatrix Potter sketching her rabbits and ducks.

It's in the 'Wiltshire Cotswolds', and even saying those words out loud feels good. I hardly know anything about them, but even the words seem to taste of scones and clotted cream and fresh summer strawberries.

The village itself, I read, is called Campton St George, and is part of the historic Bancroft Estate. Bancroft Manor was apparently in the Domesday Book, which google tells me was a property survey compiled in the 11th century – so, not just old, but really, really super-old. Even the name is perfect – Whimsy Cottage. It's like it was designed for a slightly tipsy, emotionally distraught American woman looking for a life make-over.

As I finish my super-fast history lesson, though, I learn something else – something pretty basic. The Domesday Book was a survey of *England*, not Ireland. I do a double take, and scoot back to the rental website. I check and check again, and then utter a muttered 'darn it'.

Whimsy Cottage is perfect – but it's also not even in Ireland, never mind County Cork. I probably should have realised, and feel the tug of doubt as I tell myself how stupid I am. But then I pause, stop mentally beating myself up – not many people are intimately familiar with the geography of rural England. I've made a mistake, and I'm allowed to make mistakes without throwing myself into a pit of self-loathing.

Whimsy Cottage is still smiling up at me, telling me that everything will be okay. Something about that place just calls to me, wherever it is. And maybe it being in England isn't a deal breaker anyway – after all, Nanna Nora didn't seem to ever feel homesick for Ireland. And I did always love those Jane Austen movies with the manor houses and the fancy dresses... maybe England would be fine. Maybe I should trust my gut.

I'm still not totally sure, and I haven't trusted my gut much in recent years, so I decide to consult the wisest woman in the world – Nanna Nora herself. In the run-up to her 100th, we'd filmed little interviews with her to screen at the party. The party never happened, but the clips are now even more precious.

We'd covered predictable subjects like the secret to long life, a happy marriage, that kind of thing – but the one I'm looking for is when I asked if she was scared when she moved to the States on her own as a young woman.

I see her on the screen, sitting in her recliner armchair, silver grey curls framing her amused face.

'Of course I was!' she says. 'I was terrified! But all the good things in life are terrifying, Cassie, and sometimes you have to just jump right in. Sometimes you have to take your deep breaths, and make a leap of faith. You can't live your whole life being scared, now, can you? That's not living at all.'

'But didn't you miss your home in Ireland? And your family?'

'I made my own family, and my own home, darlin'. You can make those wherever you are – the geography doesn't matter. It's what's inside that counts.'

I reach out and touch the image, blink away tears, and feel like she's there with me. Telling me to take that leap of faith. Telling me to trust my gut. Whimsy Cottage it is.

Now my mind is made up, I feel super excited. I can't believe this perfect cottage isn't booked – that it's available for a whole month. Maybe there's been a last-minute cancellation. Whatever it is, it feels like it's meant to be – and I only have the slightest hesitation as I click on 'Reserve Now'.

I say a quick prayer of thanks to Nanna Nora as I fill in my credit card details, and wonder if she actually is up there watching – telling me to go for it, or calling me a *fecking eejit*, who knows? I don't think she'd mind me decamping to England; she never spoke much about the country of her birth, despite talking like she'd swallowed the Blarney Stone. She always said her life really began when she moved to the States in the 1950s, and got a job in a hat shop. Soon after, she met my long-gone grandfather O'Hara, and the rest was family history.

If she is watching, then she's probably having a good giggle as I sit and stare at the confirmation on my screen. She'll have tears of laughter rolling down her cheeks at the shocked look on my face.

I've done it. I've really done it. I'm going to England for Christmas, all by myself.

I grab my coat, slip on my sneakers, and head out for my evening walk around the neighbourhood. I do it every night, in an attempt to help me sleep.

As I stroll the city streets, soaking in its familiar sights and sounds and saying goodbye to them, I decide to video call June and tell her what I've done.

She sings the *Rocky* theme tune and punches the air, before going very still. She bursts into tears, and says: 'I'm so happy for you – but I've just realised this means I won't see you for a whole month! That's the longest we've been apart since we were five!'

FIVE

My dad drives me to the airport, recounting tales I've heard many times before about the work trip he took to London in 1997. Decades later he remains traumatised by eating something called 'black pudding' at a hotel breakfast, and discovering it was made of pig's blood.

'They don't have air conditioning, you know,' he says, sternly.

'I know. But it's winter, I'll be okay.'

'And they're obsessed with tea!'

'That's all right. I like tea.'

'And there's a language barrier. Technically, they all speak English, but the accents, Cassie, the accents! You won't be able to understand a word of it, and they'll just think you're deaf and talk louder. And the money is weird. And you'll be alone – thousands of miles away!'

I laugh as he makes his way into the parking lot, and know he's just worried. Suzie and Mom were worried too, but for different reasons. When I broke the news, Suzie stared at me over her wine glass and suggested it might be a better idea to spend the money on a good therapist. Mom looked horrified, and held her hand to my forehead, checking for a fever.

Some of their concern is genuine – I know they love me – but they also hate not being in control. I've done something unpredictable, and that makes them nervous. Maybe they're expecting a viral video of me running naked through the grounds of Buckingham Palace, or wondering if Hugh Grant might have to take out a restraining order.

'Dad, being alone thousands of miles away is part of the appeal. I'll miss you, but I need the change. I'm stuck in a rut here. How about you tell me something good about the place?'

He looks a little misty-eyed as we walk, and says: 'The pubs. The pubs were great. And the cursing – they curse at everything!'

Mom makes him put dollars in a swear jar at home, which is a shame, because he loves a good swear – it's one of his greatest pleasures in life. Sometimes you overhear him in his den, cursing away just for the fun of it.

We make our way into the building, him walking so slowly I suspect he's trying to make me miss my flight.

'Don't forget to offer people tea,' he says suddenly, as we stare at the information screens. 'Even if they just walk past your door and say good morning, offer them tea, or they'll take it as a snub. And the weather – you'll need to talk about that, a lot. That, and traffic. Talk about weather, and traffic, and offer tea, and you'll probably be fine.'

'Probably?' I ask, grinning up at him. 'What's the worst that can happen?'

'That's not a sensible question to ask a man who watches as many true crime shows as me. Be safe, okay? Don't forget to look in the wrong direction when you're crossing the road. And make sure you come back. I think maybe that's the worst that can happen – you'll like it so much you'll stay, and I'll never see my baby again.'

'I'm thirty-seven, Dad.'

'Makes no difference. Still my baby. Now go, off with you, before I change my mind and bundle you back home again.'

I hug him, and he waves me off with his golfing umbrella. The last thing I see of him is his grey-red hair, as ever a head-and-shoulder higher than the rest of the crowd. The O'Haras tend to run on the tall side.

The trip starts well, with a free upgrade to first class – the kind of random stroke of good fortune that makes me wonder if Nanna Nora is not only up there, but has managed to charm her way into the possession of a magic wand. I luxuriate in the lie-flat bed and the free Champagne, and imagine how glamorous I look. Lone female traveller, off on a first-class adventure. The trip of a lifetime.

I have such a good feeling about it all, and can't wait to get there. To my little slice of English paradise.

FOUR WEEKS UNTIL CHRISTMAS

'May your neighbours respect you,
Trouble neglect you,
The angels protect you,
And heaven accept you.'
Irish blessing

SIX

ENGLAND

My little slice of English paradise, it turns out, is very, very wet. So wet I wish I'd packed an inflatable dinghy.

I spend a few days sightseeing in London, admiring the sparkling Christmas lights in the shopping streets, taking selfies with the bright red mailboxes, double-decker buses and the chunky black cabs. I snap pictures of the huge Christmas tree in Trafalgar Square, and send all of these to my family and to June, determined to put a brave face on things.

Truthfully, I haven't had a great time so far. Being a lone female traveller, it turns out, isn't very glamorous at all. It's actually just a bit lonely, and every time I see something fun or interesting, I wish I had someone to share it with.

Yesterday, I wandered the aisles of the famous London toy store, Hamleys, picking out gifts for my nephews. The place was packed with excited children and tired looking parents, a glimpse into a life that I will probably never have. I left the place feeling old and past my expiry date. Ted and I had always discussed starting a family quickly, but now it seems like an impossible dream. Deep down, I don't want to be a glamorous lone traveller. I want to be one of the tired looking parents.

Dad had been right about a lot of it, too, and I spend way too much time standing at busy roads, wondering if it is safe to cross. I try to pay for everything with the wrong coins, the bathrooms all feel a bit weird, and everything is loud and overwhelming.

I'm from New York – it's not like cities intimidate me – but London is a very different kind of city, and after a few days of grey skies and relentless rain I'm glad to get away. The only person I've really spoken to is the woman on reception, who is Scottish. I don't understand a word she's saying, and just try to laugh in the right places.

Today, I take my criss-cross journey by train through England to Whimsy Cottage, and it's good to be on the move. Even in the dull weather, the countryside is picturesque, and I love looking the journey up on my phone and seeing all the place names. *Berkshire, Hampshire, Oxfordshire* – it's like something out of a movie, the scenery rolling past the rain-streaked windows in a blur of green.

The little local train station I finally end up at is impossibly pretty, with white painted fences and quaint Victorian buildings. There's a tiny plastic Christmas tree behind the ticket booth, and the elderly lady serving is wearing dangling reindeer earrings. It's festive, and my spirits lift – right up until she tells me I'll have to wait for 'an hour or so' for a taxi.

My stricken face must show my disappointment, because she smiles kindly at me before picking up the phone.

'Bob, it's Linda down at the station. Got a nice young lady here needing to get to Little Ireland. I know it's your day off, but I wondered if you could drag yourself out of your pit and give her a lift?'

I'm confused by the whole conversation, partly because she has an accent so dense I feel like I'm listening to it through a bowl of soup – and partly because of what she says.

'Why did you call it Little Ireland?' I ask.

'You'll see when you get there! Now, just you have a little sit, he'll be here soon – probably not long enough for a cup of tea, I'm afraid. Anyway. My cousin lives in America. Maybe you know her?'

'Um. Maybe. Where does she live?'

'Atlanta.'

'Right. Well, no, I guess I don't then.'

'Probably for the best. She's a bit of a moody cow. Rainy, isn't it?'

I gaze outside at the torrential downpour, and nod. 'Yeah. Does it ever, you know, not rain here?'

'Oh yes! In a good year, we can get as many as four or five clear days in July! We all run around in our bikinis! I'm only joking, my love, don't worry – this is supposed to clear up tomorrow. Then we're due some blue skies, just before the snow kicks in. Hope you packed your wellies!'

I assure her I did, though in all honesty I have no idea what those are. I mean, I might have packed them, who knows?

We chat until Bob arrives, and as I leave she gives me a cheery wave, and says: 'Say hello to Ryan for me!'

I have no idea who Ryan is, but she actually blushes and looks a little dewy-eyed as she says his name.

Bob is a taciturn man in his fifties, and he shows zero inclination to chat as we drive through narrow country lanes and pretty villages. I don't mind; it gives me the chance to acclimatise, and to gaze out of the window with a big, stupid smile on my face.

Okay, so the weather is foul – I'm beginning to understand why they talk about it so much – but this place is gorgeous. So green and lush, the roads lined with dripping bushes and alive with twittering birds. The fields around us stretch on into infinity, neat little patchworks of emerald and brown, herds of cartoon black and white cows grazing contentedly.

As we wend our way through the countryside, I notice most

of the buildings are made from the same honey-coloured stone, lots of them with thatched roofs. If you took away the lights and the road signs, you could be in a different century entirely.

We have our own history in the States, but nothing like this – you can feel the age oozing from every farm house, every little pub, every row of pretty cottages. I'm living in a fantasy world, and by the time we arrive at the Bancroft Estate, I am on a natural high.

'It's so beautiful!' I can't help saying aloud, earning myself a shrug from Bob.

'Suppose. Wish it'd stop pissing it down though.'

I assume this is a reference to the rain, and if I lived here all year round, I'd probably feel the same. For now, though, it's just an inconvenience, and a temporary one. The lady at the train station promised me clear skies ahead.

We drive into the village of Campton St George itself at dusk, and it looks magical – lit up and glowing in a way that makes it seem otherworldly. Long strings of multi-coloured lights drape from cottage to cottage, from the pub to the bakery, from the tea rooms to the antiques store. They pierce the murky sky, shining optimistically in the ever-present rain, as though they're inviting me to a carnival. Golden light spills out from the pub and from the windows of the houses, chasing away the mounting darkness in a flurry of homely radiance.

The streets are cobbled, and one corner holds an ancient-looking stone cross and a trough that I guess used to be for horses but is now full of evergreens. At the far end is a small, humped bridge in the same golden stone, a little river gurgling along beneath it.

In the centre of it all is a cobbled square, dominated by an enormous pine tree almost as big as the one in London. It's dressed to kill, and even the gloomy weather can't stop it from looking gorgeous, shining like a beacon of hope before me.

I close my eyes and imagine all of this in the summer, and

then I imagine it in snow, and then in spring when the flowers are coming into bloom and the cherry trees are heavy with blossom. I can't picture anywhere cosier, or more welcoming and charming.

Bob deposits me outside Whimsy Cottage, and wishes me luck before he drives off. I can't wait to be tucked up on the couch with a glass of wine, warm from the old coal fire. Cosy and safe and happy – so far away from my real life that it won't be able to reach out and hurt me anymore.

'Ted Marshall,' I say out loud as I pick my way past some muddy puddles, 'you are not welcome here.' I channel my inner Nora, and add a hearty: '*Away with ye, now!*'

I stand at the waist-high front gate and gaze at the cottage for a few moments. It's at the end of a cute terrace of houses, attached to the bakery – I'll wake up to the aroma of freshly baked bread every morning. Suzie's idea of hell, my idea of heaven. The tiny front yard is wet and downtrodden, but I can see the outlines of the clinging ivy and the wisteria around the door, smiling as I make my way up the crooked little path.

I'd received an automated response to my booking telling me I'd find the key underneath a potted plant, which at the time had seemed a lot more quaint than a plain old lockbox. It seems slightly less fun now, as I stand here in the semi-darkness, realising that there isn't just one potted plant, there are about a dozen.

I wipe the rain from my eyes, and take it in turns lifting them all. I find some dirt, some slugs, and eventually, an old-fashioned copper-coloured key. I fumble it into the lock, then before I turn it I pause, and take a deep breath. This feels like a significant moment. It feels like I am about to carry myself over the threshold. I push open the door, and step inside.

The first thing that hits me is the smell – mouldy and musty – and the second thing is the cold. That doesn't so much hit me as sucker-punch me in the gut. I flick on the light switch, and the bulb hanging from the ceiling immediately explodes with a loud pop, a bright flash and a scattering of glass. I shriek in shock, and grab hold of the nearest piece of furniture to steady myself – a couch, it feels like, although it's covered in a white sheet that is damp to the touch.

Huh. That's strange – but maybe it's just one of those things they do here, cover up the furniture? I am, after all – like my dad warned me – in a foreign land.

I find my way into the next room, and brace myself as I press the light switch. Nothing explodes, but as I glance around the tiny kitchen, I realise I can barely move in here. If I stand in the middle and turn in a circle, I can reach everything – the ancient-looking oven, the steadily humming fridge, the sink made of solid white ceramic. Now I know why there were no pictures of this room on the website.

I find a cabinet that contains an Aladdin's cave of useful items, including cleaning products and a dustpan and brush. I make my way back into the living room, and carefully clean up the shards of glass from the shattered bulb. Okay, so this hasn't been the ideal start to my Whimsy Cottage idyll, but I'm here for a month – things will get better.

I creep around the living room, which would probably be cosy if not for the freezing temperatures and the all-pervading smell of old laundry left out too long. This place doesn't feel like it's been lived in for a while, and as I find a table lamp and turn it on, it gets even worse.

All of the furniture is covered in sheets, and the air is a dust storm. The coal fire in the hearth, the one that looked so inviting on the pictures, is dead and cold, long-burned-out ashes lying grey in the grate. The beamed ceiling is so low that I feel the need to duck, and the mullioned windows are coated in grime.

I'd hoped for more. I'd hoped for the fire to be roaring, the couches to come with soft cosy blankets. For a welcome package that included wine, maybe some home-baked cake. Maybe I'd even hoped it would be dressed for Christmas. Instead, I am standing here in the cottage that time forgot, shivering and wondering how I'm going to survive this.

Am I being a pampered American brat? I ask myself. Was I expecting too much? Is this just how things are here? *No*, I decide, as my breath clouds in the frigid air. Something has gone very wrong.

I call the number that came with the booking confirmation, and my heart sinks as I get a recorded message – a cheerful sounding woman telling me with great glee that nobody is available. If I was paranoid, I would imagine she was sitting there laughing at me while it played.

I leave my name and number, and a mumbled complaint, and try and figure out what to do next. *I am not a damsel in distress*, I tell myself, as I feel the familiar sense of anxiety start to creep into my mind. This will not kill me – it will make me stronger. Of course, by that reckoning, I should be the strongest woman on earth by now.

I am suddenly swamped with regret, with home-sickness, with the need for comfort that I know will not be coming. I am thousands of miles away from everything I have ever known. I can't just invite June over. I can't head over to my parents' house and raid their fridge. I can't even call Suzie, because I'd rather die than give her the satisfaction of knowing she was right – that maybe I should be at home, chewing down antidepressants and arranging appointments with a shrink, just like she suggested.

No, I tell myself, *I will not be defeated so easily*. Nothing is ever perfect, I should know that better than most. I look around at the grim cottage, and ask myself what Nanna Nora would do. The answer comes to me very quickly, and makes me smile for the first time since I walked into this place.

Nanna Nora, I think, would shrug her tiny shoulders, say

something both rude and wise, and go straight to the pub. I will do the same.

I grab hold of my purse, nod determinedly, and head outside. The rain is even heavier, coming down in thick, cold drops, all of which seem to find their way inside the collar of my jacket. It's like heat-seeking rain, ruthlessly finding any part of your body that might still be warm and dousing it with liquid ice.

I walk along my crooked path, already anticipating a nice glass of red or maybe even a shot of good whiskey, hoping for a log fire and friendly locals and a bag of potato chips – *crisps*, I remind myself, *crisps. Chips are fries.*

Thinking about all of it – chips, fries, crisps – makes my stomach rumble, and I realise I haven't eaten for way too long. Maybe they do food at the pub? It's a cute building with a thatched roof, a wooden sign outside telling me it's called The Red Lion. There is light spilling out from its windows, and it looks warm and welcoming – the kind of place a lost girl could find a steak and kidney pie.

I'm about to stride towards it when I hear a low, vaguely menacing yip. It's not quite a bark, not quite a growl, but somewhere in between. I narrow my eyes in the gloomy light, look down, and see a dog crouched in front of me. He's soaking wet, black and white fur plastered to an athletic body, his ears up and alert. He stares at me in exactly the same way I stare at him, then lets out another one of his yips.

I jump a little, and move to the side to get past him. He immediately scoots over and crouches in front of me again, flat on his belly, paws before him. He has striking pale blue eyes, and I swear to God he is staring me down, daring me to take him on. I move along, and he does exactly the same. I try it faster, and in different directions, but every single time, I end up looking into those piercing eyes. The damn thing is so nimble.

He yips at me, and I see that although he isn't a massive dog, he has some wicked-looking teeth.

I like dogs, but I've never actually had one – Suzie's allergies again. I'm not entirely sure what to do here. He doesn't seem aggressive or threatening, but he's also not letting me past. I murmur what I hope are comforting words, along the 'good dog, nice dog, please let me get out of the rain' line, and decide that this is stupid. He's just a dog, and I really want that whiskey and steak and kidney pie.

I stride purposefully forward, but he runs ahead, whirls around to face me and lets out a loud bark. The kind that makes me feel like if I don't do as I'm told, he might take a chunk out of me. I am trapped between Whimsy Cottage and the pub, so close I could make a sprint for it – but between us is this deter-mined hellhound. He has frozen again, ears twitching, waiting for my next move.

I swerve to the left, waving my arms and telling him to shoo, and he immediately lands in front of me, front paws in the mud, barking loudly. *Shit*. I am wet, cold, and being herded by a possessed collie. Just as I don't think it can get any worse, I hear a man's voice shout: 'Oi! Eejit!'

My eyes go wide, and the dog barely reacts. *Eejit?* On top of all of this, someone is now hurling abuse at me? I look up, and see a tall, brawny figure heading towards us.

'Eejit!' he yells again, louder. I'm torn between yelling back at him, and retreating into the relative safety of the cottage.

Before I get the chance to decide, a female voice joins in, and an elderly woman stands before me, also shouting: 'Eejit!' at the top of her voice. Before long, a couple of kids, maybe seven or eight years old, emerge from one of the cottages and add their voices to the chorus.

I am cold, confused, and a little scared – why are they all shouting at me? What have I done wrong? What stupid unwritten English rule have I broken? I'm standing in torrential rain, hemmed in by a crazed dog, surrounded by a circle of strangers all chanting the word 'eejit' at me. It's like a horror movie, but wetter.

'I'm not an eejit!' I cry out loud. 'And you can all... feck off!'

'Not you, darlin',' the elderly woman shouts back, her rich Irish accent so much like Nanna Nora's that it makes me suck in a shocked breath. 'The dog! That's his name, so!'

'He doesn't eat people!' one of the children calls out, helpfully.

'Very often,' the other one adds, giggling.

'Ignore them,' the older woman says, 'they're wee devils! Eejit won't hurt you, I promise – he just thinks you might be a lost sheep. Takes his work very seriously, that one.'

Huh, I think, vaguely reassured – maybe he's right about that. I am little bit of a lost sheep. One that very much wants to go to the pub.

'What do I do?' I ask, staring into Eejit's blue eyes.

'Don't worry, chicken, Ryan will sort him out.'

The big man – Ryan, I guess – walks to stand beside me. He nods at me once, but I barely register him. I'm keeping my gaze on the dog.

'Hold my hand, sweetheart,' the man says, his voice a calm and amused whisper of Irish charm in my ear.

'No! I don't even know you!'

'That's nothing that time can't cure – but it's for the dog. If he sees you're with me, he'll stop guarding you. If he knows the alpha dog is protecting you, he can relax and everything will be grand.'

'And you're the alpha dog in this scenario?'

'Sure I am,' he says, grinning at me. I see a flash of teeth in the gloom, and for a second wonder who the predator is here.

I reluctantly let him take my hand in his, and almost sigh out loud at the warmth of his fingers around mine. He gives me a little squeeze, and says: 'Jaysus, you're freezing!'

'I'm aware,' I reply, as he turns his attention back to the still alert dog. The creature is watching everything we do very closely, his eyes moving between the two of us.

'Rest, Eejit. Down, boy,' Ryan says, holding my hand up in his and displaying it. The dog reacts immediately, bounding forward towards us with alarming speed. I yelp, terrified at the blur of fur, and take a big unsteady step backwards. I lose my grip on Ryan's hand, and fall, right on my ass in a deep puddle of icy water and mud.

I'm so shocked I can't move for a moment, and I hear the children snickering away in the background. The dog runs over and licks my face, suddenly all affection, as the water seeps through my jeans. I stare into his blue eyes and then, on auto-pilot, I scratch his ears. The poor thing is as wet as I am, and I guess he didn't mean any harm.

'Up you come,' says Ryan, holding out his hands to me again. I gaze up, see his bulky outline against the night sky, and feel as lost as I ever have in my life. None of this has worked out like I expected it to.

I hear myself mutter: 'I think I've made a very big mistake. I shouldn't be here. This is all wrong.'

He grabs hold of me and tugs me upright. I land in a dripping mess against him, and he smiles as he steadies me in his arms and says: 'Give us a chance, darlin'. I'm sure it'll all feel right again soon. We just need to get you out of your clothes, and everything will seem better.'

Is he flirting with me? I think. Is he actually flirting with me right now? Or is it just the accent? Every word that comes out of his mouth sounds like a combination of charm and challenge.

The others rush over towards us, and the dog starts play-fully leaping around with the kids. One minute he's a hell-hound, the next he's a goofball.

'Put the wee dote down, Ryan,' orders the older woman, 'she's had enough of a shock without you manhandling her!'

I realise that I am still standing way too close to him, his hands on my waist, and I shuffle away, embarrassed. My sneakers are completely water-logged, and my feet squelch as I move.

'Come on, come on, let's be having you,' the woman says, putting her arms around my shoulders and guiding me firmly away. I don't have the energy to argue, and the thought of going back into my freezing cold cottage isn't exactly tempting. She pulls me towards the bakery next door, leads us down a small side passage and then inside.

The warmth of the place is wonderful after the day I've had. Travelling on trains, sitting on cold platforms, waiting at stations, falling in muddy puddles, the relentless rain – it's all taken a toll. I'd almost forgotten what it feels like to be warm, and the soft kiss of heat from the log burner nearly has me in tears. I've avoided crying throughout this whole ordeal, but now I feel safe, the random act of kindness of the older lady is almost enough to push me over the edge.

She ushers me towards the fire, cooing gentle words, settling me on a large armchair. I sit and wait for my body to stop shaking, and within seconds she is back, with a towel and a blanket.

'Ryan, make yourself useful. She's brutal cold, get her some magic potion, will you? And make sure the kids go back to their mammy, all right?'

I rub my hair with the towel, and then hold my hands up to the heat. It is possibly the best feeling I have ever had in my entire life.

'Now then,' says the woman, settling opposite me in a matching chair, 'I'm Eileen. And who would you be?'

'I'd... uh... be Cassie,' I reply, looking at her closely for the first time. 'Cassie O'Hara.'

'O'Hara, is it? You don't sound Irish, but you look it for sure. And why are you here, Cassie O'Hara?'

'That's a long story,' I reply, staring around me for the first time. The room is small, with the same beamed ceilings as the cottage next door, but this is clean and cosy, every surface covered in knickknacks and ornaments. A big knitting basket sits on the floor beside Eileen, and a bookcase is overflowing with paperbacks – a mix of crime and romance.

'Well, I have the time,' says Eileen, grinning at me. 'And you need to dry off anyway.'

'Oh, I know – my pants are soaking wet!'

At this exact moment Ryan reappears, and his eyebrows quirk upwards at my comment.

'Get your mind straight, Ryan Connolly, you big lug – she's American, isn't she? She means her trousers.'

He laughs, and passes me a glass of what my nose soon identifies as whiskey. I look up at Ryan, really seeing him for the first time and almost wishing I hadn't. The man is gorgeous. Over six foot, built broad and beefy, with thick, wild dark hair. His eyes are a sparkling shade of bright blue, his jaw is strong, and his mouth – good Lord, those lips are just luscious. I find myself staring at them for way too long, and blush when I realise what I'm doing. I'm a pale-skinned redhead, and I don't blush by halves.

'Linda at the train station says hello,' I mumble, suddenly understanding why she'd also gone red when she mentioned his name. This is the kind of man that conjures up sinful thoughts in a woman's mind.

'And thank you,' I add. 'For the dog thing, and for this. Both of you, you're very kind. I'll just warm up and then I'll... well, I don't know. I have clean clothes next door, though.'

'In Whimsy? You're staying in Whimsy?' asks Eileen, frowning. She is somewhere in her late seventies or early eighties, I'd say, with the same sprightly energy that Nanna Nora had. Her hair is grey and curly, a lion's mane that comes to rest on her shoulders. The face itself shows its age, with wrinkles and creases and majestic laughter lines around her blue eyes, but somehow she still seems young. Maybe it's the magic potion.

I nod, and she shares a look with Ryan. I have no idea what it means, but they're clearly surprised.

'Ryan, go off and fetch Cassie's suitcase from next door, there's a good lad.'

'Yes, Mammy,' he says sarcastically, giving her a salute before he leaves.

'Is Ryan your son?' I ask. There's no obvious resemblance but the ages and relationship seem right.

'Not in blood, no – he was just being a cheeky pup. I've known Ryan since he was a baby, and was best friends with his actual mother, may she rest in peace. She was originally from Dublin like me, moved away to a different part of Ireland when she met his dad. It's a good job I'm here, he often needs a slap around the back of the head, that one.'

As I take all of this in, I realise that for the first time since I landed in London, I don't feel like everyone around me is speaking a foreign language. I've struggled with all the regional accents, but this one – this one is like coming home for me. Against all odds, I actually smile.

'You sound just like my Nanna Nora,' I say, sipping my excellent whiskey.

'Ah. A fine woman, I'm sure. Would she be the O'Hara?'

'Kind of. She married an O'Hara. She was originally a Murphy. From County Cork, maybe? She didn't talk about it much, which is weird, because she talked about everything else all the time. She moved to the States in the early fifties.'

'Ah, Cork – same as Ryan, so! Well, it was tough times during the war in Ireland, and maybe she wanted a fresh start, eh, Cassie? I take it from the past tense that she's no longer with us.'

'No. She died earlier this year. She was... well, we were very close. I'm using the money she left me to have this adventure.'

I sound weary as I say the words, because I am – I'm exhausted, mentally and physically. Eileen leans over and pats my now-thawed hand, and says: 'Not the best of starts, was it? You must forgive that dog Eejit, now. Nobody even knows who he belongs to. He appears and disappears at will, and Ryan is the only one he's listening to. He must recognise a kindred spirit!'

'Does he live with Ryan then?'

The dog has followed us in, and is curled up in a slinky ball in front of the fire. Every now and then his pale blue gaze flickers up towards me, like he's keeping a careful eye on me.

'No, the poor yoke doesn't seem to live anywhere. Most of us open our doors to him, and he doesn't go short – but so far, he keeps his distance. He belongs to everyone and no one. Much like Ryan, now I come to think of it…'

Just as she says this, the man himself reappears, wheeling my suitcase into the room. I notice that his black T-shirt is soaked through, clinging to his strong shoulders and solid torso in a way that makes me blink and look quickly away. I'm sure a man who looks and sounds like him is used to women falling at his feet, and I'm in no rush to add my name to the list.

'Thank you,' I say, 'that's very kind of you.'

'Sure, it's not a problem – at your service, Cassie. I'll be leaving the two of you for a while now – I have an urgent appointment to get to.'

Eileen makes a 'tsk' sound and flaps her hands at him as though she's chasing him out of the place.

'Get gone, you hallion! I don't think it's altogether "urgent" that you prop up the bar in the pub, now, is it? Will the sky fall in if you stay away?'

'It won't fall in, but maybe it'll slip just a shade? Truth be told, Cormac had just pulled me the perfect pint of Guinness, and it's terrible rude to leave it there all alone, pining for my lips.'

Eileen picks up a ball of wool from her basket and throws it at his head, saying: 'Not everything is pining for your lips, Ryan Connolly!'

Ryan laughs, nimbly dodging out of the way, and disappears through the doorway. I find myself staring in that direction, blinking and slightly bewildered.

'That man never met a living creature he wouldn't flirt with,' Eileen announces, the crinkled laughter lines gathering around her eyes giving away her fondness. 'And to be fair, I reckon he'd have a go at charming the kettle if he was bored enough! Has a heart of pure gold though, he does. Anyway. How are you feeling now?'

I sip my magic potion, and realise I am very slightly tipsy, quite sleepy, and still hungry. It's a weird combination, and I need to move away from the comfort of the fire before I drift off. I'll just drool all over my face and wake up ravenous enough to eat my own arm.

'Better, thank you,' I reply, automatically relaxing at the gentle lilt of her voice. 'I can't tell you how much I appreciate you rescuing me. It's freezing in Whimsy Cottage, and it doesn't smell great, and it wasn't exactly what I was expecting when I booked it.'

'No, I can imagine, you poor thing. I'm sure it can all be sorted – the owner is a decent sort, so don't be worrying. Need be you can spend the night here with us.'

'Us?' I echo.

'I live down here and run the bakery. Ryan has his own rooms upstairs. It suits us both – our own space, but company when we fancy it. I just pop in my wee earplugs and I'm away.'

My eyes widen slightly as I wonder what he could be getting up to that's so loud, but decide it's probably better not to know. Since my ill-fated wedding day and the ensuing collapse of my life, I've not really thought about men, and definitely not in a sexy or romantic way. It's like that part of me just switched off – I don't feel the urge to get out into what seems like a scary dating world, and I don't have the self-confidence to go and meet people the old-fashioned way in bars.

If I'm being honest with myself, the little spark of interest I felt when I really noticed Ryan was the first I'd felt in a long while. I'm not quite sure whether to smother it or kindle it – my instincts say smother, but then again, aren't I supposed to be using this trip to recreate myself?

It's all too complicated, and I'm exhausted at the thought. Instead, I think, I will simply do what I intended to do all along – go to the pub in search of sustenance.

'Eileen, do they have steak and kidney pie in the pub across the road?'

She grins at me, and replies: 'Ah! A woman after me own heart, now, aren't ye? They do a steak and Guinness pie, and I promise it's the best you'll ever have. I know the one who bakes the pies. She's a rare talent.'

'Right,' I say, clocking her mischievous wink, 'well, I'm starving, and if I stay here a minute longer I'll be asleep. So I'm going to do what my Nanna Nora would do, and head to the pub. I love English pubs.'

'I hope you like Irish pubs, too. Now, head through that wee door there, you'll find the bathroom and my bedroom, where you can get changed. I'll call Cormac and tell him to get your dinner in the oven!'

I nod gratefully, and drag my suitcase away with me. As I root through it for fresh clothes, I realise that the bedroom smells like Nora as well. A combination of lavender and rose – an essence of something from childhood. I sit on the pretty patchwork quilt, and gaze around at the unfamiliar room that somehow feels like a place I already know. I spot a huge 'Happy 80th Birthday' card that stands in pride of place on top of a dark wooden cabinet crammed with knickknacks and pottery ornaments.

I can't help but smile, and I feel a sense of warmth and contentment spread over me. It's almost physical, that sensation – a sweeping presence of reassurance and wellbeing. Like my nanna really has come back to me, for this one precious moment, just to tell me: 'Don't worry so much, angel – everything will be as it should.'

SEVEN

On the outside, The Red Lion is the very picture of a quaint English countryside inn. It looks quite prim and proper, the kind of place Agatha Christie's Miss Marple might visit for a swift sherry on her way back from solving a murder at the vicarage.

Inside, it's a different matter. As soon as I step through the door, my senses are assaulted – the room isn't that big, but it is a riot of colour and sound, a melting pot of music and mirth and mouth-watering smells.

All of the scattered tables and little alcoves are filled, and in one corner a small group of people are playing lively music on a variety of different instruments. I spot a couple of energetic fiddlers, a flute, a penny whistle and a banjo, all going with great gusto, filling the room with a melodic but playful backdrop.

There's a roaring fire in a hearth so big you can imagine a hog roasting there, and the place is filled with a dazzling array of what my mother would call 'tat', and I call 'character'. There are flags and brass horseshoes, stacks of books and board games. It's the kind of place where you could sit out the zombie apocalypse and never get bored.

The walls are decorated with stunning framed photographs of the coast and countryside of Ireland. Moody and magnificent, they draw the eye in so deeply that you almost feel like you're there, standing on the Cliffs of Moher. They're so good they could be in a gallery.

Hanging above us, dangling from the ceiling, are crisscrossed glittery Christmas decorations, and way too many bunches of mistletoe. The long wooden bar is decorated with string lights, and a small tree twinkles away in one corner.

The bar is lined with tall chairs and stools, along with more types of 'stout' than I've ever seen in one place before – not just the familiar black and gold of the Guinness harp, but pumps that offer Beamish and Murphy's and what appears to be the pub's own brew, Cormac's Porter.

I get a few curious looks, a couple of hand waves, and a raised bow from one of the fiddle players. Ryan, tucked into a window seat, meets my eyes and gives me a wide grin. He looks so devilish with his wild hair and his sparkling eyes that my stomach takes a little leap, and I remind myself that I am not the same Cassie as I was a few weeks ago. I am not panic-attack-in-Macy's-Cassie; I am international-jet-setter-Cassie. I surprise myself by maintaining eye contact and grinning right back at him. He looks a little taken aback, and I find that I like it.

Behind the bar is a glamorous blonde with huge hair that wouldn't look out of place on an old-school Charlie's Angel. She's currently managing about five different pints of black ale, scooting along pulling the pumps, letting creamy heads settle and topping up, all in a perfectly synchronised rhythm. She chats to each customer as she works, and has several older men gazing at her in adoration.

'You must be Cassie!' she exclaims as I approach, her Irish accent not quite as pronounced as Eileen's, but very much still there. 'What's your poison?'

'Umm... what do you recommend?'

'Well now, that depends, doesn't it? Are you looking to get ossified?'

'I don't know. What does that mean?'

'It means so drunk you forget your own name.'

'Ah. Well, in that case, no thank you – not tonight at least. Maybe a glass of red wine? A Merlot if you have one?'

Her pretty face creases in sadness, and she replies: 'Oh, I'm so sorry. We only sell stout and whiskey. Anything else is a bit too fancy for the likes of us.'

Before I get the chance to respond, she bursts out laughing and waves a dishtowel at me, clutched between impeccably manicured nails.

'I'm just acting the maggot!' she exclaims. I've not heard that one before, even from Nanna Nora, but I can figure it out from the context. 'A nice glass of Merlot, coming right up! I believe someone booked you into Whimsy by mistake?'

'By mistake?' I echo, as she pours my drink. This is the first I've heard of it, and it sets alarm bells ringing in my head. I only booked it a week ago, paid in full, and flew thousands of miles to spend the next month here – all on the basis of a mistake?

It does explain why the cottage was so cold, so unwelcoming, so dirty. Why the place felt abandoned. I gulp down half my wine in two mouthfuls, and she says: 'Oh, don't be listening to me – I never know what I'm talking about! It's nothing that can't be fixed. I'm Orla, by the way. I run this place with my fella, Cormac. He's just sorting your food for you, Cassie. It was stir-fried octopus with raspberry sauce you were looking for, wasn't it?'

She says this perfectly seriously, with one arched eyebrow quirked upwards. If I hadn't just been caught out by her, I might have fallen for it.

'You're acting the maggot again, Orla, aren't you?' I say, narrowing my eyes. She laughs out loud and nods, clearly delighted with having a new playmate.

Just then Cormac himself emerges from the back room with a plate. He's an enormous man in every way, tall, with an impressive beer belly nestled beneath his green Ireland rugby shirt. His brown eyes are kind and his smile is welcoming.

'The woman of the hour!' he says, laying the plate down in front of me. 'I'm just after getting this for you – pie, peas, and our finest colcannon.'

I suck in a breath, and can hardly contain my delight. Nanna Nora used to make colcannon for me, and I haven't had it since she died. She called it 'proper Irish comfort food', made of buttery, creamy mashed potato with cabbage. It tastes much better than it sounds, and she used to serve it up with bacon chops. The rigours of the day seem to drop away from me – my usual response to butter and carbs.

'Are you okay there, Cassie, or do you want me to chase off some of the hooligans so you can have a proper table?'

I assure him I am fine where I am, mainly because I can't bear the thought of waiting even a moment longer. I go into some kind of trance-like state as soon as the first taste of colcannon hits my tongue, and follow it up with a mouthful of pie that is, as Eileen promised, one of the best things I've ever eaten.

I realise, after a few minutes of deeply concentrated enjoyment, that Orla and Cormac are staring at me in amusement. I'd completely blanked them – and the rest of the world – out while I started my meal.

'What?' I ask, smiling and refusing to feel embarrassed. 'Can't a woman enjoy her food?'

'She can, sure,' Orla says, laughing. 'But you're enjoying your food an awful lot, there, what with the sound effects. Feels a bit like the priest should be reading the marriage banns for you and that pie.'

'It's like that scene in *When Harry Met Sally*,' adds Cormac.

He raises his voice to sound like a woman, and pronounces: 'I'll have what she's having!'

'Well you're out of luck, big fella,' replies Orla. 'Because that was the last pie standing! Will you have another glass, Cassie?'

I nod eagerly. It really has been a day of contrasts, I think, as I sip my refreshed Merlot. I've gone from the depths of despair to being warm, welcome and well fed. I know I have to deal with my accommodation, but right now this is enough. The music in the background is buoying my mood almost as much as the meal, and I find myself tapping my toes and clapping along.

I recognise the song from Nanna Nora's house – 'The Wild Rover'. She had a recorded version by a band called The Dubliners, even though she told us it was an old folk tune. As kids, Suzie and I would spin around to it like tops, and Nanna would let us stand on her green velvet couch and jump off into the air as we sang the 'no, nay, never' chorus.

It makes me smile to remember her, and for the first time since she died, I find that the happy childhood memories are starting to balance out the pain of losing her. She, I decide, looking around at the crowded pub, would love it here. It's a place full of people who seem to share her zest for life.

The little band is hammering away at the rousing end of the song, and Orla and Cormac are dancing an enthusiastic jig behind the bar. There's not a lot of space, and their spins end up knocking over a stack of menus and sending a wicker basket full of peanuts flying into the air.

Several people are standing up, either dancing or singing along. One of them, I notice, is Ryan. He has a powerful voice, as you'd expect from a man of his size, but he can hold a tune as well. He raises his glass at me, our eyes meeting once more, and I feel a hint of a blush creep over my cheeks. I nod at him in acknowledgement and sing along quietly myself.

Orla jigs towards me and tops up my glass again, and I don't stop her. If I end up freezing to death in Whimsy, at least I'll die happy.

The band are given a hearty round of applause, then start something much slower and sweeter – it sounds like a sea shanty, with its haunting tones and mellow pace.

I am so lost in the sailor's song of love and loss that at first, I don't notice when someone sits next to me on one of the tall chairs that line the bar. In fact, it's the smell that first alerts me – a delicious cologne that makes my nostrils twitch in delight with its bewitching mix of wood and spice. It's subtle and sophisticated, but still utterly male – the kind of scent June would call a 'panty-dropper', because she's classy like that.

I turn around, and see the profile of an absolutely stunning man. His features are aquiline, with a strong nose, high cheekbones and a wide mouth. As he turns to face me, I'm floored by the combination of his golden blond hair and deep green eyes. He looks every bit as good as his cologne smells, and I fear for a moment that I might actually fall off my chair. What is it with this place and the hot men?

He's dressed in a stylish charcoal-grey tweed suit that has clearly been tailored to his lean body, and a crisp white shirt that is open at the top few buttons, displaying a hint of sun-kissed flesh. The kind that comes from winter trips to the Caribbean, or skiing in exotic places.

I see his gaze flicker over me in exactly the same way mine flickered over him, and he gives me a full-wattage smile that could power the whole of Manhattan.

'Hello,' he says, offering his hand in such a formal gesture that I'm momentarily unsure how to respond. 'I'm Charles.'

He's the first non-Irish person I've met since I arrived here, but his accent is pure cut-glass English, and easy to follow. I place my hand in his, and the shake goes on for a few seconds too long.

'Hi, I'm Cassie. Cassie O'Hara.'

He frowns slightly, and asks: 'American? Not that I'm complaining, but what are you doing in our little village, Cassie O'Hara?'

'Ah. Well. That's a long story – and I've no idea if I'm even staying. I might not even make it through tonight.'

'Really? That would be a terrible pity. What could possibly tempt you to change your mind about that?'

He says this completely deadpan, but there is a little upward quirk of one side of those lips, and a sparkle of mischief in those green eyes that tells me he is flirting with me. He's just doing it in a very English way. In fact, I realise, biting back laughter – he's flirting with me in a very Hugh-Grant-in-the-90s kind of way. I can't wait to tell June about this encounter.

'Well, a good start would be accommodation that isn't covered in mould, freezing cold, and as welcoming as a root canal without the anaesthetic. I checked in to my alleged vacation home this afternoon, and honestly? It's like the place that Christmas dreams go to die.'

It's a slightly longer rant than I intended, but his eyes crinkle in amusement, and the laughter lines around them make him look older but no less delectable.

'Oh no! That bad, really?'

'Yup. That bad. It looked so nice online, but in reality, it's not fit for a dog to live in. Even Eejit – he's a homeless stray – would probably give it a one-star review on Tripadvisor. I'm not picky, and I didn't expect luxury, but basic cleanliness isn't too much to ask, is it?'

'Certainly not. Sounds dreadful. I assume this was in Marshington Grange, the next village over? I hope you've complained to the owners?'

'I tried, but I only got an answering machine, and nobody's called me back. I'm not quite sure which clowns they've got running the circus at the Bancroft Estate, but I'm not impressed.'

He stares at me for a moment, his face suddenly still. I wonder what I've said wrong, and am about to ask when Cormac delivers him a glass of brandy. Charles nods his thanks, and turns his attention back to me.

'You booked a holiday cottage with the Bancroft Estate?' he says. 'And it wasn't... habitable? No fire lit, no welcome package? No wine or chocolates, no Christmas decorations? And it was cold and dirty, you say?'

'Very cold, and very dirty. And the only welcome package was an exploding lightbulb and a lungful of dust. Why? Do you know them?'

His eyes narrow slightly, and for a moment he looks almost intimidating – or at the very least, very authoritative. Like a man who is used to getting his own way. Then he runs his hands through his slightly floppy hair, sighs, and says: 'Perhaps I should introduce myself in full. My name is Charles Alexander Bancroft.'

'Oh! Um... *that* Bancroft?'

'Yes. One of the clowns, at your service.'

I feel embarrassed and awkward, but also slightly defiant – which might, of course, be because of the wine. The old me – the stay-at-home me – might have spluttered an apology and shuffled off into the shadows, but I am determined to not behave like that.

'Right. Well, it's nice to meet you, Mr Bancroft – any chance of a refund? The place I rented really isn't fit for habitation.'

He nods, and stands up. Wowzers, he's tall – much taller than me, and even than my dad. I get another waft of that cologne and try not to inhale too deeply. It will definitely affect my bargaining powers if I pass out from lust.

'Ryan!' he shouts, gesturing from the table in the window to the bar. 'Could I have a word with you?'

Ryan looks over from the chat he was having with an elderly

man with wizard-length grey hair, and stares at us both. His usual mischievous smile is nowhere to be seen, and it takes him several moments to move. For a second, I think he's going to simply ignore him.

The two men stand facing each other, and as I look on, I spot the unmistakable signs of tension. Ryan has his hands shoved into his jeans pockets, and Charles is frowning. I see Cormac and Orla exchange a look, and have no clue what's going on. The whole tableau reminds of me of nature shows, when you see stags fighting with their antlers.

'Yes, *sir*?' says Ryan, his flippant tone at odds with his tense body language. 'Did you command my presence?'

'Pack it in, Ryan. I'm just back from three long days in London and I'm not in the mood. This is Cassie, she booked one of our holiday cottages.'

Ryan nods in my direction, and winks at me in a way that can only be described as 'saucy'. In other circumstances I might feel a little flutter, but right now I'm aware that I'm actually irrelevant – I just happen to be caught in the middle of a situation that existed long before I arrived.

'We've met already. Old friends.'

'Well, be that as it may, Cassie tells me her cottage was in an unacceptable condition when she arrived. Not only was there no welcome package, but it hadn't been cleaned, and the fire wasn't ready. Between you and Mary Catherine I expect higher standards for my guests. It's your job to maintain Waverley and Waterfall, Ryan, you know that.'

There's a flare of anger in Ryan's blue eyes, but he quickly clamps it down. He nods slowly, and rubs his hand over his chin, as though he's thinking hard.

'I do know that, Your Lordship – but Cassie here wasn't booked to stay in Waverley or Waterfall. She was booked to stay in Whimsy.'

'Whimsy...?' repeats Charles, looking confused. 'But Whimsy isn't available. Whimsy is being renovated. How did that happen?'

He looks at me and I simply hold my hands up in surrender.

'Don't ask me,' I reply. 'I filled out a booking form online, paid my money for a month-long trip, and flew across the Atlantic. I have a confirmation email if you don't believe me.'

The two men look at each other again, and I can almost feel the conflict in the air. Then Ryan seems to relent, and his gaze softens as he says: 'Charles, Eileen's been trying to speak to Allegra since we found out, but she hasn't called back. The other two cottages are both booked, and I don't know what happened here – I thought you'd taken it off the booking site until the work was done?'

Again, something is going on that I don't quite understand, because suddenly all of the machismo has drained out of both of them. Charles sighs, looks sad, and answers: 'Well. It should have been, yes, you're absolutely right. I'll have to speak to her about it. I know it's all a bit much for her to deal with, but she insists she can cope, and I don't want to make her feel...'

'Useless?' Ryan supplies, his face sympathetic.

Charles nods tersely, and then turns to me.

'Cassie, I'm so sorry. It appears there's been an error, as you probably just gathered – Whimsy should never have been available, and I can only apologise for the inconvenience. Ryan, how long will it take for you to get Whimsy ready, if you make it your top priority?'

'If I give up sleeping, eating and all my other bad habits, maybe five days, a week?'

He smiles at me as he speaks, making it clear that he's not taking this too seriously. I suspect he doesn't take much too seriously.

'Right. Very well. If you could, I'd very much appreciate it,' says Charles, nodding firmly. 'And in the meantime, Cassie, I'd be honoured if you'd be my guest at Bancroft Manor. It's the very least I can do in the circumstances.'

EIGHT

I feel like I've been transported to a movie set when we arrive at the manor. It's only a few minutes' drive away, high on a hill that overlooks the village down in the river valley. The golden stone buildings seem to shine in the moonlight as I gaze down at them, and I sigh at how magical it all is.

Charles drove me here in his slinky racing green Jaguar, which I'd climbed into with a few doubts. I was raised to be cautious of strangers, and here I am, driving off into the night with one. But he's clearly genuine, Ryan knows him, and anyway, I'm desperate to see a real-life English manor house.

He was full of apologies as we curled our way through the winding hedgerows and one-track paths. Eventually, we passed through wrought-iron gates and along a wide gravel road.

I see the house from a distance, but when he pulls up in front of it and I climb out of the car, I still stand and stare in amazement at the building before me. It's stunning, lit up by ground-level lights dotted around the grass. It's three storeys high and built of the same honey-coloured stone as the village cottages. That's where the similarities end, though, because this is a mansion – huge, imposing, studded with mullioned windows, the massive front door guarded by carved statues of lions on either side of the steps.

The rain has finally been banished, and the night air is surprisingly mild. I feel like I could gawk at this place for hours.

'Oh, my,' I mutter. 'This is your home? How old is it? It's so beautiful.'

'It is,' Charles replies, lifting my case from the car, 'very beautiful – until you see the heating bill! There's been a house here at least since the Domesday Book, but there's nothing much left of that version, of course. What you see now is Tudor, and the rest evolved over time.'

'And you've always lived here?'

'Well, not since Tudor times – I hope I don't look that old! But my family, in one form or another, yes. It's survived civil war, two world wars, and numerous complicated family dynamics... but there's been a Bancroft here for as long as anyone can remember.'

I nod, taking in the grand sweep of the surrounding gardens.

'And... well, Ryan called you "Lordship". Was he just being sarcastic?'

'Ah. Well, he was being sarcastic – it's his default setting – but technically, it is correct. I don't use it in everyday life as it's a bit of a mouthful, but my full title is Charles, Viscount Bancroft de St George.'

He grimaces slightly as he says it, as though he's embarrassed at the formality, and then shrugs as we gaze at the house.

'It's all I've ever known,' he says quietly. 'And it's not as perfect as it looks.'

'I'm sure. Nothing ever is. But... tell me, Charles, if you're a viscount, does that mean you've met—'

'The King? Well, yes, at formal events of state and the like. But it's not like we're bosom buddies.'

'I was actually going to ask if you'd met Hugh Grant...'

There's a little silence, and he laughs – loud, full, hearty. It relieves all of his stuffiness, and makes him look like a completely different person. A far happier one.

'As it happens, yes. Once. Very nice chap.'

Now he's mentioned the King, though, I can't help asking: 'Wait – so, are you, like, in line for the throne?'

'Only if several hundred people have some very bad luck first. Including my uncle, who's an earl. Now, are you ready to go inside? Maybe a nightcap, and then I'll get you settled? You must be exhausted.'

Oddly, I'm not – in fact I feel energised by the strange twist my journey has taken. But I nod, and he politely gestures for me to go forward. As we approach the grand, formal front door, it swings open, and I jump back at the sight of the man who greets me.

He's very tall, very bony, and about seven hundred years old. His face looks almost as aristocratic as Charles's, and his bearing is stiff and regal. The effect is spoiled by the fact that he's wearing a tatty plaid dressing gown, striped flannel pyjamas and moccasin-style slippers.

'Ah, Lord Charles. You're finally home. I thought you were avoiding me – you know it's your turn to put the rubbish bins out!'

Both men laugh, and hug each other in a way that speaks of a long familiarity.

'This is Roberts,' Charles says, introducing us. 'He's pretty much a one-man band around here – butler, housekeeper, groundsman, all rolled into one. Roberts, this is Cassie – she'll be staying with us for a while. She was accidentally booked into Whimsy.'

The two share a serious look, and Roberts replies: 'Ah. Well, these things happen. And Cassie, he forgot to tell you about my most important role – making sure His Lordship here doesn't get too big for his boots.'

'Pleased to meet you, Roberts,' I say, noticing that he raises an elegant eyebrow at my accent.

I follow them through into a grand hallway, dominated by a sweeping staircase that is lined with what I presume are family portraits of Bancrofts through the centuries. My eyes widen when I spot an actual, real-life suit of armour in the corner. I really want to whip out my phone and take a selfie for June, but I remind myself to keep it classy.

The men lead me through towards the left, and I immediately notice the difference in temperature. The room we find ourselves in is much warmer, and I remember his earlier comment about the heating bill. I suspect they only heat the parts of the house they actually use.

'This is where we spend most of our time,' Charles says, confirming my suspicions. 'We call it the Blue Room, for obvious reasons.'

It is, in fact, obvious – the walls are all painted in differing shades of blue, and the windows are draped in midnight-blue velvet. The ceilings are high, decorated with ornate plaster-work carved into elaborate floral designs, all flowing around an extravagant chandelier. Despite the formality, it feels warm and lived-in, with comfortably shabby sofas and a roaring log fire in the huge hearth. There are bookshelves laden with paperbacks, and stacks of newspapers and magazines scattered over a large dining table.

'Cassie, can I tempt you with a drink?' Roberts says, making his way to an antique mahogany cabinet. 'Whiskey, brandy, or our local delicacy, crème de badger?'

He sounds completely serious, but I narrow my eyes at him. Roberts is, I think, acting the maggot.

'Are you messing with a poor American gal, Roberts?' I ask.

'Heaven forbid!'

'I'll take a small brandy, thank you.'

He nods, and pours drinks for all three of us. He definitely

doesn't have that *Downton Abbey* 'below stairs' feel to him –
Roberts is clearly part of the family.

He holds up the crystal decanter, and announces: 'Lady
Georgina seems to have been sneaking the booze again,
Charles.'

Charles rolls his eyes and explains: 'Georgina is my
daughter – although I sometimes wonder about that. I think it's
entirely possible my ex-wife had some kind of liaison with
Satan. You'll meet her in due course. I suggest adopting the
brace position at all times.'

The words are harsh, but his tone is indulgent – Georgina is
clearly the apple of his eye. We sit on the couches closest to the
fire, and the two of them catch up. I half-heartedly listen as
Charles describes his business meetings in London, and Roberts
fills him in on 'estate matters'.

I'm happy enough just looking around, noticing something
new and interesting everywhere my eyes settle – a Bakelite
phone with a rotary dial, a magnificent chess set with a game
half-played, a giant dinner gong made of dimpled copper. It's
like sitting in an especially comfortable museum display.

'Where's the dog?' I ask, when I spot a basket in one corner.

'That was Jasper's,' replies Charles, staring at it in a slightly
mournful way. 'He was the last of a long line of Springer
Spaniels, and sadly went to the great walkies in the sky a few
months ago.'

'Oh, I'm sorry!'

'No need to be. He was almost seventeen, and it was his
time. I keep thinking we need a puppy to liven the place up, but
it's quite a commitment.'

'True. I get stressed by keeping my house plants alive, never
mind an actual living creature. Though I got herded by a dog
called Eejit earlier today.'

'Ah, the stray who knocks around the village?' he says, smiling. 'Poor thing seems happy enough, I suppose, but nobody can

find his owner. No tag, microchip – nobody seems to be missing him.'

I nod, and start to ponder Eejit a little more deeply than I should. He seems like a good dog, a useful dog – why *isn't* somebody missing him? Has he been thrown out, replaced by something younger and shinier? And am I even thinking about Eejit now, or just imposing my own feelings on a random pooch? Anyway, I remind myself, Eejit is, as Charles says, happy enough, even if he doesn't have a conventional life.

I'm pulled out of my reverie when I hear Roberts say: 'Alexa, play Ella Fitzgerald.'

Within seconds, the singer's rich, bluesy voice fills the room, and I can't keep the surprise from my face.

'All mod cons, as you see,' Roberts adds. 'We even have flushing toilets, and a Netflix account.'

'No television though?'

'Of course not – that would be dreadfully common!'

I'm happy enough here, but I know I'm also not quite ready to sleep. I am not great at sleeping. Since things ended with He Who Shall Not Be Named, I've constantly struggled to drift off. At home I've got into the habit of walking every night before bed, and I've kept that up in England.

'Would you mind,' I ask, 'if I went for a little stroll? Just around the outside of the house. I won't wander off into the woods or anything stupid. I just... well, it's part of my routine.'

I feel slightly embarrassed as I say this, as though I am admitting weakness, but Charles meets my eyes and says: 'Not at all. We all have our routines, don't we? The things that help us get through the day. Do you want any company, Cassie?'

I am tempted to say yes, because I am only flesh and blood. It's been a long time since I took a night-time stroll with a hand-some and attentive man, and I know it would be potentially quite romantic. But instead I smile gently, and say: 'Thank you, but no. I won't stay out for long, if you need to pull up the portcullis or anything.'

He grins at me, and replies: 'Not a problem. Stick to the paths, and we'll leave the lights on. Here, take this...'

He stands up, and pulls a large fleece jacket from a crammed coatrack. He helps me into it like the gentleman he is, and I am enveloped in that gorgeous cologne of his. I try not to sigh out loud, and make my farewells.

I head back outside, my feet crunching on the gravel as I wander around to the side of the house. More windows, more statues, more doors. The place is a warren. The lights play over the grass and the trees, casting shadows and creating a sense of mystery as I explore.

I find a vast formal garden laid out behind the house, with closely trimmed lawns and neat rows of bushes and plants. The landscaping flows up to the wide steps of a stone terrace. The room behind the floor-to-ceiling windows is in darkness, but the glimpses I catch suggest that it is enormous, possibly some kind of ballroom. The mansion looks even more magnificent from the back, and I snap a few pictures of the house and grounds, thinking that even my mom and Suzie will be impressed.

I continue my walk, seeing vegetable gardens, flower beds, a small orchard of apple and pear trees and a collection of buildings that look like tiny cottages from a fairy tale.

I've just decided to head back inside when I spot something intriguing tucked away at the side of the orchard. It's a wooden door set into an old stone wall, and as I get closer I see that it is slightly ajar. I push it forward, feeling slightly guilty, and find myself inside the most amazing place.

It's surrounded on all four sides by higgledy-piggledy walls that look as ancient as the land, and I can't help reaching out to touch them, feeling the rough, aged brickwork against my palms, trying to imagine the lives of the people who built them.

Enclosed within their protective shield is what I can only

describe as a secret garden. Unlike the rest of the place, it's lush and wild, even in the darkness of a winter's night. I use the torch on my phone, following a winding path through the greenery. There are tall pines that reach up to the stars, and a massive monkey puzzle tree. Rows of old tree stumps have been scattered about like impromptu chairs, and every inch of the place is covered in something weird and wonderful.

Much of it is dormant at this time of year, but the little hand-written tags tell me that I am walking through camellias and rhododendrons, Japanese dogwood, jasmines of every kind – trees and shrubs from every corner of the globe.

I sit on one of the tree stumps, snuggled deep in a jacket that smells like Charles, and gaze around, letting the peace and quiet settle over my mind. I feel like a zen master, perfectly at one with my surroundings, and just know that I am going to sleep well tonight. This is the most calming place I've ever been.

At least it is, right up until the point when a determined woman's voice growls at me: 'Stop right there! I have a shotgun, and I'm not afraid to use it!'

I jump up in terror, dropping my phone to the ground. The torch shines up into the face of my assailant, and it is not what I expect. She's dressed in a large raincoat that dwarfs her petite frame, and her white-grey hair is loose and wild around a face that is a portrait of faded beauty. Even here, even with her pointing a gun at me, I can see that she is stunning – and also very, very upset.

I hold my hands up in the universal gesture of surrender, and stammer: 'I'm s-s-sorry! I didn't know I wasn't supposed to be here! Please don't shoot me!'

She shows no sign of relenting, and I wonder if I could make a run for it – do a duck and roll like they do in the movies, grab my phone and hide beneath the branches of the Chilean lantern tree.

'Don't move an inch!' she shouts, her tone imperious. 'I

know what you're about – poaching! Well, I'm not having it, you hear? You're trespassing!'

'I'm not poaching, I promise! Charles brought me here. Charles Bancroft? I was just with him and Roberts in the house, and I came for a walk, and I really, really don't plan on stealing anything!'

I see a flicker of confusion pass over her aristocratic features, and her nostrils flare slightly.

'Well... you would say that, wouldn't you? Come on. Let's be having you. We'll soon see the truth of it. Quick march!'

She orders me in front of her, and stoops to pick up my phone, slipping it into her coat pocket. I'm terrified that she will accidentally fire, but she keeps her aim steady and gestures for me to move.

I don't see that I have any choice, and even though my legs feel like Jell-O and my heart is racing, I stumble along in front of her. She points towards the wooden door with the barrel of the gun, and I pray that I don't unintentionally do anything to spook her. I really don't want to die like this – blasted to death in a foreign land by a woman who seems to think I'm here to illegally hunt game.

She mutters as we go, and yells at me when I trip, but eventually we reach the entrance to the mansion. I stand there before her, frozen on the spot, my hands still high.

'Roberts!' she screams at the top of her voice. 'Phillip! Get out here now!'

Within seconds the big door swings open, and both men appear, silhouetted in the light of the lobby. I meet Charles's eyes pleadingly, and they both leap into action. Roberts jumps straight between me and the crazy woman, blocking me physically with his body in a way that suggests her shotgun holds no fear for him.

Charles mutters a few apologetic words, and goes right to

her side. I risk looking over my shoulder, and see him gently prising the gun from her clenched fingers.

'Phillip!' she says, gazing up at him. 'You need to call the police – I found her in Vanessa's secret garden, up to no good!'

'It's Charles, Mother. I'm Charles. And this is my guest, Cassie. She's come to stay with us for a few days. She meant no harm, and I told her it was fine to look around. Shall we all go inside and have a warm drink?'

He has the gun in his hands now, and I see him do something with the mechanism, and then sag slightly as he says: 'It's not loaded.'

'Of course it's not bloody loaded!' the woman snaps at him. 'What do you think I am, a lunatic?'

Nobody answers that question, and she strides off ahead into the house. I have no idea what's happening here, and I say quietly: 'Who is Phillip? Is that another one of your names?'

He shakes his head sadly. 'No. Phillip was my father. He's been gone for six years. She's... well, she's in the early stages of Alzheimer's. I'm so sorry that happened to you, Cassie. It's really not been the greatest of days for you, has it?'

He sounds so shaken, so distressed, that I don't have the heart to do anything but comfort him. I lay one hand on his arm. 'Don't worry about it. I live in New York. I get held up at gunpoint every time I go out to buy milk.'

I'm very obviously joking, and he manages a wan smile of gratitude as we follow his mother inside. We find her in a massive kitchen at the back of the house, making a pot of tea as though nothing untoward just happened. My phone has been left out on the counter.

The huge room is dominated by a giant pine table that has been battered by generations of use, pots and pans hang from racks on the ceiling, an ancient looking Aga stove taking up most of one wall. I can imagine how busy it must have been in here in days gone by, when there was a full staff and house guests. Now, although everything is perfectly clean and tidy, it feels a little neglected. The appliances look old, the chairs are mismatched, and the dented fridge makes an alarmingly loud humming noise that seems to vibrate through the stone floor.

'So, Cassie,' the woman says as she prepares a full tea service – china cups and saucers, dainty squares of sugar in a bowl, tiny spoons for everyone – 'my name is Allegra. I'm Charles's mother.'

She sounds confident and assured, which I suspect comes from years of training in her social strata – but as she passes me my cup, her hand is trembling. Tea, as my dad had warned me, is the glue that holds the English together, and she is using this ritual as a way of calming herself down.

'I can only apologise,' she says, her voice straight out of *The Crown*, 'for my uncouth behaviour. A terrible misunderstanding, and not the way I normally greet guests. So, are you one of Charles's London friends?'

She says 'London friends' in a way that suggests they are an exotic species, as unexpected a sight in her kitchen as a snow leopard or a ring-tailed lemur.

'Ah, no – in fact I only met him today, um... Lady Bancroft?'

'We don't use titles in the kitchen, dear.'

'Right. Allegra. Well, Charles has been very kind.'

She raises an eyebrow, possibly at my accent, possibly at my words, and responds: 'Well, yes. He's a very kind boy, my Charles. Always has been. And there'll be no judgement from me about the sleeping arrangements – you young people should grab life while you can!'

Although her pale skin is lined and creased, and she is maybe somewhere in her seventies, she is still incredibly beautiful. Her features are delicate, and her eyes a startling shade of blue that is so deep it's almost violet. She's looking curiously from Charles to myself, and I decide to let him handle that one.

'No, Mother, it's not like that at all. Cassie is staying with us because she came all the way from New York to stay in Whimsy Cottage.'

'Why would she do that? Whimsy's getting a make-over, isn't it? That handsome young Ryan is supposed to be doing it, isn't he?'

I see a muscle twitch in Charles's jaw, and he answers: 'He is, yes. But perhaps mistakenly, I left it available to book online.'

Everyone very politely sips their tea, and I see Allegra process the information.

'Right. Well, that'll be my fault then, won't it? Nice of you to try and take the blame, darling, but I'm not so doolally that I don't see what's happened. I manage the booking system, and I've obviously stuffed things up. Cassie, in that case, double apologies – I drag you all the way from America to stay in a dilapidated cottage, and then hold you hostage at gunpoint. I'm like the opposite of your fairy godmother! I hope I get the chance to make it up to you over the next few days.'

'It's absolutely fine,' I promise her. 'I love an adventure.'

Of course, that is usually far from the truth – but as I stand here in this strange place with these strange people, I realise that I am enjoying myself. I am enduring circumstances that are out of my control, but for some reason I don't feel the familiar spiral of anxiety and tension that usually accompanies me.

Allegra nods, and announces that it's time for bed.

'I'll walk you up, ma'am,' says Roberts, holding out his arm for her to link. 'Make sure you don't decide you're a ninja and try to assassinate the chandeliers.'

'You're a dreadful man, Roberts,' she says, haughtily.

'I know, ma'am, I know.'

The two of them leave the room in an oddly stately way, like a couple heading to a ball, and Charles and I are alone. He leans back against the counter and sighs. His blond hair is ruffled, and his shoulders are slumped in defeat.

'I'm sorry,' I say, once Allegra and Roberts are out of earshot. 'This must be so hard for you.'

'Yes, but not as hard as it is for her. A lot of the time she's absolutely fine, her old self. It's torture for a woman like her, who has always been in charge of her own destiny.'

'Are you the only child she has? Are there any siblings to help you?'

'Not anymore, no,' he says, in a tone that closes down that line of conversation very firmly. He draws in a breath, stands up tall, and says: 'Anyway. You really must be tired after all of that. I'll show you to your room.'

NINE

I am being buried alive, and I smell smoke.

These are the first thoughts that run through my brain as I start to slowly wake up. Well, they don't so much 'run through' my brain as 'attack it with a sub-machine gun', and my adrenaline response kicks in. I start to flail my arms and legs, trying to fight my way out of my bonds, and let out a desperate, strangled shout.

Little by little, reality starts to take hold and I realise that I am not being buried alive after all. I am just buried in especially heavy bedding. I take a few deep breaths, slide one arm out, and begin to dismantle my cocoon jail.

Once I've escaped, I lie back on the pillow, reminding myself of where I am. I am in a bedroom at Bancroft Manor. I am a guest here, and seem to have accidentally become pals with a British aristocrat. Last night, after his mother attempted a citizen's arrest, he escorted me here to this large, ornate and fairly cold room.

The bed is a four-poster, the wallpaper is red and gold fleur-de-lys, and I can actually see my breath puff out clouds in the frigid air. Charles had apologised for the temperature, explaining that they only 'keep up' the rooms they use, and left me with enough blankets and bedspreads to keep me cosy.

I actually slept exceptionally well by my standards, and the deepness of my sleep probably contributed to my mind getting confused and thinking I was buried alive. That primal fear has now dissolved but I realise, wrinkling up my nostrils, that I can still smell smoke.

I sit upright, shivering slightly as the cold hits my bare shoulders, and sniff the air as I look around.

It doesn't take long – I hadn't noticed it last night, but the room actually comes with its own balcony. The French doors leading out to it are wide open, which explains the chill, and a young woman is sitting outside with a cigarette, which explains the smell.

'Morning!' she says brightly, as I pull the comforter up to my chin. 'I brought you a coffee, but then I drank it. Sorry. I'm Georgina. Everyone calls me Georgie, or sometimes George. Sometimes a few other things but we won't go into that!'

Georgina – Charles's daughter, I recall. She's somewhere in her late teens, I'd say, with a lean build, long legs, and shining blonde hair that shimmers over her shoulders like a golden curtain. Her naturally wholesome good looks are a bit at odds with the Ramones T-shirt she's wearing, peeking out from beneath a shaggy, hole-ridden cardigan.

'Right. I'm Cassie. And could you either stub out that cigarette or close the doors, ideally both? I'm freezing.'

I wonder if I'm being rude, but decide I'm really not. I might not know much about the etiquette of the English upper classes, but I do know that it's impolite to sneak into someone's room, open their windows and blow smoke at them while they sleep.

'Aye aye, Captain!' she replies, giving me a little salute before she flicks the cigarette into a large pottery jug.

She strolls into my room and closes the doors behind her,

standing at the end of my bed and biting her lip as she assesses me. She passes me my robe, then sits at the foot of the mattress. She curls her long legs up beneath her, and gives me a killer smile. I can imagine it gets her out of a lot of trouble, that smile – or possibly into it.

'I'm sorry I possibly freaked you out a bit there,' she says. 'My room is actually next door, and this used to be my mother's domain. I've been climbing between the two balconies for years. You weren't awake, even at this very civilised hour, so I just... opened the doors to give you a bit of a nudge. It's quite rude, really, I know – but as soon as Dad told me you were here, I was bursting to meet you! I've been home for weeks and I think I'm almost *dead* from boredom.'

I'm taken aback by so much of that small speech that I simply stare at her as I process it. Charles mentioned his ex-wife... but this was her room? Maybe they were sleeping separately before they divorced. Maybe that's normal here, when you have so many rooms. Or maybe it was all super-amicable and this is where she sleeps when she visits? Maybe – in fact definitely – it's not my business. I'm also slightly alarmed at the thought of Georgie clambering between rooms on frosty mornings, and wondering what time she considers a 'civilised hour'.

I go with the last one, check my phone, and do a double-take when I see that it's after ten a.m. I never sleep in this late, even when I'm on vacation. I slip on my robe and look around for my case. Everything feels strange and unfamiliar, and my body is aching in some weird places. Probably from the journey, or falling over outside Whimsy, or stumbling through the darkness with a shotgun at my back. I'm spoiled for choice.

'Will there be more coffee downstairs?' I ask, concentrating on the important stuff.

'Yes! There's always coffee. And once you're up and about, Roberts will get the fire sorted in here, and then you won't need so many covers, and maybe tonight you won't have nightmares about being buried alive...'

'Are you a mind reader?'

'I could be, couldn't I? Or it might be that a few seconds before you woke up, you were shouting "Help, I'm buried alive!" Would you like to come and get some breakfast with me? And would you like me to drive you around for the day – I could be your chauffeur, and take you to the village, and show you all the best places?'

Her blue eyes are shining with excitement, and her hands are so animated they're flying around and clapping together mid-air. I notice her fingernails are painted black and chewed right down to the skin, and wonder why a girl who looks so perfect has so many bad habits.

'Please, please, please?' she asks, trying on a little-girl expression that makes me laugh out loud.

'How old are you anyway? Have you actually passed your driving test?'

'Of course I have – I wouldn't be offering to drive you around if I hadn't, would I?'

'I'm not so sure about that.'

'Okay, fair point – I don't suppose I've exactly shown myself up as Sergeant Sensible so far. But I assure you, I can drive – I'll even show you my licence if you like. And I'm seventeen.'

'Right. Shouldn't you be, I don't know, in school or something?'

She fidgets around, twisting her hair around her fingers, chewing her lip again before she answers: 'Um, well, probably – but I'm dyslexic, and also a total nightmare, so I kept getting kicked out of them. The local schools, boarding school, all of them. I... uh, well, I don't like being told what to do, you see, and that's kind of a big deal at school.'

'Yeah. I remember that part. I didn't mind it – it was easier than deciding what to do by myself. I'm trying to change that.'

As I speak, I unzip my suitcase and start to unpack. I can feel her sharp eyes on me, and eventually she says: 'Is that why you're here? Have you run away to England to try and grow a backbone?'

'I'm starting to see why you kept getting kicked out of places.'

'Yeah. Sorry. I'm frightfully inappropriate, I know. Granny's been horrified at me for years, but now she finds my lack of filter amusing – probably because of the Alzheimer's, and the fact that she's losing her own filter these days. We can be awful together now. Would you like me to help you unpack?'

'No, thank you,' I say firmly. 'In fact, I need to get dressed now, so maybe you could scram?'

'Scram! I love how that sounds in your accent! See you downstairs? You've missed cooked breakfast in the kitchen, but second breakfast will still be out in the Blue Room. We're like hobbits, we always have second breakfast. Byeee!'

As soon as she leaves – thankfully by the door and not by the window – the room feels empty. She's an absolute force of nature, and truth be told I already kind of adore her. As the least perfect member of my own family, I've developed a healthy appreciation for people with flaws. Beneath the chatter and the bravado, I suspect there's a sensitive soul who finds the world a difficult place.

I look around the room, now swathed in sunlight pouring through the windows. Dust motes dance in the air, fluttering in the vast space between floor and ceiling. The Persian rug beneath my feet is a little threadbare, and I see no signs of recent habitation other than a few abandoned items of women's clothing hanging in a huge closet.

By the time I've finished my morning necessities, I feel much better. I lie on the bed for a few minutes and message June, as promised, keeping her up to date on everything that's happened. I send a much smaller message to my dad:

Here and settled. I've drunk tea, and been to a pub. Love you, say hi to Mom and sis for me – more later xoxo

As I leave the room, I notice that even the door is made to an enormous scale – everything in this house seems to have been built for giants. In the hallway outside, I am greeted with more family portraits. There's an especially dour-looking dude with a big ruffed collar and a floppy hat at the bottom of the stairs, and I stick my tongue out at him.

'That's Earl William Carruthers de St George,' Charles tells me, suddenly appearing at the foot of the staircase. 'I don't think he's used to such disrespect!'

'I can imagine – he'd probably have me burned as a witch. But come on, he looks like such a bore! You can't tell me that when you were kids, you didn't do exactly the same? Or slide down this shiny banister? Or try and fit inside the suit of armour and walk around pretending to be a knight?'

'Pretending? How insulting! That's one of my ceremonial titles! And yes – of course. Many generations of Bancroft bottoms have slid down that banister – though you have to be very careful of the carved wooden pineapple at the end, or the family line could come to an abrupt and painful halt. How are you this morning? I believe you met Georgina?'

'I'd say "met" is too subtle a word... she's great, isn't she?'

I add the last few words partly because they're true, but also because he looks concerned. He moves in different circles than me, ones that are potentially less tolerant. Georgina looks every inch the posh young English lady, but her personality and behaviour seem quite out of synch with that role. Added to that the problems with discipline, and I can guess life hasn't always been easy for her dad.

'She is. It's good to have her home again, and now all I need to do is find a tutor who can tolerate her for more than a day.

She's actually very bright, and with adjustments the dyslexia shouldn't hold her back, but I think perhaps she worries about it more than she lets on, and there have been a few family issues, and... well, that's more than you probably want to know!'

'Not at all. I'm super-nosy. But whatever her deal is, I'm sure she'll be fine, Charles – being a teenage girl is never easy, and she'll find her way through it all. Not everybody has to be perfect, do they?'

He smiles at me, and his deep green eyes meet mine. He's dressed more casually this morning, in well-worn Levi's and a pale blue shirt that emphasises the golden tone of his skin. He is, to channel my own inner teenage girl, totally dreamy.

'That's very kind of you to say. Does it come from experience? Were you an awkward teenager?'

'I wasn't too bad as a teen actually. I was always a good girl, always wanted to please. But these days, I'm pretty much the family loser. I had a thing happen to me – not even that serious a thing compared to other stuff that goes on in the world – but it... well, it kind of derailed me for a while. I basically lost my mojo, you know?'

He reaches out and lays a comforting hand on my shoulder. His touch is warm, his fingers firm, and I resist the urge to lean into him like a cat looking for affection.

'I do. Mojos are rare and precious items, surprisingly easy to lose. Is that one of the reasons you're here? Searching for it?'

'Yeah. And to be honest, I think maybe it's working a little? Or maybe I've just been busy. I definitely haven't been thinking about the stuff that normally upsets me anywhere near as much.'

This is true – since I arrived in the Cotswolds I haven't had a minute where I've felt ashamed of myself, or worried that I'm a waste of space. I've felt plenty of other things – angry, confused, like I'd made a mistake by coming here – but never quite the same toxic self-loathing stew.

'Well, that's good news. Maybe I should build it into one of my business proposals,' he says, leading me towards the Blue Room. 'Bancroft Manor – mojo hunting a speciality.'

'Business proposals?'

'Yes. I'm trying to drag this place into the 21st century – if we're going to survive, we need to diversify our income streams. The upkeep on this place is tremendous, and my only other alternative would be to put the rents up for the villagers, which I very much do not want to do. I was in London discussing it all with a few possible backers.'

'Well, it's a beautiful place, and it has a lot of potential. With a little TLC you could use it for retreats, or wellness events – people love those! You could hold special weekends for different interest groups – people who are into gardening, wildlife, whatever. You could hire in some experts to run classes – art, photography, writing, that kind of thing – and offer it with luxury accommodation packages. Cooking classes could be a hit – people love learning how to cook, and your kitchen is big enough for a masterclass. You could hold events – it would be beautiful for a wedding or a party – or even hire it out as a movie location...'

I realise that he has stopped walking, and I am talking too much. He stares down at me, frowning slightly, and says: 'Where did all of that come from? I've been thinking about this for years and didn't come up with all of those!'

'Oh. Uh. The top of my head, I guess?'

'What do you do, Cassie, as a job, if you don't mind me asking?'

'I'm an event planner. Once quite high level, now more of "make sure the clown is booked and don't forget the piñata" kind of girl. But I can see exactly how fantastic this place could be – I'm sorry if I over-stepped.'

'Not at all. In fact, I'd love to hear more. Maybe we can

carve out a little time to chat? I know you're on holiday so I wouldn't want to impose, but perhaps dinner one evening?'

I feel a little rush of warmth, and know that at least some of it is spreading to my face. Sometimes being a redhead really sucks. I remind myself that he's not asking me out on a date. Men like this do not go on dates with women like me. He's just looking for some free business inspiration – which I am happy to provide.

'That would be amazing, Charles. I'm sure I won't come up with anything life-changing, but, well, glad to help.'

'Splendid, I shall look forward to it. Now, we'd better go through – Georgie will be swinging from the chandeliers.'

We walk into the Blue Room, and actually find her lying flat out on one of the couches, giggling at her phone.

'I'm watching a TikTok of a Great Dane getting chased around by a dachshund! It's hilarious, he's enormous but he's terrified!'

She wipes tears of laughter from her cheeks, and adds: 'How on earth did you old people pass the time before you could look at videos online?'

'We watched black and white movies and went to tea dances,' Charles replies. 'And Cassie isn't old, so don't be rude!'

'Soz – a thousand apologies, Cassie! I meant my dad – he's forty-four, so definitely old. He was probably around when they built Stonehenge. Have you been to Stonehenge? Shall I take you?'

'No I haven't, and maybe. I'll go for a shorter drive with you today, and see how terrifying it is first.'

The big table has been cleared of its newspapers and magazines, all of which are now in an untidy heap on one of the chairs. In their place is a gorgeous spread of breakfast food – flaky croissants, delicious-looking pastries, home-made bread, a thick slab of butter, jams and marmalades of every kind. I pour coffee and snag a cinnamon roll.

I perch in one of the window seats that line the room, and gaze outside as I eat. I'm met with a view of the gardens and the terrace at the back of the mansion. It stretches for miles, so much further than I could make out last night – a glorious landscape as far as the eye can see.

I am yet again completely awed by how beautiful it all is. Blue skies, no rain, and vivid yellow sunlight bringing the whole world to life. Everything looks so bright, so perfect. The grass is a vibrant shade of green, the terrace is perfect golden stone, the scattered statues almost seem to glitter.

I sigh out loud, and ask: 'Who does all of this? Who takes care of it? It's so gorgeous!'

'It's all me,' announces Georgie, feigning sadness. 'Child labour! He sends me up chimneys as well!'

'I'm often tempted to send you up a chimney,' says Charles, 'when the fire's already lit.'

He's sitting next to his daughter, her legs now across his lap, reading a huge newspaper. I love the fact that they have actual printed newspapers.

'But to answer your question, Cassie,' he continues, 'it's a joint effort. Georgie is a talented gardener, and does indeed help. My mother, Roberts, myself, we all chip in, and a couple of men from the village come up and help out too. It's quite an effort, but it's important – once you start letting grounds like this go wild, you're in trouble. We keep parts of it as natural as possible – there's a wildflower meadow, whole sections we let go to grass. It's better for the environment, and better for us – less time on the mower!'

It is, I can see, a mammoth job – and my mind briefly wonders if Ryan is one of the men from the village, or if the two of them avoid each other at all costs. Then I wonder what happened to make them dislike each other so much, because from what I've seen, neither of them is especially difficult to get along with. A mystery for another time, I guess.

'Well, maybe the gardening classes are the way to go, Charles – you'd get free labour as well as paying guests!' I say.

'Indeed. I rather suspect I've accidentally invited a business genius into my home.'

'Ha! Believe me, you haven't,' I reply. I turn to Georgie, and say: 'Right. I'm caffeinated and now capable of functioning. Should we start our magical mystery tour? Assuming that's all right with your father?'

'Please, take her,' he says, 'for as long as you want, I beg you.'

He clearly doesn't mean a word of it, but she playfully punches in the back of his newspaper anyway.

'Don't forget you have an appointment at two, though, Georgie!' he shouts as we leave.

'I *know*, Dad!' she yells back. She leads me around the side of the house, and towards a garage. Inside I see Charles's Jag, an ancient mud-spattered Land Rover, and a small electric Fiat 500 that is plugged in and charging.

'I'll give you a quick spin around the estate,' she tells me, 'and then we'll take the scenic route to the village.'

'As opposed to the ugly route?' I say, gazing at the picture-perfect countryside around me.

As we drive she provides a commentary, telling me that as well as the house and grounds, the Bancrofts also own the village of Campton St George. There used to be farms, too, she explains, but they were sold off because the family was 'land rich, cash poor'. It's interesting to imagine people like these struggling for money – they seem to be so golden.

None of this seems to bother Georgie, because she is seventeen, and boring things like finances and stability rarely concern seventeen-year-olds. There's clearly more to her than meets the eye though, and as we pass a large set of buildings all based around a yard, she goes uncharacteristically quiet.

'What's that?' I ask, pointing across her.

'Oh. That's the stables.'

'Right. Do you have horses?'

Maybe it's a stereotype, but I imagine they must. Georgina is the type of girl who should definitely have a pony.

'We used to, but not anymore. Do you fancy going for a pint?'

It's a very polite shutdown, but a shutdown nonetheless. I accept it, and say: 'Well, it's not even noon, and you're definitely not twenty-one, so I'm going to say no.'

'Twenty-one?' she says, sounding shocked. 'Do Americans have to be twenty-one before they can drink?'

'Yep. You can get married and vote at eighteen, though – and you wouldn't want to do either of those things when you were drunk.'

'True. But you're in England now, and we're allowed to drink when we're seventeen. We're much better at drinking than you Yanks, obviously.'

'That might be the case,' I reply, as my fingers fly over my phone, 'but us Yanks are just as capable of using google, so I know you're lying. The legal drinking age seems to be eighteen. Maybe you forgot.'

'Well, it was worth a try!' she says, flashing me a dazzling grin that immediately makes me forgive her.

'Was it hard to pass your driving test, with your dyslexia?'

'Um, yeah. A bit harder to pass certain parts of it – there's a thing called a theory test that was tricky. But I got some support and there are different ways I can learn. Plus, I know what all the road signs mean, so don't worry that I'll see one that says "no entry" and do the opposite!'

'I wasn't worried about that, I promise. But I am a bit worried about how fast you're taking these turns.'

'I do it every day. I could do it with my eyes closed!'

'Please don't.'

She laughs again, and carries on tour guiding. She pulls over and we follow a path to a beautiful steep-sided pond where, in summer, she comes to watch dragonflies skim the water and listen to the skylarks sing as she lies in the long grass. It sounds idyllic, and I have a flash of sadness that I won't be here by then.

She takes me to Marshington Grange, the next village over, which is a bustling metropolis compared to ours – there are two pubs, and a place for take-out. The main street is built of mellow yellow stone, and we stop for pictures. She looks amused as she perches on a garden wall and smokes. I guess I must look like a crazy American, snapping shots of a place that she sees as mundane. I always feel the same about tourists taking selfies in Times Square.

I get shown the local school – 'to be fair, they took over a year to kick me out' – and the church and the farm where Ollie Kerr lives. Ollie Kerr, I learn, is the coolest boy for three counties, and has mini-raves in his barn when his parents are away. Sounds like trouble.

Eventually, we arrive back in the village of Campton St George, and she parks the car outside the inn. It's interesting to see the village in full daylight during a working day, and the atmosphere is very different. The tea rooms are busy, the windows steamed up, and I assume that the bus brought visitors. The hair salon is also open, although it looks like no salon I've ever visited – it's basically one room inside a very old, very pretty cottage.

Inside, I see Orla wielding a dryer and chatting to an older lady in the chair.

'Huh – does Orla run the salon as well as the pub?'

'Ah, yeah – everyone here does a bit of everything. You never know where someone's going to pop up next. Cormac doubles up as a community police officer, and Mary Catherine does cleaning but also works as a delivery driver. Eileen just has the bakery, but she supplies loads of places. Everyone's always very busy here, and when they're not busy, they're having fun.'

'I see. And what about Ryan? Does he have more than one job?'

She grins at me, and pokes me lightly in the ribs.

'Do you fancy him? He's yummy, isn't he? I didn't notice that until a few years ago when the hormone soup kicked in, and then I was suddenly like, who is this God-like creature? Muscles in his muscles, the twinkly eyes, that accent... obviously he's way too old for me, but that doesn't mean I can't appreciate a fine example of manhood. He's single, too, so you wouldn't be treading on anybody's toes if you made a move.'

'I am not going to be making a move on Ryan!' I say, maybe a little too quickly. 'Or in fact any man.'

'Oh. Right. Are you gay? Because if you are, I can take you to some bars in the bigger towns.'

'No, I'm not gay. I'm just not interested in men right now.'

'Why?'

'None of your business.'

'Okay,' she says, shrugging, not at all offended. Clearly straightforward speaking is the way to proceed with Georgie. 'Shall we go and see Eileen?'

As we cross the road, I notice that Eejit is curled up beneath the Christmas tree, where someone has placed a bowl of water. He flicks his ears backwards and forwards when he sees us approaching, then slinks to his feet, trotting over and licking my fingers. I give him a scratch behind the ears, and he follows us to the bakery.

The small storefront is laid out with baskets of bread, pies and cakes of every description – tiny cupcakes in a rainbow of colours, slabs of lemon drizzle, gooey-looking chocolate brownies, and a spectacular carrot cake that's already down to one slice.

I love baking, and I love eating, and I love absolutely everything about this place. I must go into some kind of trance, because as I stare at the mouth-watering display before me, I hear Eileen say: 'Earth calling Cassie – is there anybody out there?'

'Oh! I'm so sorry! I think I temporarily slipped into an alternative universe there – 2001, a Cake Odyssey! Eileen, would it be greedy to buy one of everything?'

'It's been done before, so it has, but I wouldn't recommend it! How about I put you a little taster plate together? I have spare out back – the ones that came out a wee bit wonky – so you can try a few? And your usual, Georgina?'

We both agree, and Eileen bustles away to the back. When she returns, she has a box for me, and gets a cupcake for Georgie. She slides a couple of slices of bacon in Eejit's direction as well, and he gobbles them up. Looks like she's feeding all the strays, and more are on their way – a group of women who probably arrived on the bus are heading in our direction.

Eileen nods at us, and quickly bags up a nice-looking pie – a smaller version of the steak and Guinness I had in the pub. She passes it to me, and says: 'Looks like the rush is here! Be an angel and pop this round to Ryan at Whimsy Cottage for me, will you? He's elbow deep in the work, and I know he won't stop unless somebody makes him.'

We leave her to it, and move as a trio – woman, girl, dog – next door. It looks just as adorable as it did yesterday, and I feel surprised when I realise that I only arrived here the evening before. A lot has happened.

The door is open, and as we walk through Georgie shouts: 'Oi! You've got company, put your clothes back on!'

Already, after only a morning, I can see the difference in the place. Someone – Ryan, or the mysterious Mary Catherine – has given it a thorough scrub, and it's clear of dust and cobwebs. The musty smell has been replaced by one of lemons, and all of the furniture has been cleared out.

There's the sound of music playing upstairs, and within seconds I hear the thud of big feet on the steps, then Ryan jumps down the last few. He's dressed in shorts and a T-shirt, despite the cold weather, and a pair of paint-spattered steel-toed boots. His dark hair is wild, and he's brandishing a cordless drill. His face breaks into a big smile when he sees us, and I can't help it – I blush. Again. Helpless in the face of a man bearing power tools.

'Ladies!' he says, ushering us inside. 'I'm giddy with excitement to see you both – and am I mistaken, or is that one of Eileen's pies you have there?'

'It is. I am a bringer of joy,' replies Georgie, passing it to him. 'Do you have anything we can sit on or should we just go to the pub?'

'Nice try, whippersnapper,' he answers, grinning at her. 'But you know your da would kill me if I enabled any under-age drinking, now, don't you? Give me a second, would you?'

He disappears out through the back, and returns with two chairs he's clearly fetched in from outside. He wipes them down with a towel, and gestures for us to sit. I feel slightly strange with him hovering over above us, his bulk taking up so much of the room, but he solves that problem for me by simply sitting on the floor, his long legs spread out before him.

He pretty much inhales the pie, but makes sure to save a crust for Eejit. The dog settles at his side, his lean furry body snuggled into his thighs, and promptly falls asleep.

'So, how was your night at the big house, Cassie?' he asks.

'Interesting,' I say, casting a look at Georgie. 'Especially when I woke up this morning to find a stranger in my bedroom.'

'I'm not a stranger!' she protests, as she nibbles her cupcake. 'We're old friends now!'

'Really? We know nothing about each other!'

'Well,' she says, rolling her eyes, 'I'm Georgina. I'm a Scorpio, I enjoy long walks on the beach, listening to punk music, and smoking. My favourite food is spaghetti and meatballs, and when I grow up, I want to be an astronaut.'

I laugh at her tone, and it only encourages her.

'What's your favourite colour?' she asks.

'Green.'

'Favourite flower?'

'Um, roses. Maybe lilies.'

'Favourite human – fictional and non-fictional?'

'That's a tough one. In real life, it was my Nanna Nora. Fiction? Lots of them, but possibly a mash-up between Jo March from *Little Women* and Joey from *Friends*.'

'That would be a weird mash-up,' she says, frowning as she tries to visualise it.

I glance over at Ryan, who winks at me and says: 'How *you* doing?'

I try not to laugh, but it sneaks out anyway. It's a terrible impression, coming out more Irish than American-Italian. I see Georgie looking between the two of us, and wonder what conclusions she's coming to.

'So,' I say, deciding to move the conversation on a less flirtatious level, 'what's the plan then, with the cottage?'

He runs his hands through his hair, thinking. 'Well, mainly the place is grand – it just needs a good clean and re-decorating, new furniture, a proper spruce up. That was always the plan – I'll just be doing it a lot more quickly than expected. I'm hoping to have it sorted for you by the end of the week. Ideally, I'll be all done by Saturday night.'

'What happens on Saturday night?'

'It's Ryan's date night,' Georgie supplies, pointing at him in accusation. 'It's when our Irish lover boy turns on the charm, and no woman between here and Cornwall is safe.'

'Ach, you're exaggerating, Georgie – I've only roamed as far as Devon. What's a man to do? I have a lot of love to give, and I don't want the poor ladies of the county to go lonely now, do I?'

'Ah,' I say, remembering another of Nanna Nora's phrases. *'You're one of those feckless playboys, are ye?'*

I manage the accent well enough, and he nods enthusiastically.

'That's the idea, darlin', yes. But don't you worry, there's plenty of me to go around, sure.'

'Thanks for the offer, but feckless playboys aren't my type.'

'You don't know what you're missing,' he says, grinning at me in a way that leaves me in no doubt that he's right. I have no idea what I'm missing, because Ted is the only man I've ever been with. Thirty-seven years old and a born-again virgin. I know what June's view on all this would be, but I'm not sure I'm ready – for me, sex has always been tied up with love, and that's definitely not what Ryan is offering.

'Is there anything I can do to help?' I ask, changing the subject. 'With the cottage, I mean? I'm pretty good at manual labour.'

He nods, and looks around at the stripped-back room.

'Maybe, if you've a mind to. I need to get the wallpaper off upstairs, and the bathroom needs a good scrub, and a million other jobs. It'd go all the quicker with two pairs of hands.'

I find myself strangely enthused at the thought of getting involved – of doing something useful and positive, something that has a tangible result at the end of it.

'I'm up for it,' I say. 'I'll start with a couple of hours, maybe? I'm free now.'

Georgie gets to her feet and stretches. She ducks under the beams, and walks towards the door.

'I need to get back,' she announces. 'As Ryan knows, I'm too much of a lady to get my hands dirty.'

'You're as much of a lady as I am,' he retorts. 'You're just lazy!'

'That may very well be true – but I have an appointment with my counsellor at two. I think I've almost persuaded her that I'm beyond help, and am hoping for a resignation before

Christmas. Ryan, will you get Cassie back to Bancroft safe and sound?'

He agrees that he will, and she gives me an unexpected hug before she leaves. Once she's gone, Ryan stares after her, a sad look on his face.

'She likes you,' he says, shaking his head.

'Is that so hard to believe?'

'No, no, I didn't mean it like that – I mean she doesn't like many people. I know she seems all shiny on the surface, but the girl's been through a lot in her life.'

'I got that feeling. I know her mother isn't around, and she told me about the dyslexia. I picked up on some stuff at the house as well. What happened?'

He meets my eyes, and seems to be having some kind of internal debate.

'That's their story to tell, Cassie, and not mine. Now come on – let's be getting to work!'

TEN

The two hours turn into three, and then into four, and before I know it, night has fallen. Ryan has set up a cosy base camp in the living room of Whimsy, the floor lined with comforters and blankets from the upstairs cupboards. He assures me they're all being replaced as part of the renovation, and although they're perfectly clean, they are on the shabby side.

I lean back against the wall, and bask in the simple act of sitting still. A couple of little lamps are bathing the room in gentle light, and Ryan has cleared the hearth and got a fire burning.

I watch him use the old-fashioned poker, then slide the guard into place. The crackle and hiss of the coal is so soothing, and the heat is wonderful – but I'm not sure how capable I'm going to be of building my own fire. It looks a lot more complicated than I expected.

Ryan settles opposite me, and passes me a can of Guinness. Eileen called round with some sandwiches earlier, which we shared with Eejit, and although the surroundings are a lot less glamorous than Bancroft Manor, I feel a deep sense of contentment.

Some of it is the physical exhaustion. Nothing like a few hours of real work to make you appreciate the simple things in life. I've cleaned and scrubbed and taken endless trips up and down the stairs. Ryan was treating small damp patches with a product that involved him wearing a mask that made him look like a space alien, and I have worn rubber gloves for so long that it felt like peeling my own skin off at the end of the day.

We had music playing on his phone hooked up to a speaker, and sang along to Motown classics from our respective spots. He really does have an amazing voice, and during an especially intense performance of 'When A Man Loves A Woman' I had to stop what I was doing and just listen. He must be a hit on karaoke night.

He told me they were planning on ripping out the kitchen and replacing all the units, but now he's just going to do a 'cheat version' and install new surfaces and doors to save time. The whole cottage will be re-decorated, the thatched roof serviced, and the leaky shower fixed. Once he points it out, I see a stain on the downstairs ceiling where the water has pooled. Then there'll be new curtains, furniture, and bedding to install before I can move in.

This isn't exactly how I'd planned to spend my vacation, but I realise it's all worked out for the best. When I was alone in London, seeing the sights as a solitary tourist, that's exactly how I felt – solitary. Deep down I yearned for company, for someone to talk to, for someone to see those sights with. I think that if the rest of my trip had followed the same route, I'd have flown home early with my tail between my legs and Nanna Nora's nest egg wasted.

Since I arrived here, though, I've been swamped with company, and I've felt busy, engaged in both my own life and other people's. It's a good feeling, and I'm even relishing the aches and pains in my back and shoulders.

As I rest, my phone pings, and I see an excited message from June, asking for pictures of everything and everyone.

I send some of the ones I took earlier in the day, then look over at Ryan and ask: 'Can I take a picture of you for my friend June?'

'I don't know about that. I'm not sure I'd like to be, what do you call it, objectified?'

He gives me a wink to show he's joking, then flexes his arms so his muscles pop. I snap a pic, and quickly press send. It's around midday back home, and I know she'll be waiting. I laugh as her response lands.

'What does she say?' he asks.

'She says you look like a ride!'

'Fine taste, your friend June. If you're needing any more poses, just let me know.'

Once I'm off the phone, he holds his Guinness can up, clears his throat, and says: 'May the roof above us never fall in, and those gathered beneath it never fall out!'

I smile as I recognise the toast from Nanna Nora, and join him in finishing with a hearty: 'Slainte!'

We pop open our drinks, wait until the first hiss has passed, and glug away. It's an acquired taste, Guinness, but one I have already experienced many times.

He grins as I finish my first pull, and says: 'I didn't expect an American woman to be so fond of the black stuff there, Cassie!'

'Ah, well, that's because beneath the accent, I'm mainly Irish. My grandma was a Murphy, and my dad is an O'Hara. Guinness was one of the first drinks I ever took. My friend June and I stole a few cans of it from Nanna Nora's stock, and guzzled it down in the neighbourhood park. We were fourteen at the time.'

'And how did that end?'

'About as well as you'd expect. Black puke, terrible hangovers, and a ferocious telling off from my dad.'

'That sounds like fun. Be careful now, we don't want a repeat performance.'

I assure him I am much better at drinking these days, and we sit in companionable enough silence for a while, listening to the music.

'So,' he says, after a few minutes, 'what's your story, Cassie O'Hara? Why are you here?'

'Oh, I don't have a story, Ryan. I'm just on vacation.'

'For a month. On your own. Nah, there's definitely a story there – I can see it in your eyes. I'd say you had a bad case of the heartbreak.'

I laugh, and reply: 'Well, who doesn't? And I'm not about to tell you my life story, I barely know you.'

'Well now, that can only be fixed one way – how about we take a leaf out of Georgie's book. One question each that we have to swear to answer truthfully, as God is our witness.'

I narrow my eyes at him, and answer: 'Just one? And I get to ask anything?'

'Anything at all. Cross my heart and hope to die. Come on – we've bonded over the smell of cleaning products, woman! And Eejit wants to know, too, so he does.'

The dog is curled up in a cosy ball between us. He lifts one eyebrow at the sound of his makeshift name, and lazily thumps his tail on the floor.

'Okay,' I say, smiling at how peaceful he looks right now, this yipping beast that had me corralled like a sheep the day before. 'Only for Eejit though.'

I drink a little more, and take a deep breath. I rarely talk about my life to anybody outside it, and that is a very small circle – basically June and my family. I don't really have work friends, and never did – my whole social circle revolved around Ted, and when he left me, I never quite had the confidence to build a new one. But why shouldn't I tell him? I've felt ashamed and embarrassed about what happened for years, and maybe it's time to stop. Maybe it's time to try and make it an anecdote, and drain it of its power over me.

'Well,' I begin, feeling nervous but also a little exhilarated, 'I guess it's a story as old as time. Boy meets girl. Eighteen years old, and in love. Ted was his name, and we were together for a long time. All the way from college until we were thirty-four.'

I pause, and he says gently: 'So, most of your adult life, then, was spent with this Ted fella?'

'Yep, it was. We lived together, did everything together. And we were getting married. In fact we almost did get married, but he called it off at the last minute.'

'How last minute?'

'As last minute as it comes,' I say. 'Right at the altar. In front of our family, all our friends. I stood there in my wedding dress, looking into his eyes, and he told me he couldn't go through with it.'

'Jaysus wept! What a terrible thing to do someone – especially someone you claim to love. Why would a man do such a thing?'

He looks shocked, sympathetic and a bit angry all at the same time. He shakes his head, and adds: 'Ted was clearly a fecking eejit!'

I laugh and reply: 'That's exactly what my Nanna Nora said! As to why, I guess now, a few years later, I kind of understand. Even though we were in our thirties, we'd only ever known each other. We'd met too early, maybe, and dived in too deep when we weren't quite ready for it. I don't think he planned it, I don't think there was any intention to jilt me so brutally – he just realised, as he stood there, that it was wrong. That he wasn't ready. And maybe, by that stage he had his eye on somebody else... maybe, in his own way, he was trying to do the decent thing.'

'Well, you have a different idea of decency than me, Cassie. So was that it? The end?'

'Apart from a lot of weeping, wailing and downright begging on my part, yes. He moved out. He moved on. He got married this year, actually. And I... I guess I stalled. I put my whole life on pause, because I was so ashamed, so shocked.'

'Of course you were! This was the man you were expecting to spend the rest of your life with. The man you thought loved you and cherished you, who you trusted – and he abandoned you. Splitting up would have been tough enough at any time, but the way he did it? I'm surprised you're still standing!'

'Ha! Well, I wasn't, for a long time, Ryan. Then my Nanna Nora – the Murphy – passed away, and left me a little money in her will, and this is what I decided to do with it. Make my great escape. June told me it would be good for me, and she's never wrong.'

As I speak, I feel tears stinging the back of my eyes, and try to shake it off. It's not even that I'm sad about Ted anymore – I'm sad about myself, and how badly I let myself down. Ryan, clearly a man well-attuned to such things, immediately scoots across to my side of the wall. He puts a beefy arm around my shoulder, and roughly tugs me close until I'm nestled into his chest. He smells of paint and wood and hard-working man, and I feel like I could stay there forever.

'Come on, now, let it all out – it'll be good for you!' he says, dropping a gentle and entirely non-predatory kiss on top of my head.

I do as he instructs, and have a good old cry. He rubs my arms, and holds me close, and murmurs comforting words that make me feel safe. It feels good to have talked about it all, and to be consoled without judgement.

It also feels, I realise, as I start to compose myself, a little too intimate. My hands have crept around his torso, and I feel the hard, flat outline of his abs beneath my fingers, and his breath on my skin. I haven't been this close to man since Ted, and I'm not sure how I feel about it. My body says yes, but my mind says no.

I know I need to extricate myself and put some distance between us, but I like it here, in his arms. The fire is warm, the lighting is low, and the music is mellow.

Just as I think that, the song changes – and we leap from the end of Bruno Mars singing 'Just The Way You Are' to the brain-crunching opening to 'Firestarter' by The Prodigy.

I laugh into his now-soggy chest, and he says: 'Well now. That was a mood-changer, wasn't it? Serves me right for my mixed-up play-lists. I'll get us another Guinness from the fridge.'

We both have plenty left, and I suspect he is simply giving me the time to gather myself. He walks back in, passes me the can, and takes his earlier position on the opposite side of the room. I am grateful for the simple courtesy, and for the fact that despite his self-confessed playboy tendencies, he didn't take advantage of the situation. Grateful, and possibly a tiny bit disappointed.

'Thank you,' I say. 'For listening, and for being so... nice. You need to be careful, that kind of thing might ruin your image.'

'You may be right. But I have six sisters – three older than me, three younger – so I've wiped away many a tear in my time. You okay?'

'Yes,' I say firmly. 'I am. I feel much better. So, my turn – I can ask anything?'

He nods, but does look a little wary.

'What's the story with you and Charles? Both of you seem like great guys, but it's clear that you don't get on. Why is that?'

He tenses slightly, and says: 'Ah, well, that's simple enough, Cassie. Another story as old as time. He thinks I slept with his wife.'

I do a double take, and splutter out: 'What?'

'His ex-wife, these days. Leonora. Quite the one, is Leonora.'

'And did you?' I ask. 'Sleep with his wife?'

'Absolutely no, I did not. I may be a feckless playboy, but I have rules – and I don't mess with married women.'

'So why does he think that?'

He takes a quick drink, and his expression is hard to read.

'Probably because she told him I did. I don't know why – to hurt him, maybe, by saying she'd been screwing the help? Or to hurt me – because she tried her best, she did. She made no secret about what she was after, and it was quite the task to keep saying no. I have my rules and I stuck to them, but she's a beautiful woman. She wasn't used to being rejected, and she never quite forgave me for it. So before she finally left for her new life in the South of France – as you do – she put the boot in.'

I turn this information around in my mind, suddenly understanding the sense of underlying conflict between the two men. Charles's pride has been injured, and he blames Ryan for at least part of that.

'Haven't you, I don't know, just told him it's not true?' I ask.

'He's never asked. He just believed her, and I'll not be lowering myself to the lord of the manor and begging forgiveness for something I never did.'

Ah, I think. Charles isn't the only one who is proud. I shake my head, amazed at the stubbornness of them both.

'Well, that sounds insane to me, but what do I know? I'm just a visitor. I hope you figure it out anyway.'

He shrugs, and is obviously ready to change the subject.

'It's no big deal. Now, darling Cassie, I still have work to do, and I plan on doing plenty of drinking while I do it. It's time for me to get you back to the big house.'

ELEVEN

Dressing the Bancroft Manor Christmas tree is like a military operation, with Allegra as commander-in-chief.

The tree is positioned in the grand lobby, and is so tall we need ladders to reach the top. Allegra is moving between the ground floor and the landing at the top of the stairs, where she can gaze down from the banister, get a bird's eye view of matters and tell us loudly where we're going wrong.

It's actually a lot more fun than it sounds, and I'm now fairly used to hearing her cut-glass voice raised to screeching levels as she informs us we need 'more lights to the left, less robins to the right!'

The whole place smells deliciously of pine needles, and Roberts has set up a CD player with traditional Christmas songs to put us in a festive mood.

The decorations themselves were packed away in wooden chests, which themselves smelled of pine as soon as their heavy lids were lifted. Inside we found a charming mix of old and new, battered and pristine, and I look on in delight as each new treasure is produced.

Some of them are clearly Victorian, and I have no idea how

such delicate items have survived for all this time. I hold one of the beautifully painted glass baubles up to the light, admiring the way it seems to shimmer with an iridescent purple sheen.

'There used to be twelve of those,' Roberts informs me. 'But over the years, there have been grave losses. Now we're down to two. You can blame Lord Charles for the demise of three of them. He buried them in the vegetable patch, then dug them up the next day pretending they were ancient artefacts he'd discovered. Seemed very confused when they were in smithereens.'

He glances over at the man himself, who is on ladder-climbing duty and looking delightfully scruffed-up today – hair ruffled, a light golden stubble on his face.

Charles laughs, and replies: 'What can I say? I was going through my Indiana Jones phase. I think I stole all the Champagne and wine glasses and set them up in the barn as well, so I could pretend I was finding the Holy Grail...'

'You did do that!' shouts Allegra from her spot on the landing. 'And you almost blinded yourself trying to use a whip! Frightful child!'

'Thank you, Mother, for that glowing endorsement. Now, am I going to be stuck up here all night? How are the upper branches looking?'

'We need more!' Georgina cries, holding up extra baubles. They're a lot less classy than the Victorian glass, but in their own way just as sweet – obviously hand-made by children, little papier-mâché angels with huge, cartoonish smiles and pipe cleaner arms. Some look older than others, some have two wings, some have one, and a couple have lost both. I suspect this is a family tradition – that each child makes their own contribution, and they're kept and cherished for as long as possible.

Georgie passes them up one by one for her father to attach to the tree, and Allegra immediately shouts out that he needs to move them to a different spot. I spot a grimace from my angle, but he remains stoical and does as he is told.

It is a huge privilege to have been asked to join in with this particular Christmas ritual, and not one I'd expected. I wasn't at all sure of the etiquette of my stay in the Bancroft home – at the end of the day, I am merely a paying guest who got lucky with a spectacular upgrade. I'd assumed I'd be spending evenings in my room – now much warmer thanks to Roberts's interventions – to avoid intruding on their private time. But as I'm fast learning, this family might be posh but they are not sticklers for protocol.

This will be my fourth night here, and it's been a lot of fun. When I got back from helping Ryan a few days ago, I was invited to bake with Roberts in the vast kitchen. Despite my fatigue, I loved every moment of whizzing, mixing and pounding, and between the two of us we made light work of producing a small feast.

'I wonder if they'll be as good as Eileen's,' I'd said, gazing at a tray of apple tarts.

'Well, that would be expecting a miracle, Cassie,' he'd replied as we started to clear up, 'Mrs Devlin is in a class of her own. But these will keep us going for a few days, and I do find baking clears the mind wonderfully, don't you?'

Last night was pronounced Games Night, and the big table in the Blue Room was cleared to make way for a variety of board games – an ancient version of Monopoly with London streets and landmarks, checkers, Buckaroo, and sets of Top Trump cards ranging from sports cars to Lord of the Rings to dinosaurs.

It got quite competitive, with Roberts and myself the only ones not taking it very seriously. Georgie was vicious at all of them, Charles was way too invested in Buckaroo, and every time Allegra lost any of the games, she'd fold her arms across her chest and say: 'Well, it's because of my Alzheimer's, isn't it?' instead of admitting she was beaten. I guess if you're going to be stuck with a terrible disease, you might as well use it to your advantage. It didn't really work though, because Georgie would simply reply: 'No it's not! You're just crap at games, always have been!'

It is loud and raucous and disrespectful, and not at all how I would have expected the British aristocracy to behave. I wonder if it's this riotous round at Buckingham Palace?

Tonight, after a laid-back dinner in the kitchen, has been dominated by 'doing' the tree. I can tell that we're nearing the end when Allegra shouts down at us: 'All right, squadron, ready for the cherry on top!'

I assume she is simply using a turn of phrase – but no, there is an actual cherry. It's huge, made of shiny red plastic, and is passed from Roberts to Georgie to Charles. He hooks it by its bright green string over the very top of the tree, and it dangles there, looking absolutely ridiculous and yet somehow also perfect.

Allegra trots down the stairs, Charles descends the ladder, and Roberts switches on the plug. The tree is transformed, the multiple strings of lights sparkling and twinkling, playing through the glass baubles and casting red-and-gold glimmers on the various bows, plaid ribbons, miniature reindeers and draping candles that we have spent the last hour hanging.

It is absolutely glorious, and all of us are grinning.

'If you don't mind me asking,' I say after a few moments of silent admiration, 'why a cherry?'

'No idea,' Charles says, grinning. 'It's been there every Christmas I remember, though.'

'Your great-grandfather brought it back with him from his travels in Australia,' Allegra replies, her violet eyes misty. 'He'd spent a month there, in Adelaide I think, on business. Apparently cherries are a thing at Christmas there, and this was being used as part of a display in a shop. He knew I'd love it, and persuaded the shopkeeper to part with it. I was only a little girl, and thought that cherry was the finest thing I'd ever seen. I remember it very vividly, despite the fact that this morning, I got up ready to take Rupert for a walk around the estate. Rupert was the Springer we had before Jasper, Cassie dear, so you can see why I found it confusing when neither of them was there to greet me. Every day is a grand adventure now.'

And every day brings repeated loss, I think, imagining how awful it must be to face up to such pain every time you remember that a loved one has actually gone. Suffering that emotional shock over and over again.

'We should get a new puppy,' Georgie announces firmly. 'I promise I'd look after it!'

'We'll see,' replies Charles. 'Perhaps I'll put the word out in the new year, and we'll see if there's a local litter we can go and visit.'

She throws her arms around her father, squealing in glee, and despite her height and age, she suddenly seems like a young child again.

'Now,' says Roberts, clapping his hands together, 'I've got a buffet ready, as usual. I'll lay it out in the Blue Room, and we can reconvene in an hour for movie night. I'll bring the television through. The usual, I presume?'

Everyone nods enthusiastically, Roberts departing for the kitchen and the women heading upstairs, arm in arm. Charles and I are left, me still gazing in wonder at the tree.

'It's beautiful,' I murmur. 'Strange, but beautiful.'

'Ah. That should be our family motto.'

'What is your family motto?'

'Something awful in Latin to do with defeating your enemies even if you pity them.'

'Oh. Yeah. That does sound awful! What's your usual movie night film?'

I'm entranced with all of their beautiful family traditions, and not at all missing my own – whatever it is they're planning to screen, it will be a lot more fun than my wedding video, that's for sure. Even if it's the latest *Saw* flick.

'Every year, after we do the tree, we watch *Home Alone* together.' He shrugs and adds: 'It's a classic.'

I laugh out loud, because they've done it again – completely subverted my expectations. I'd thought maybe *It's A Wonderful Life*, or one of the old versions of *A Christmas Carol*. Instead, it's Kevin McCallister and his perilous paint cans.

'You have a marvellous laugh,' he says, gazing at me in a way that makes me both warm and self-conscious. 'It always makes me want to join in.'

'Thank you – and I seem to be doing a lot more of it since I came here, Charles.'

'That's good. All part of the Bancroft service. Now, as we have a little time, would you like to see the rest of the house? Maybe cast your professional eye over it?'

I nod enthusiastically, because I've been desperate for a tour. I've popped my head around a few corners, but didn't want to be too invasive – this place might look like something out of a Jane Austen novel, but it is their family home after all.

I follow him around as he displays room after room, all of which are named after colours, all of which are magnificent but cold. It's clear they're not really used, and need a spot of love – but the potential is vast. There are big rooms, perfect for dinners, and smaller rooms that could be set up for meetings and talks. There's one called the Amber Snug that is absolutely delightful – tiny by this building's perspective, but still large enough to hold a group of ten. Then he shows me the library, which has been better cared for – free of dust, walls lined with glorious mahogany shelving, tables and chairs scattered about for reading.

'This is gorgeous,' I say, walking around and surveying it. 'If you went for the writing classes, people would freak over this. You could sell packages to Americans for a small fortune.'

'That's excellent news. I wouldn't mind a small fortune. This is one of my favourite rooms, to be honest. I have an office upstairs, but this is where I come to let my mind roam free, unencumbered by thoughts of rents and taxes and bills and duty.'

I'd never really considered how much of a responsibility running a place like this would be. Normal household tasks in my small apartment take up enough of my time, and that's just for me. Charles is dealing with not only a historical legacy, but the burden of ensuring his family's future. That can't be easy.

I spot some books about ancient Rome on one of the tables, and ask: 'Is that what you're reading? You like history?'

'I do,' he says, running his hand over the covers fondly. 'The Indiana Jones phase wasn't really a phase. I studied Archae-ology at Oxford, and I would have dearly loved to pursue it as a career. I did, for a few years, and I had the time of my life on digs in Zambia and Greece. Never happier than when I was grubbing around in a trench, searching for the perfect pot. But then my father's health took a turn for the worse, and it was time to come home and grow up.'

'That's sad,' I reply, hearing the yearning he is trying to hide. 'Having to give up your own dreams like that.'

'Maybe – but that's all it was, a dream. And besides, this is hardly torture is it? By most people's standards I lead a gilded existence, so I don't want to complain. What about you? Did you always dream of being an event planner?'

I stroll around the shelves as we speak, stroking the spines of the ancient leather-bound texts, smiling at the odd unexpected romance novel crammed between the tomes. Allegra's, probably – or maybe Roberts's, who knows?

'Well, kind of,' I say. 'I mean, I know it's not a vocation like being a doctor or a lawyer, which my sister is. But I always loved organising things. Tea parties for my dolls, that kind of thing. I never really enjoyed going to parties, or being at the centre of my own, but I got a real kick out of making them happen. I love tending to all the little details that go into a great event. It's hard work, but seeing people enjoy it, seeing people have a great time when everything goes well? That's satisfying, in its own way. I might not save any lives, but I like to think I've created a few good memories.'

'I'm sure you have, Cassie – and as I'm learning as I get older, and as I see my mother decline, creating memories is quite a gift. No matter how big your home, how impressive your title, at the end of the day it's the memories that matter.'

He sounds melancholy, but then gives me smile so dazzling that it feels like the sun coming out.

'Come on,' he says, 'Enough lollygagging. I've saved the best 'til last – the ballroom.'

I'm not at all sure what lollygagging is, but I murmur the word as I follow him, enjoying the feel of it on my lips.

He leads us down another hallway, then sweeps open huge double doors, gesturing for me to go inside. At first I simply stand still and stare at my breath-taking surroundings. The room is vast, the high ceiling dotted with stunning chandeliers that sparkle into life when he presses a switch.

One entire side is made up of windows and doors leading out onto the terrace, with a to-die-for view of the landscaped gardens sweeping away into the distance. The night sky is so clear that every star looks like a jewel suspended in the air, and the moonlight turns the grass silver.

At the moment, it is largely bare, just a few items covered in dust cloths. I can tell that one of them is a grand piano, and when I pull another away I reveal an enormous cherry-wood cabinet that stretches almost as long as the wall it's laid against.

'Oh my goodness,' I mutter, looking around me. It might be barren right now, but its bones are perfect. I can already see it restored to its rightful glory, a string quartet in one corner, tables with crisp white linen, vases of lilies scenting the air. I can picture a wedding, a party, a formal event – it's big enough for anything at all. I can almost hear the chatter, feel the excitement, smell the flowers.

I walk to the middle of the room and start to spin, my arms out and flying, around and around and around until I'm giddy and giggling.

Charles stands and looks at me, a lopsided grin on his face as he watches my reaction.

'It's nice, isn't it?'

'Nice?' I repeat, letting my head steady. 'It's not *nice*. Hot chocolate is nice. Baby bunnies are nice. This is... *staggering!* When was it last used?'

'As a ballroom? Gosh, that's going back a while. I vaguely remember there being an event when I was a child, maybe about nine or ten. I'm not sure what it was for, but it was packed – family, friends, everyone we'd ever met. But I was a kid, and the grown-ups all seemed frightfully stuffy and boring. I was more interested in sneaking off to watch TV, but was forced to endure it for an hour, all smartened up in my own suit and tie. My sister Vanessa – she was a few years older than me – was a terror all night, dressed up like a lady but acting like a monster. She spent the whole evening sneaking wine, then swiped a decanter of port to take back to her room.'

He smiles as she says this, but it is another puzzle for me to ponder. Allegra said she'd found me in 'Vanessa's secret garden' when she first met me, but Charles also said he had no siblings. I can only imagine that for some reason, she is not part of their lives anymore. There are smatterings of framed family pictures in the Blue Room, but I haven't as yet fully examined them – maybe I'll find her there.

He seems to realise what he's said, and quickly changes the subject. 'So, this could work, couldn't it? For events?'

'Of course! It's wonderful. In summer, everyone could spill out onto the terrace. In winter, you might get snow and it would look amazing. Everything about it works. It just needs a little spruce up. I think you could even just use it for dancing – you have that show here, don't you, where celebrities learn how to foxtrot and tango? It's called *Dancing with the Stars* back home, and it's made the whole ballroom thing popular again.'

'Yes, it's *Strictly Come Dancing* here – beloved of millions. Maybe you've got a point. If we could get the funding, we could even perhaps hire some of the professionals, offer weekends with lessons and dance parties?'

'Exactly! I'd be up for that – I've always wanted to learn to dance, and I'd feel like a princess if I got to do it in a room like this.'

'I see. Well, Princess Cassie, your wish is my command – I happen to be an expert ballroom dancer. Part of my education. It's an excellent way to clear your mind, I've found.'

He takes out his phone, and frowns in concentration as he looks at the screen. I see a smile break out on his face, and he presses play. I'd expected some strings or something classical, but instead it's a song that I quickly recognise from one of the *Twilight* films, 'A Thousand Years' by Christina Perri. It's deliciously tender, and I feel a little thrill run up my spine as it begins.

I was technically way too old for the *Twilight* films when they came out, but I'd been sucked into the book series a few years earlier, when I was still clinging to my teens. The movies might not be considered cool these days, but they're a guilty pleasure, and I can't help feeling swept away in the music.

Charles moves closer, and tells me we're going to try a waltz, and that he's put the music on repeat so we have plenty of time. His right hand goes to my back, and he gently pulls me close. He takes my left hand, and places it up on his shoulder, and holds my other one high.

He grins at me, and says: 'We're in hold. You've made it through step one.'

'The trouble will start when I move,' I reply, laughing.

I've watched the show, and I've danced around on my dad's feet – though not for many years obviously – so I have a rough idea of what the waltz is, and know that it is done to counts of three. Still, watching it and doing it are two very different things.

'Just trust me,' he says, 'and follow my lead. I'm going to move my left foot forward, so you move yours back. Then sideways with my right, and we close the gap. So, left forward, side right, close, then the opposite. Whatever I do, you mirror it. It's a lot less complicated then it sounds, honestly. Don't forget to breathe!'

I look up into his deep green eyes, and wonder if breathing might be too tall an order. There is something so intimate about this, the way our bodies are pressed together, the touch of his fingers against mine. He is holding me firmly, so I feel safe and secure, and I am swamped with the delicious smell of his cologne.

He waits for the right beat in the song, and we begin. To start with I stare at my feet, and inevitably make mistakes. He deftly avoids stepping on my toes even when my foot is in the wrong place, and laughs off every error.

'Look up,' he says, 'not down. Or am I so unbearable?'

No, I think, as I lift my gaze. Far from unbearable. In fact he's gorgeous, and I am only human, and I am starting to feel warm for all kinds of reasons.

'That's it,' he says, as we move around the room, 'you're getting the hang of it. Just stay relaxed, and listen to your body.'

I'm not sure my body would be talking any sense right now, even if I was capable of listening to it. I am being whirled around an actual ballroom in an English manor house, clasped in the arms of a very handsome man, listening to incredibly romantic music. My feet seem to have disconnected from my mind and taken on a life of their own – moving with more confidence, trusting my partner, letting him guide me as we twirl together.

I'm not sure how long we are dancing for, or what time it is in the real world, because I am lost in this one – the world where love can last for a thousand years. My eyes are locked on his, and his hand is solid and present on my back, and our fingers are curled together – whatever our other worries, we are both lost in this one magical moment.

He seems to pull me even closer, or maybe it's me who moves – but suddenly there is no distance between us, and my face lies against his chest. I feel his touch move higher, flowing slowly and smoothly up my back until his fingers tangle into my hair.

We slow, settling in the centre of the room, abandoning the waltz hold, now barely moving – just the tiniest of sways, locked into each other's arms. My hands are around his firm shoulders, my hips against his, and I daren't look up. I know that if I look up, I will want him to kiss me. And if he doesn't kiss me, the spell will be broken – and I never want this spell to be broken.

I sigh, lean into him and the music, inhaling his scent and wondering if there is a way to make this dance last for the rest of my life.

'Hey!' someone yells. 'Look, it's snowing!'

I jolt back into reality, and my eyes blink rapidly, as though I'm waking up from a dream. It's Georgie, I realise after a few seconds. It's Georgie, and she is running excitedly past us and towards the terrace.

'Stop doing old people dancing, and come and see!' she shouts over her shoulder, so wrapped up in her own excitement that she doesn't notice how wrapped up her father and I are in each other.

He smiles down at me, his lips quirking in a question, and he slowly moves his hands away from me. I immediately miss them, and smile back. I wonder if he's going to turn into a stereotypical English gentleman and stammer an apology, but the expression on his face is more intrigued than sorry.

'See – I told you it was a good way to clear your mind. I don't know about you, but my mind was definitely not in control for a few moments there.'

'Mine neither. In fact I don't think I have a mind right now. Thank you – that was... special. My first real waltz.'

He laughs, and replies: 'I'm not sure either of is quite ready for the rumba! Come on, we'd better go and see what she's so excited about.'

We find Georgie outside, doing her own dance – arms extended, spinning and jumping, shrieking in delight at the thick flurries of snow that are pouring down on us. Her hair is already covered in it, and she looks genuinely overjoyed at this simple act of nature.

'Snow!' she yells. 'Snow snow snow snow snow! I bloody *love* snow!'

I look up, see the brilliant white of the snowflakes falling from the starlit sky, feel them fall on my upturned face.

Is any of this real?

TWELVE

Later that night, when I am tucked up in bed after a fun evening of snacks and screen slapstick, I do my duty and send a couple of pictures to my family on our group chat. One is of Charles, standing beside the decorated tree, an enigmatic smile on his face.

Suzie replies immediately with just two words:

MARRY HIM!

I laugh quietly, snuggled beneath the covers – it looks like I've finally done something that my sister approves of.

After that, I call June. It's just after five at home, and she is finishing up her work for the day. I've been wanting to talk to her for hours, because I am feeling odd. Not odd in a bad way – quite the opposite in fact. But something is stirring in me, something is changing, and I need to hear my best friend's voice. I am thrilled to see her face, and remind myself to speak quietly – Georgie is in the next room, and she might have a glass to the wall.

We spend a while catching up on her end of things, and I

smile as she carries her phone around with her, seeing the familiar backdrop of the home she shares with her boyfriend, Neil. It's a nice place in Brooklyn, and looks like an artist's hangout even though they both work in finance. Her fat ginger cat, Mr Potato Head, sits on her lap when she settles on the couch with a mug of tea, purring so loudly I can hear him all the way from England.

'So,' she says, grinning at me devilishly, 'you seem to be surrounded by hot men right now. Ryan is a ride, but so is Charles, in a totally different way. Ryan's all big and bear-like and he could probably kill you a woolly mammoth before he fixes your plumbing, if you know what I mean by "fix your plumbing".'

Her tone leaves me in no doubt as to what she means, and I reply: 'But he's a player, and unashamedly so. I'm not sure I need that in my life.'

'Well, then, what about Charles? My God, woman, he's like a fairy tale Prince Charming – and he waltzed with you! To "A Thousand Years"! I'm practically swooning just thinking about it!'

She pretends to fan her face, and I laugh at her antics.

'Seriously, Cassie, they're both gorgeous. What are you going to do?'

'I'm not going to do anything, June. This is just a silly conversation between friends, where we pretend we're fifteen again. I'm not arrogant enough to think that either of them is interested in me that way. Ryan is constantly on auto-flirt – he'd even try and charm Mr Potato Head if he got the chance. And the thing with Charles... it was just a moment, that's all.'

'Yes, but what a moment! Come on, be honest – you fancy him, don't you? And I think you probably fancy Ryan too... you've gone from zero to sixty in a few days!'

'Look, I'm not going to lie – they're both super attractive. But I'm sure I'm not their type.'

She shakes her head, and frowns as she speaks: 'Why not? You're funny and kind and hard-working and gorgeous. Why have you forgotten all of that about yourself?'

I think we both know why. I think we both understand the pathology of my lack of confidence, and even though I hate to admit it, it's not like all of the pain and injuries of the past few years have magically healed just because of one trip abroad. I'm here, thousands of miles away, but I carry it with me – I carry Ted's betrayal with me.

I've definitely been thinking about him a lot less, and even when it started snowing he wasn't my first thought – he usually is, back home, when the season changes and everything looks white and perfect and so much like our wedding day. But thinking about him less doesn't mean that it's over, or that I'm ready to throw myself back into the dating pool.

'I'm trying to remember all of that about myself,' I reply honestly, 'but it's not going to be an overnight fix. This has been good. This has been a distraction, and I do feel better – like I've changed course, you know?'

'I do know, and I think you're right. You're so lucky to have a best friend to steer you in the right direction! And okay, I get it – much as I'm enjoying your second-hand romance, I know this isn't anything permanent, and I know how risk averse you are. But perhaps you need to change course even more, babe – perhaps a fling with a handsome stranger might do you the world of good!'

'It might. But it might also hurt me. I'm getting stronger, but I don't think I could handle another rejection, just as I start to feel okay again. It's not worth it.'

'Really?' she asks, sounding incredulous. 'Are you telling me that you didn't enjoy your cosy night in with the hot Irish handyman, or being twirled around a ballroom by a prince?'

'He's not a prince, he's a viscount. And... yeah, I guess I did enjoy both of those things. But underneath enjoying them, there was still a layer of terror. Still that little voice telling me that I'm imagining any connection. Telling me that I'm not good enough.'

'You need to stop listening to that little voice, and listen to mine – you *are* good enough. For Ryan, for Charles, for Hugh Bloody Grant. You're good enough for anyone, and you need to start seeing yourself the way I see you, the way other people see you, instead of through your Ted lens.'

'What about my mom and Suzie lens?'

'Get rid of that, it's distorted too. Look, I'm not saying you should be thinking of a long-term commitment here – but would it do you any harm to at least loosen up and have a little fun? As a special Christmas treat to yourself? You deserve it!'

I sigh, and tell myself that she's right – but it's a big leap from my previous life to what she's suggesting. Maybe a Christmas treat to myself would be safer if it was something smaller, like a nice massage or some new shoes. Baby steps.

'Well, I'll see,' I reply. 'It's not like anything's actually happened with either of them, and it probably won't.'

'Yeah, okay – but don't rule it out, all right? Go with the flow – just like a waltz...'

'I will, I promise. And before you ask, yes, you'll be the first to know if anything changes.'

'Pinkie swear?'

'Pinkie swear,' I say, and we touch the phone to mimic the action.

'Good,' she replies, 'because Mr Potato Head and I plan to live vicariously through you for the next few weeks.'

We say our goodbyes, and I realise that I am not yet tired. It's like speaking to June has somehow swept me back into New York time, and I'm wide awake now.

I gather up one of the blankets, and wrap it around my shoulders, grabbing a pillow. I open the French door, and take a tentative step out onto the balcony. It's sheltered out here, I find, as I settle myself on one of the wrought-iron chairs. I wrap myself up, and smile as I see Georgie's impromptu ashtray – the jug is actually pale blue Wedgwood.

The balcony is at the front of the house, and as I gaze outwards I am again astonished to be in this wondrous place. The snow has settled, a coating of white on the gardens, sparkling in the moonlight. I can see all the way down the hill and to the village, a collection of shining lights and a distant curl of smoke from a chimney.

I wonder who the lights belong to – if the pub is still open, if Eileen is awake and reading one of her crime novels. If Eejit has found somewhere warm to sleep. If Ryan is up in his rooms, listening to music, or lying in bed and flirting with someone on his phone.

I wonder what they are all doing, how their lives are going, and how amazing it is that mine has intersected with them.

June said she wanted to live vicariously through me, and for the first time in years, it feels like my life is something worth watching.

THREE WEEKS UNTIL CHRISTMAS

'May peace and plenty be the first to lift the latch to your door
and happiness be your guest today and evermore'
Irish blessing

THIRTEEN

BANCROFT MANOR

I'm woken up the next morning by the not-so-subtle sound of a child, stage whispering: 'She's not dead, see? Her foot just moved – she's just asleep, you eejit!'

I risk opening one eye, and see two little boys and one girl standing at the bottom of my bed. All three of them have red hair and blue eyes, and the ruddy cheeks of kids who have been out in the snow. They stare at me intently, shoving each other around, and all jump back in shock when I suddenly sit up straight. A real Frankenstein moment.

We eyeball each other for a second, and then the girl steps forward. She's clearly the bravest of the bunch, with long, messy plaits that drape over each shoulder.

'Sorry we woke you up,' she announces, her Irish accent there but subtle. 'It was an accident.'

'Oh,' I reply, swiping sleep from my eyes. 'All three of you accidentally opened a closed door and came into my room, did you?'

'We did, yeah,' she answers, her tone defiant despite the fact that she can't be more than ten. I try not to smile – this is the kind of girl who lives with eternally scraped knees and doesn't take crap from anybody. 'Kind of. We're here with Nanny. She's doing the cleaning, and she told us to make ourselves scarce and keep out of trouble. This room is usually empty, and we jump on the bed.'

She sounds deeply aggrieved that I have deprived them of their fun, and I say: 'Right. Well, I'm sorry about that. Who's your nanny?'

'Mary Catherine, of course,' she answers, as though I'm the stupidest person on the face of the planet. 'Are you the American lady who fell on her arse in the puddle?'

I'm slightly taken aback at her use of the word 'arse', and see the boys' eyes widen in surprise. She's clearly out to impress. Also, exciting that my fame has spread – Cassie O'Hara, the incredible falling woman.

'Yep, that would be me. So what's your name?'

'I'm Molly. These are my brothers, Daniel and Patrick. My daddy's called Patrick too, but everyone calls him Paddy. He does the gardens, and mends the cars. Our mam is Sarah and she runs the tea rooms.'

I'm reminded again of how useful everyone here seems to be, and how busy their lives are. I wish I had a practical skill to offer, like being a high-flying nail technician or having a knack for repairing clocks.

'Are you going to get up?' Molly asks, frowning.

'I am, yes. And you're going to leave while I get dressed, and then you're not going to come back in and jump on my bed, are you?'

I put some steel into my voice, and see her battle with the urge to argue. She's quite a handful, this red-haired sprite, but eventually she concedes.

They're just turning to leave when a middle-aged woman rushes into the room, a feather duster in her hand and an actual real-life baby strapped to her chest in a papoose. He's all tufty red hair and pale skin, pudgy arms sticking out at right angles.

'There you are!' she says, sounding flustered. 'You wee horrors, I'm just after telling Allegra how well-behaved you've been, and then you disappear off and start causing mayhem!'

Her eyes fly to me, and she says: 'I'm so sorry – no manners, rascals all! I blame the parents!'

'I'll tell Mam you said that,' Molly pipes up, earning herself a stern look.

'You be sure and do that, so. And I'll have plenty to tell her as well, won't I?'

All three of them look suitably chastened by this threat, and I'm guessing that their mam is not to be messed with.

'It's fine,' I say, reassuring her – she looks like she has enough to deal with. Her hair is a faded red, much like my dad's, and she is clearly harassed. 'Not a problem. I'm Cassie.'

'Oh, I know that already – talk of the village, you are! I'm Mary Catherine, and this here is Connor. Another little monster to add to the clan.'

I climb out of bed, throw a robe on over my pyjamas, and go over to peer at the baby. He opens his eyes and stares at me in that unapologetic way that babies do. I smile, because he is adorable, and reach out to chuck his chin. He chortles at me, and I am smitten – totally in love. Forget Ted, forget Ryan, forget Prince Charming – Connor is surely the man for me.

'Can I hold him?' I ask, hoping that I'm not overstepping. A few of my old school friends have kids, and some of them were quite precious with them.

'Be my guest!' she replies, unhooking the harness and passing over the bundle. 'Six months old and already full of deadly charm!'

I gather him my arms, and he immediately reaches for my hair. He manages to clasp some of it in his chubby little fist, and chuckles – this is clearly the most amusing thing that has ever happened to him. I dance around with him, relishing the feel of his solid little body in my arms, lost in the simple pleasure.

'Ah, that's grand,' Mary Catherine exclaims. 'Look – he likes you. Will you keep him a while, do you think? I'm already behind... he's fresh changed and fed.'

I glance across at her, see that she looks stressed and a little desperate, and reply: 'Of course I will. We'll go for a little wander together, won't we, Connor? See what's what in the world?'

Mary Catherine stretches her back, and then turns to the other three.

'Now,' she says firmly. 'You'll be helping me, won't you? I've got three scrubbing brushes with your names on them!'

'They don't really have our names on them, do they, Nanny?' asks one of the boys, looking confused.

'That's for me to know and you to find out, Daniel Kelly. Come on, now.'

I find myself alone with Connor, who doesn't seem at all distressed by the situation. He's clearly a confident boy who is maybe used to being handed around – I suspect the phrase 'it takes a village' was invented for a place like this. It's a million miles from my own life, where I live in a crowded city but barely know a soul. Everyone here matters in a way that fills me with yearning.

I kiss Connor's fuzzy ginger locks, and slip my feet into my sneakers. I risk a quick glance in the mirror, and see that I am a disaster zone – bed head to the max, groggy eyes, and my second-best PJs with little yellow ducks all over them.

'Ah well,' I say to Connor in my best Nanna Nora voice, 'I'll be breaking no hearts, for sure!'

He sticks his finger up my nostril, which I take as encouragement, and we make our way down the grand staircase. I can see that Mary Catherine has been at work, and the wood is shining and smells of lavender polish.

I walk carefully down the steps, showing the baby the portraits on the way. He pulls a face at the last one – miserable old Earl William – and his lips start to wobble, as though he's considering having a cry.

'Yeah,' I murmur soothingly, quickly moving on, 'that's exactly how he makes me feel.'

I pause and admire the Christmas tree again, and have to keep a tight grip of the wriggling baby as he seems intent on grabbing handfuls of pine needles. Onwards into the Blue Room, and I find the usual assortment of breakfast delights. I grab a pastry topped with chopped apricots, and nibble it as we sway around the room – anything more complicated would be impossible. I have no idea how mothers manage this full-time.

Connor makes a bewildering range of gurgles and splutters as we move together, trying to communicate in his baby way. I realise after a few moments that we are waltzing – that I am waltzing this tiny creature around in my arms. Huh, I think, smiling at the memory of the night before. Connor is definitely someone I could love for a thousand years.

'Should we look at some pictures?' I ask, waltzing towards one of the walls. The pictures here cover a range of eras, the frames spanning the very old to the very new. I see a large sepia shot of days gone by, a collection of staff standing on the grand steps at the rear of the house, the presumed then-lord of the manor and his wife before them.

Everyone has that stiff and frozen look you see in old pictures. I gaze at them, laughing at some of the expressions and the formal Sunday best clothes, and wonder who they all were – not just the lord, but the staff. Cooks, maids, groundsmen – over forty of them. Each of these people were just as important in their own lives, even if they didn't have a title. They'd have all had dreams and loves and heartbreaks as well, and now here they are, frozen in time inside a gilt-edged picture frame.

I move along, jiggling Connor as he reaches out to try and touch everything we pass, and see one that I think is Allegra as a child, holding that silly plastic cherry in the air, gaps in her front teeth. Another on her wedding day, looking stunning in white, Charles's father handsome in a military uniform pinned with medals.

I see Charles as a little boy, with a Springer Spaniel who could be Rupert, and later a more modern picture of a dog that could be Jasper. I see the family at formal events, and yes, even one of them at a royal wedding. I'd love to snap a pic of that and send it to everyone back home, but I'd feel a bit like a snooping paparazzi.

There are some of Georgie when she was younger, but none of a woman who could be the mysterious Vanessa. There are, though, a few lighter patches on the blue-painted wall, where possibly pictures have been removed – or maybe my mind is getting carried away with itself.

Connor is starting to weigh heavily, perched in my arm, so I scoot him over to the other. He laughs delightedly, and nuzzles into my hair. We continue to wander, to look at the pictures, until a voice from behind says: 'Good morning to you both.'

I recognise it as Ryan's voice right away, because he sounds melodic when he's speaking as well as singing. I wonder how long he has been standing there, and for a split second I am self-conscious, aware of my shabby hair and less-than-stylish clothes. I push that down – it is morning, I am in my temporary home, and I am caring for a baby. It is fine to look less-than-stylish, and it's not like I normally look like a supermodel anyway.

I turn around, and see him walking towards us. He's wearing paint-spattered jeans and a white T-shirt that sculpts the shape of his muscles, throwing a heavy fleece jacket on the back of the couch as approaches. His thick dark hair is scattered with snowflakes, which answers at least one question about the day ahead – it is still snowing.

'That looks good on you, Cassie,' he says, grinning in that way he has. The way that makes me feel slightly nervous, like I'm fizzy inside.

'What? My rubber duck PJs?'

'No, darlin' – the baby. You look like a matching set.'

I glance down at Connor, who is now waving his chubby arms at Ryan. They are clearly old friends. He's right, I think – it's the colouring. This could be my baby, in another world. But that feels like a world that is beyond my reach now. I know I'm technically not too old to become a mother, but it still feels impossible – too many hurdles in my way. Maybe that's simply not for me, and that's okay, I tell myself – not every woman has to have children. Many women have successful and fulfilling lives without being moms.

Even as I repeat that to myself, even though I know it's true, I don't feel comforted by it – because I did always want this. I always wanted to have children. Ted and I were so busy establishing our careers that we always assumed we'd be able to do it later – except that 'later' never happened for us, and I was left alone with that shattered dream.

'You okay?' Ryan asks, and I assume some sign of these sad thoughts has shown on my face. He is, after all, a man with six sisters.

'Sure. Just tired.'

'Let me help there,' he replies. 'I'll take Connor while you get a coffee. Weighs a ton for his age, doesn't he? Going to be a rugby player, this one!'

He plucks the baby from my arms, spinning him around until he laughs. Coffee is probably a very good idea. Ryan joins me and takes a pastry, effortlessly juggling the child – he is a natural, it seems. Connor keeps making grabs for the food, and Ryan says: 'Are ye hungry, fella? Will I find you a snack?'

'Is that okay?' I ask, suddenly aware of my responsibilities. I told Mary Catherine I'd look after him. 'Can babies eat at this age? I... well, I don't know much about babies, really.'

'They usually go onto solids at about six months, but this monster started earlier. He's a big fan of the bananas.'

He finds one in the fruit bowl, and peels it halfway down. Connor grabs hold of the bit with the peel still on it like it's a handle, and immediately begins to smash his mouth on the top. It's a very messy and curiously fascinating process, and I laugh as he starts to slam it against Ryan's chest, covering his top in yellow blobs.

Ryan just laughs, not at all bothered, and says: 'Comes with the territory, doesn't it? Spend enough time around one of these wee creatures and you soon find yourself covered in all kinds of stuff. Some of it a lot less appealing than banana.'

I assume, from his easy familiarity, that those six sisters of his have maybe produced a lot of 'these wee creatures', and he is an experienced uncle.

'Are they all back in Ireland?' I ask. 'Your sisters?'

'They are. Some in County Cork, some in the city – Eileen mentioned that's where your nanny was from.'

'Yes. We're probably related, Ryan.'

'Sweet Jesus, I hope not!' he replies, winking at me. The man is a flirt machine, even when he's covered in squashed fruit and baby slobber.

'What's the deal with this place,' I ask. 'With the Irish? When I was at the train station Linda behind the ticket counter called it Little Ireland, and apart from the Bancrofts, everyone I've encountered has been Irish – some more than others. The kids – Mary Catherine's grandchildren – not so much.'

'Ah, you met the terrible trio, did you? You seem to still have all your body parts and nobody's drawn a fake moustache on your face, so they clearly liked you. Well, they were born here – but their whole family is Irish, as you've gathered. Everybody in the village is – it's a historic thing.'

'What do you mean?' I ask, frowning in confusion as I sip my blessed coffee.

'It dates back a few hundred years or so. Lots of poor Irish came over to England to find work at harvest time. Most of them just went back afterwards; it was a cycle. But here, a few of the single lads stayed – they had little to go back to, and from what I know, the people who lived in the big house back then were decent sorts who treated them well. So it started like that, but for some reason it grew. Brothers joined them, and sometimes brought wives, and babies were born, and over the generations more and more came over.'

'And that still happens now? With people like you? Why would people come now – Ireland isn't so poor anymore, there must be opportunities to keep younger ones there?'

He takes the now-destroyed banana from Connor's hand, and throws it into the bin. He takes a paper towel, damps it with water from the jug, and wipes his squirming little face clean. All done in a matter of seconds, with utter ease.

'Yeah, sure – in many ways it's a thriving place now. But the tradition was already set, you see. The links have got stronger over the decades. Everyone here has family back there, and sometimes they leave here and go back home, and sometimes family leaves home and comes here. Some of the young ones just come for a little while, for the experience. Some, like Eileen, came later in life. The reasons are different for everyone, but it shows no sign of slowing down – this is a good place to live. His Lordship and I might not see eye to eye, but he's fair with the rents, and always finds a spot for people, a job, something to make them feel part of the community, you know?'

I nod, and start to understand even more about the pressures that Charles is facing. He'd mentioned having to increase rents, and how much he didn't want to do that.

'And what about you?' I ask, feeling curious. 'Why are you here? You're not at the start of your life looking for an experience, and you're not at the other end either – how old are you anyway?'

'That's terrible rude of you, Cassie. In our culture you don't go around asking men their age!'

'That's a lie isn't it?'

'It is. And I'm thirty-nine if you must know. As to why, well, that's a story for another day – I wouldn't want to spoil my man-of-mystery image now, would I?'

I screw my eyes up at him, and say: 'Are you on the lam? Are you wanted by Interpol for a daring art heist, and hiding out in the English countryside?'

'Maybe I am, darlin' – all part of the mystery!'

At that exact moment, Connor belches loudly, and spits up a chunk of banana onto Ryan's smirking face. Instant karma, right there. He remains stoical while he wipes it off, but I find the whole thing deeply amusing, and laugh for a very long time.

'Ha! Not so much a man of mystery now, are you, Ryan Connolly?'

'If that's even my real name...'

We're still laughing when Charles walks into the room, and I feel suddenly strangely guilty. Their drama is exactly that – theirs, not mine – but his presence still makes the atmosphere palpably different. It's frostier in here than outside in the snow, and I see both men transform before my eyes. Apart, both are easy-going in their own unique way – together, they feel like a ticking time bomb of icy politeness.

Charles's gaze takes everything in, including the jacket that Ryan had oh-so-casually flung onto the furniture – designed, I suspect, purely to annoy Charles if he happened to walk in.

'Good morning, Cassie,' he says, sounding deeply formal. 'And to you, Connor,' he adds, walking over to pat the baby's head – Connor is, after all, irresistible.

'Ryan. What can I do for you?'

The words are fine, but the tone implies that he has no desire to do anything for Ryan other than beat him to a pulp. These two should be fighting a duel or something – they have the setting for it, I think, gazing out at the snow-covered grounds.

'It was actually Cassie I was wanting to see, Your Lordship. Due to my impressive skills, and the fact I had a helping hand, Whimsy is pretty much done. Still smells of paint, but looking grand.'

He digs in his pocket, balancing the baby on his hip, and passes me a set of keys.

'Better late than never,' he says, as I accept them. 'Let me know when you're moving in, and we'll all meet you in the pub, give you a proper village welcome.'

I nod, and thank him, and he passes me Connor. He gives us both a nod, and says he has to be on his way. The temperature goes up a few notches as soon as we hear him drive away – you can almost see Charles relax.

'So,' he says, making himself a plate and pouring a cup of tea, 'that's good news, I presume?'

'Yeah, I guess,' I reply, shrugging. Truthfully, part of me will be sad to leave this place – to leave the beautiful gardens, the historic building, and, more importantly, its eccentric residents.

'You don't have to go, you know,' he adds, speaking quietly. He looks uncertain, which isn't an expression I've seen on him before.

'What do you mean? I paid to stay in Whimsy, and I'm guessing the rental fee on this place would be considerably more!'

'I simply mean that if you'd like to, you'd be welcome to spend more time here. Georgie has enjoyed having you around, as has Allegra. And, just possibly, so have I.'

He gives me a small, sheepish grin as he adds the last part, and it's very cute – like he's admitted a weakness and is now concerned as to how the world will see him. I am tempted, but I also know that this trip was about me learning how to be happy alone – not about living a fairy tale fantasy in the English castle.

'How about I stay tonight?' I respond, untangling Connor's vice-like grip from my hair. 'It's very kind of you to offer, but I don't want to overstay my welcome. I'd be more than happy to carry on discussing your projects with you, though. I know you're looking for investors, and I have a few ideas about how to make this a more attractive proposition for them.'

There is a flicker of disappointment, but being the kind of man he is, he hides it almost immediately. I wonder how hard it must be to constantly be on alert, constantly watching what you say and how much of yourself you let creep out into the world. I guess it's part of his upbringing, this stiff upper lip – his normal way of functioning. It must be exhausting, especially when you'd rather be knee-deep in mud on an archaeological dig.

'That sounds marvellous, Cassie, and is very much appreciated. Now, I have to take my mother for a hospital appointment this morning, but perhaps I could ask Roberts to prepare us a celebratory dinner? A kind of last supper? What's your favourite meal?'

I feel like I should say something location-appropriate, like pheasant or quails' eggs or caviar, but in the end I shrug, and say: 'I'm a sucker for a good mac and cheese.'

He laughs, and as ever the simple act of being genuinely amused transforms him.

'Mac and cheese it is!'

FOURTEEN

The next afternoon, Roberts gives me a lift down to the village with my luggage. The snow is still falling, thick and heavy, and every country lane we drive through is a picture of rural winter charm. Bright-eyed birds perch on thick white boughs, the fields spread out around us, and the village itself is transformed.

It was rain and mud and grey skies the night I arrived, and it still looked gorgeous. Now, it is like something from a Christmas card. The tree sparkles snow, and the warm glow coming from the windows casts a golden shimmer over the central square. Everywhere I look I see tiny touches of beauty – the strings of lights bright against the darkening sky, the mellow stone of the buildings dusted with white, the cobbled streets coated with fresh snow. It is perfect, and I sigh out loud. Roberts quirks one amused eyebrow as he parks outside the inn.

'It is rather pretty, isn't it?' he asks.

'Beyond pretty,' I reply, smiling. 'Thank you – for the lift, for the hospitality, for the baking. I've had a wonderful time.'

'The pleasure was all ours, Cassie. It's been a delight having someone new in the old place. Allegra seemed much better for it, too – it gave her the incentive to strive.'

'How was the hospital appointment?'

'As well as can be expected. Unfortunately it's a one-way street, and there will be many bumps in the road ahead for her.'

'I know, and I'm so sorry. But at least she has you, Roberts.'

'This is true,' he says, climbing out of the Land Rover in a sprightly way that belies his obvious age. 'She will always have me.'

There is nothing inappropriate in his tone, nothing scandalous, but I do wonder about his feelings towards the lady of the house. Theirs is much more than a mistress and servant relationship, and he seems totally devoted to her. It might never develop into romance – that is not the way people like these behave – but it is very clearly, in its own way, love.

He hauls my bags out of the car, waves to a few passing villagers, and toots his horn as he leaves. I roll my cases across the square, struggling to fight my way through the inches of snow, relieved when Ryan appears to help me.

'Thank you!' I say, as he hoists the biggest one up effortlessly.

'You're welcome. I could never resist a damsel in distress.'

I snort with laughter, and together we make our way down the terrace to Whimsy. Smoke is curling up out of her chimney – I have decided that Whimsy is very much a 'her' – and the little front yard is blanketed in snow. I pause outside, and smile. She looks absolutely perfect.

Eejit emerges from the bottom of the path, the one that leads to the little flowing river and its golden stone bridge, and licks my fingers. I scratch his ears and say: 'Hey there, boy. Want to come into the warm?'

I fit the key in the lock, and we step inside. I have now seen this place in three separate incarnations – the dank and miserable first night, then the midway part of the process when I helped Ryan with his work. Now, she looks different again.

The fire is roaring behind its guard, and the heat it throws off is a delight. The new couch is in place, a simple shade of very pale blue, resting against the newly painted white walls. There are fresh flowers in a vase on the mantelpiece, and on either side is a gorgeous scarlet poinsettia in a pot that gives the place a Christmassy feel. Everything is fresh and cosy, exactly how I'd imagined it would be when I first arrived.

The tiny kitchen is gleaming, and a gorgeous looking layer cake has been left out for me. I smell coffee, and see walnuts, and know that it will taste as good as it looks. Next to it, beneath a dish towel, I see a loaf of soda bread – my absolute favourite.

'I assume this is from Eileen?' I say, taking in the bottle of Merlot next to it, and wondering if it would be anti-social to simply spend my first night here in glorious solitude.

'The cake and bread, yes; the wine is from Cormac and Orla, though they're hoping to see you in person. Orla says she has your stir-fried octopus in raspberry sauce ready to go, whatever that means. Do you want to see upstairs?'

I nod eagerly, and we leave Eejit lounging in front of the fire, looking like he's always been there. The bathroom has been fitted out with a new shower curtain and towels in matching shades of pale yellow, and the tub now comes complete with a giant bottle of rose and geranium scented bubbles I cannot wait to soak in.

Ryan leads me across the landing towards the bedroom, and I freeze on the spot when I see what he's done with it. He lurks behind me as I gaze around, speechless at the sight. The entire room has been painted in the most gorgeous shade of pale green, and the big bed with its brass frame is coated in comforters and blankets and cushions, all in other shades of green. I feel like I'm inside a fairy tale forest – and the absolute best part is the flowers.

The wall the bed rests against is covered in an exquisite painted garland of flowers – lilies and roses, I see, as I move closer. Their leaves and stems and petals intertwine, an endless flow of beauty. Reds and pinks have been used to pick out spots of colour, and the whole thing creates a floral arch that soars over the bed.

I reach out and touch them, my fingers tracing the fine lines and perfect petals, not quite believing what I'm seeing. It's like one of the frescos you see in old Italian buildings, but made entirely of blooms.

'Ryan, this is amazing!' I say, turning around to find him watching me. 'I don't think I've ever seen anything so beautiful! Who did this?'

He shrugs, but looks pleased – almost embarrassed at being caught out in such an act of kindness.

'I did,' he replies simply. 'You said your favourite colour was green, and these were your favourite flowers. So, I just thought...'

It is such a nice thing to have done that I can't help myself – I throw my arms around him and hug him. His hands go to my waist, and he lifts me off my feet for a second. I look up into his eyes and say: 'That is possibly the kindest thing anyone has ever done for me.'

'Well, you've led an altogether sad life if that's the case, Cassie, but I'm glad you like it.'

'I don't just like it – I love it!'

I realise that I am still in his arms, and he grins at me playfully. He pushes a stray lock of hair back from my face and says: 'You'd better be moving on, darlin', or I'll start to think I'm irresistible...'

There is a moment – a split second – where I wonder what would happen if I didn't move. Would we make love beneath the flowers?

The thought of it is enough to make me blush, and I quickly disentangle myself from him. I stick my hands into my pockets to make them behave, and say: 'It's truly beautiful, Ryan. You're very talented. Are you an artist as well as the village's Mr Fixit?'

'I am many things, Cassie, and had a whole different life before this one.'

There's a story there, but the closed down look on his face tells me it's not one he's eager to share. In fact the mood darkens slightly, and I decide to lighten it back up.

'But what will happen when the next people come to stay? What if they have really serious hay fever, or they hate roses and lilies?'

'I suppose I could paint it again. Or maybe I'll have a word with His Lordship, ask him to make it part of the booking process to ask what their favourite flowers are! Now, will you be coming to the pub with me for a quick celebratory pint or seven?'

'Maybe a pint or two,' I say firmly. 'I know I don't have far to walk home, but the roads are slippery, and I have a bad track record for staying on my feet in this place. Just give me a minute.'

He nods and disappears off downstairs. I go into the bathroom, and splash cold water on my face – because I most definitely need it. I run my fingers through my hair to smooth it down, and smile at myself in the mirror. I look dishevelled but happy, and decide that's a good look on me.

Within minutes we are tucked away in the pub, with a big corner table, pints of Guinness, and packets of potato chips called Taytos laid before us. The sides of the packs have been ripped open and spread out to create little foil plates, so everyone can help themselves.

The musicians aren't here tonight, but the place is still busy, bustling with happy energy as people eat and drink and chat. I hear a mix of accents – some thicker than Nanna Nora's, some just a subtle twang, and it all makes a lot more sense now Ryan has explained the history of Campton St George and the generations-old links between the Bancrofts and Ireland.

Various people come over and introduce themselves,

including Connor's super-pretty mother, Sarah, and I soon realise that everybody here already knows who I am.

Eventually Eileen joins us, smelling of sugar and vanilla, which is the very best perfume a woman can wear. Her grey hair is clouding around her face, and her sparkling blue eyes are merry as she sits.

'Be a good boyo and get me a pint,' she says to Ryan, who quickly obliges. 'I'm terrible parched. Started on my Christmas orders today and I'm ragged with it all.'

'I could always help,' I offer. 'I'm good in the kitchen.'

She pats my hand and says: 'Sure, and that is kind of you. I might take you up on it. So. How was your stay at the big house?'

'It was interesting, and fun, and like nothing I've ever experienced before.'

'Well now, that's good news. Bit of come down, being in Whimsy, is it?'

'Gosh no! It's gorgeous and I already feel at home. Ryan did such a wonderful job, and he even painted my favourite flowers on the bedroom wall. Tonight I'll be sleeping beneath roses and lilies!'

'Did he now? Your favourite flowers?' she says, her eyes narrowing a little. 'That's new behaviour, there!'

'Should I be worried?'

'No, no. Ryan has his rules, and I should imagine you're covered by them.'

The man himself returns laden down with more drinks, and more bags of Taytos gripped in his teeth. He settles back in, and Eileen nudges him.

'I was just telling Cassie here about yer rules, Ryan. The ones about the women.'

He pauses, drinks the creamy head of his pint, and sighs in pleasure. There's a wisp of cream left on his top lip, and my cheeks flame as I imagine kissing it off. What is wrong with me?

I'm turning into some kind of sex demon. I imagine what June would say to that – she'd say that I've gone without for so long that I have a lot of that energy stored up, desperate to escape.

'Ah. My rules. Well, there'd be three main ones, Cassie. The first,' he says, counting them off on his fingers, 'is no married women. Too complicated, and too wrong on all levels. Two, nobody from the village, because that could get messy. Three, nobody I suspect I could fall in love with.'

'What?' I repeat, frowning. 'But why not? Isn't that kind of the point of dating? To find someone special?'

Eileen snorts, and says: 'In Ryan's case, he finds someone special every weekend! They stay special right up until Sunday!'

She pauses, and adds: 'Sure I've just realised, Ryan, it's actually a Saturday – why are you even here? Don't you have hearts to be breaking?'

'Even a feckless playboy needs the occasional night off, so he does,' he replies, laying the accent on thick and winking at me. 'And besides, I wanted to make sure Cassie got settled.'

Eileen looks at him suspiciously, and he throws a crisp at her face. I giggle out loud, because they are quite the double act.

'Thank you for the cake, and the bread,' I tell her. 'Soda bread is the stuff of dreams for me. I used to make it with my Nanna Nora, which was almost as much fun as eating it!'

'No problems, Cassie, you're very welcome. So, your Nanna Nora then – she was from Cork, you say?'

'Yes. As far as I know. She'd never really talk about it though, and didn't seem to stay in touch with family either.'

She thinks it over, and replies: 'You should talk to my cousin Moira. She's one of them yokes, what do you call them? Gynae-cologists?'

I can tell from her barely repressed grin that she's joking with me, but I still say: 'Genealogist?'

'The very fella! Traces family trees for people all over the world, she does. Makes a good living from it too, what with all the Americans keen to connect with their roots. Maybe if you could get me some basics, like her birthday, she could find out a bit more for you?'

I nod, turning it over in my mind. I loved Nora so much, and missing her has been a constant dull pain ever since she passed. Maybe this could be a way of feeling closer to her, and I know my dad would probably be interested.

'I'm off to Cork for Christmas,' Ryan adds. 'For my annual pilgrimage to the rural hovel.'

'Hovel my arse!' interjects Eileen. 'Your sisters are all very respectable married women, and you'll be staying at Sinead's place – it has five en-suite bedrooms and a hot tub!'

He laughs, thoroughly caught out, and says: 'All right, it's not so bad, I'll admit it. Plus I get pampered, like the family prince come home from his travels. I'll be fat as Santa by the time they're finished with me.'

He rubs his perfectly flat stomach, and I can see how fond he is of them. I wonder why he's here, across the sea, when he could be at home with people he loves.

'See how you go, Cassie,' he says. 'If you fancy it, you could come over. It's a short plane ride away, and it seems a shame to have come all the way from New York and not see something of the place now, doesn't it?'

'I'll think about it. And I'll talk to my dad, see what else I can find out about her.'

He's right, though. It does seem like a waste not to take a quick detour to Ireland, because I'm not likely to be so close again. Before long, I'll be home, back in New York, back in my real life. Living in my little apartment, going to work, trying to find a place for myself in a world that seems entirely made up of couples. I fight back a sigh, because the thought does not fill me with joy.

I don't have time to go down that melancholy rabbit hole,

because Cormac decides that it's time for some dancing. He announces this after he rings a bell that's placed over the bar, and everyone whoops and claps as the room fills with what Nora always used to call 'fiddle-di-dee' music – the kind of fast-paced tunes that have your feet tapping and your heart rate pumping. It blasts out of speakers until the whole room is shaking with it.

Everyone gets up and starts doing what I can only describe as a lively and totally chaotic jig. I look on as people of all ages descend on the centre of the room, which Orla has cleared of chairs, and start to dance. There are children and teens and parents, all the way through to one man who looks so old I fear for his life as he swirls and hops.

Ryan grabs hold of my hands, and tugs me towards the madness. Eileen is with us, her earlier fatigue forgotten as we all join in.

I don't know if it lasts for ten minutes or an hour, because there isn't any way to keep track of time – all I can try and do is keep up. We whirl around, linking arms, clapping our hands, swapping partners, all the time to the frenzied beat of the music. Everyone is laughing, a few people spin off into chairs and the walls, and it is absolutely insane – a primeval celebration of simply being alive.

We end up slumped back in our original seats, glugging our drinks and laughing. I wipe sweat from my eyes, and know that my hair is now just a big, messy tangle of red around my over-heated face. I suck in air, laugh as Eileen fans herself with a beer mat, and glance over at Ryan. He was already watching me, and he raises his pint glass in my direction. I lift mine, clink it against his, and we both say 'Slainte!'

I am both exhausted and exhilarated, and can't stop laughing at what just happened. It's a far cry from my romantic waltz in the ballroom, but in its own way, just as perfect.

FIFTEEN

My first night in Whimsy cottage is also perfect. I am blissfully happy as I lie in bed, stretching and luxuriating in the space. Before I came up I ate soda bread slathered in butter – because some kind soul had also stocked the fridge with basics – and poured myself a glass of wine.

I did a quick video call with June, where she laughed at me for most of it, especially when I told her I might be a bit 'ossified'. I messaged my dad asking for some info on Nanna Nora, and when I finally made my way upstairs, I knew I was going to sleep well – my insomnia seems to be a thing of the past, and I was filled with a deep sense of everything being right in the world.

That lasted until about two a.m., when I was woken up by a noise outside. I'm from New York, and usually go to sleep to the urban lullaby of sirens and breaking glass, but here in the English countryside it's usually quiet and peaceful – apart from the occasional hoots of owls or the rain pelting against your windows. I sit upright and rub my eyes, not at all sure what woke me until I hear it again.

It's a bark, I realise, and the sound of furious scratching

against my front door. I drag myself out of the warmth, and pull the drape back. Sure enough, outlined in moonlight, I see Eejit in my snow-covered front yard.

I make my way downstairs, and as soon as I open the door he slinks past my legs. He's coated in snow, and when I touch his fur he is icy beneath my fingers. I grab the dish towel and give him a quick rub dry, which he endures stoically, his pale blue eyes seeming to say: okay, I'll let you do this, crazy human, but I am descended from wolves, and this is an affront to my dignity.

'You okay, boy?' I ask afterwards, scratching his ears the way he likes. 'You want a snack?'

I pour him a bowl of water, and come up with a pack of chicken slices from the fridge. He devours it all, and I wonder if he'll leave again now. I've been told that he never spends the night in anybody's house, despite multiple offers, so I expect he'll turn tail and run. Instead, he simply gallops up the stairs, leaving me with an empty packet of cooked meat and cold feet.

I shrug and follow him, and smile when I see him curled up in a ball on my bed. I end up crawling in around him, not caring one jot that he'll be making the sheets damp. I climb under the comforter, and feel the solid lump of his body pressed against my legs.

'Goodnight, Eejit,' I say, flicking off the bedside lamp. 'Sweet dreams, pal.'

I'm out like a light, and when I wake up, he's licking my face, his tail wagging furiously as I finally start to move. He yips at me, clearly wanting me to get up, and I find myself staring into a pair of insistent blue eyes.

'Okay, okay, I get the message,' I say, pushing him gently aside as I extricate myself from the comforter. I have a moment of confusion where I reacquaint myself with the room, looking behind me and smiling again at the beautiful arch of painted flowers over the bed.

We make our way downstairs, and he heads into the kitchen, sniffing hopefully at the fridge.

'Right. Breakfast. You may be out of luck.'

I rummage around in my supplies, and find nothing especially dog-like to give him. He ends up with a small chunk of cheese and a piece of soda bread, which might not be recommended by vets but seems to keep him happy. After that, he goes to the door and scratches it.

'You're off then, are you? Typical. Worm your way into my bed, then leave without a word the next morning... you'll probably ghost me now, won't you?'

He shoots away, off to who knows where. I look out at the peaceful village square, and a quick sniff of the air tells me Eileen is already up and about next door, baking bread even though it's a Sunday, and I wonder where Ryan is. Maybe he's in his room upstairs – maybe his room even adjoins mine. I could knock on it in code, like I do with June.

I close the door against the cold, and realise that I have no idea how to start the fires up – I really must ask for a tutorial or I might freeze to death.

I take a quick shower, get dressed, and have a tiny slice of coffee and walnut cake. The breakfast of champions.

Charles and I have exchanged numbers, and I ask if he's up for a chat – a business-type chat. He replies immediately that he is, and says that he'll pick me up later. I realise that I am actually quite excited to try and help, that my mind has been working away in the background, coming up with plans and suggestions. I feel a sense of enthusiasm that I know I've been lacking in my actual workplace, and suspect that my reduced hours and demotion back to children's parties probably aren't just down to the economy – they're also down to me.

I used to be a dynamo, full of energy and professional pride, but over the last few years that has waned. It's hard to be a dynamo when inside, you feel like a failure. Losing Ted in such a dramatic way made me question everything about myself, it made me see myself as unworthy, and some of that defeatist attitude has definitely bled into my work.

No more, I think, as I grab my coat and wander around to Eileen's. I will go home filled with new ambition. And possibly cake.

I find her fist-deep in kneading, her blue apron covered in flour, singing along to 'That's Amore' by Dean Martin as she works – she's very loudly crooning along to the bit about the moon and the pizza pie.

'Morning!' I say brightly, raising my voice to be heard. 'Anything I can do to help?'

'Ah, Cassie, love! You're looking fine today – thought your poor head might be banjaxed!'

'Nope, which is basically a Christmas miracle. I did get a late-night visitor, though.'

She stops what she's doing and stares at me intently.

'He didn't go and break his rules, did he, the devil?'

I'm momentarily confused until I realise she thinks my late-night visitor came in the form of Ryan. I laugh, and say: 'No! Don't worry, my virtue is safe. My visitor had four legs and goes by the name of Eejit. He spent the night with me in Whimsy.'

'G'way! He didn't, did he? Now that *is* a Christmas miracle! Poor fella's been straying around for ages now. You must have the appeal!'

'Yep, that's me – irresistible to stray dogs the world over. Anyway, it was nice. The whole night was fun.'

'It surely was – there's always a good craic around here. Now, don't be dawdling – go and get the kettle on!'

I spend the next few hours in her company, brewing the tea, fetching and carrying, loading loaves into the ovens and generally making myself useful. She tells me about her life back in Ireland, and her late husband, Donal. They 'weren't blessed' with children, and when he died, she felt like she'd lost her place in the world. Here, she tells me, she found it again, and she's been in the village ever since. She's an easy woman to talk to, and the time flies over quickly.

By the time I see Charles's dark green Jaguar pull into the square, I feel like I've already done a day's work – but it was good, honest work, and I have plenty of energy left to spare.

I make my farewells, and she watches me as I leave. I can still feel her knowing eyes on me as Charles clambers out of his car, coming around to the passenger side and opening it for me like the gentleman he is.

'I've been thinking,' I say, as soon as I have my seatbelt on.

'Oh. That sounds serious,' he replies, grinning. He's wearing what I now think of as his casual outfit – smart jeans and a perfectly pressed shirt in a shade of blue that complements his blond hair.

'I was thinking that what we need to do – well, what you need to do – is come up with some absolutely killer marketing materials.'

'You mean like a website? Because we already have one of those.'

'I know, but at the moment it focuses on the holiday lets. If you want to attract backers, you have to make Bancroft Manor look as good as it can. You need to show them exactly what's on offer, and what its potential is. At the moment, you have a good family name, and a beautiful house in a gorgeous location, which is a great start – but, forgive me for saying this, it needs some work.'

'No apologies necessary,' he replies, as we drive through the now-familiar country lanes and up the hill. 'I have eyes. I can see that it's all very genteel, but most definitely on the shabby side. I'd hoped that my meetings would yield more fruit, to be honest. At the moment we're surviving, with rentals and the tenants and a few other income streams, but long term, we need to either find a new way of making more money, or look at selling the estate. Which of course would be awful.'

'It would. Not just for you and your family, but for the whole village, and all of these people who depend on you.'

He nods, and again I am struck by how heavy a burden he carries – which makes me even more determined to help.

'How did you leave it, with the people you met?'

'That we would reconvene in the new year, and that I'd come up with a more robust business plan. They seemed interested but not sold, if you know what I mean.'

'And what did you have to show them, as well as your charming smile?' I ask. 'How did you try and convince them that you were a good bet?'

'I'd hoped the charming smile might be enough, but obviously not. With hindsight, I didn't show them an awful lot. I had financial projections, and I had comparators – examples of similar places that had successfully diversified. But what I didn't have was anything unique, or anything that really made them sit up. I did a presentation, but a lot of it was about the history of the place, when I think I needed to focus more on the future.'

'Did you have visuals?'

'I did. We have some glorious shots that were taken of the exterior over the summer, the grounds and gardens, and they looked magnificent. The inside, not so magnificent. The cloth sheets in the ballroom probably didn't exactly give off the right image.'

'Exactly! And in this game, image is everything. Look, don't be disheartened – I don't think it's unfixable. But you need professional pictures, and you need to show it in action.'

'What do you mean, in action?'

'I mean that if you want to market yourselves as an events space, you need to show events – tables set for dinner, musicians in place, a party going on! You need to bring it all back to life again – even if it's just for one day. Then, Charles... *then* you have something to sell.'

We discuss it all further as we drive, and I am amazed at how quickly my ideas are coming – it's like something's been switched back on inside me.

When we arrive back at Bancroft Manor, Georgie and Roberts are waiting to greet us. Georgie hugs me enthusiastically, seemingly full of youthful exuberance, but I can smell the cigarette smoke on her clothes.

'How's Allegra?' I ask, looking around the lobby.

'She's not having a good day,' Roberts replies simply. 'So she's resting in her rooms. I hope she'll feel up to joining us later.'

I pat him on the arm, and say: 'I hope so too. She'll remember this place when it was a social whirl, and I'd love to talk to her about it.'

'I'm sure she would love that too, Cassie – remembering the past doesn't seem to be a problem for her. Now, what is it that we're all meeting about? Or could you simply not stay away from my second-breakfast pastries?'

'I'm sorry to say this, Roberts, but I've spent the morning in Eileen's bakery. I couldn't eat another pastry if you offered me a million bucks. I'm here to talk to Charles – and you guys – about your plans for this place.'

'Cassie has some marvellous ideas,' Charles adds. 'Why don't we discuss them as we walk?'

He fills the other two in on what I've suggested, and Georgie gets it immediately.

'We need to dress it all up!' she says, fizzing with energy. 'We need to stop it looking like a dusty old museum, and make it look like the kind of place someone would want to get married in! Like it's a stage, and we need to set it!'

'Exactly that,' I say, as we walk through the various rooms of the house. 'Like this – the library. Here, we stage it like someone is giving a talk. We scatter books around, get a whiteboard, fill the room with people – find someone to pretend to be the guest speaker. Someone who looks like an author or a playwright!'

'Jack Mullaney,' Roberts suggests. 'He actually is a poet, although I always think he looks rather like Gandalf.'

'Yes, wizard man – I saw him in the pub, first night I was here. Stick him in a tweed suit, perfect! And you can do the same in the other rooms. Show them how they could be used. So, for example, an art class – stage it so it's full of people with easels and paints. A meeting room – tables, screens, jugs of water, people having a conversation while they make notes on their tablets.'

They all follow me into the hallway as I speak, like a strange string of eager ducklings.

'The kitchen,' I say, 'that could be so good! Someone demonstrating their baking skills, a few huge cakes scattered around, that whole olde worlde country kitchen thing! Don't just tell potential investors what it could be – show them! I know from my job that the right marketing sucks you in. Of course you'd go and check the place out in person, but if the look and feel is right, you'll give it a chance – and honestly, if we're clever with what we've got and find the right photographer, we could do it all in one long day!'

'But what would happen when they did visit, and saw that all was not as it appeared? That none of it was real?' asks Roberts, clearly a little daunted.

'There would be time,' Charles replies, rubbing his chin and nodding thoughtfully. 'Time to actually make it real. If we could get the investment, that would allow us to improve things, and by the point we went "live", as it were, it wouldn't be fake anymore. Cassie, that's genius!'

He grins at me as he says this, his mind now very clearly engaged.

'I don't know about that, but I am here to help, in any way

you need,' I reply, as we go into the ballroom. It is cold and dusty and empty, but it still shines with star power – or at least it could. 'And this would be the centrepiece. You need to fill it. You need to make it glow. You need to give it what it needs, no matter how temporarily, to look like the dream venue.'

Georgina heads straight towards the piano, and pulls its dust cover off with a flourish. She lifts the lid, and starts playing something jazzy and fun, maybe Scott Joplin. I shake my head in amazement – this place and these people are full of surprises.

'There you go – you've got your pianist already!' I say.

Charles is walking around the room, stopping every now and then and tapping his toes to the music as he thinks. By the time he comes back to me, he clearly has questions.

'It's a great idea,' he says, 'but frankly I wouldn't know where to start. I mean, even simple things like how to set up a room for a corporate meeting, or how many tables I'd need to hire to fill this place? The logistics feel overwhelming.'

'Gosh,' I say, smiling up at him, noticing that his hair is in unruly tufts where he's been worrying at it. 'If only you had someone around who was, you know, a professional events planner? Wouldn't that be useful?'

He laughs, and replies: 'Well, yes, that would be frightfully useful. Do you know any of those?'

I punch him playfully in the arm, answering: 'You can do this, you know. It's not even that big a deal – a lot of it is smoke and mirrors, and I've done this before, for the company I work for. Some of the pictures and video we use to promote our services are from genuine events, but some are completely staged. The food doesn't need to be edible, the guests don't really need to be drinking actual wine... there ways of doing it quickly and cheaply. There will be some costs, but we can keep them minimal – and at the end of the day it's an investment.'

'Where would we get the people?' Roberts asks, frowning. 'Do we hire *actors*?'

He says this with such dread that I have to smile. Maybe Roberts had a bad experience with an amateur dramatics troupe that has left him bitter.

'Well, you can – or models at least. But look, I've been thinking about this, and I suspect you have more on your doorstep than you think you do. You have a whole village, and from what I've seen of the people in that village, there are a lot of skills to go around. You have bakers and cooks, you have people who know how to run hospitality. You have musicians, and you have a poet, and you have so many people who could probably help...'

There's a definite stiffening of upper lips at this suggestion, from both men. Only Georgina seems to be taking it in and running with it.

'Ignore Dad,' she tells me, 'he's just tripping over his own importance. It's a pride thing – asking for help doesn't come easily to him. You're right, Cassie – the people in the village are brilliant. Cormac used to run a posh bistro in Dublin, and Eileen's obviously a genius, and everyone has something to offer – Orla could do hair and make-up, and Mary Catherine would help get it all sparkling. Her daughter Sarah doesn't just run the tea rooms, in the summer she does catering for outside events, so she'd have the right contacts for hiring tables and all that boring stuff. And Ryan could take the photos.'

'Ryan?' I repeat in confusion. I'd anticipated him having a role, but it was more along the lines of brawny general labourer than man behind the camera.

'Yeah. Ryan. He used to be a photographer, had exhibitions in galleries and stuff. He took all the pictures that are up on the walls in the pub?'

I remember those pictures. I remember thinking how good they were, how they brought the beauty of Ireland to life – that they were gallery quality. I assumed they'd been bought for the pub, and I never would have expected the artist to be Ryan.

I don't even give Charles the chance to over-react to Georgie's suggestion, though – I just jump on it.

'Perfect. Those photographs are excellent, and you need someone top quality. Plus if they were up for it, the rest of the villagers could be our wedding guests, or our business people, or our art class! I honestly think, Charles, that if you explained the situation they'd be happy to get involved – and if they do, I think we can get this done in time for the New Year.'

Charles still looks hesitant, and I know Georgie is right – this is his pride at work. He doesn't come across as a snob or as a man who thinks he is better than everyone else, but he is the latest in a long line of people at the top of the social tree. Accepting that he now needs to ask for help from the lower branches might not come easily to him.

'I know you don't want to wash your dirty linen in public, Charles, but this does affect them as well, from what you've said to me? You've mentioned putting their rents up, or even selling the estate, which would mean they'd have a new landlord who didn't have any of the personal connections. Maybe it's only right to give them the chance to avoid that?'

He seems to be giving it a lot of thought, and eventually nods, abruptly.

'Okay. That's a fair point. But we'll need to move quickly – a lot of them go home for Christmas. We'd need to get the ball rolling straight away.'

'Shall I call around, Charles?' Roberts asks, once the decision has been made. 'Invite a few key players up for a chat?'

'No,' Charles says firmly, 'if I'm going to ask them for their help, then I need to be honest about it – and I need to do it on their turf. Set it up for the pub, and spread the word – if nothing else, I'll definitely be needing a drink afterwards.'

SIXTEEN

Georgie and Roberts disappear soon after – Roberts to arrange the meeting, and Georgie to 'raid the Dressing Room'.

This, I'm told by Charles, is a chamber at the top of the house where clothes going back decades are stored.

'I've no idea what's even up there,' he says, shaking his head. 'There could be everything from a Jacobean ruff to the awful sailor suit they dressed me up in as a baby. I suspect Georgie is planning to put together splendid outfits for our fake party guests to wear.'

'That's not a bad idea, Charles – I'm sure there are some classy garments to choose from.'

He shrugs, and I can tell he is worried.

'Are you okay with all of this?' I say, placing my hand on his arm. 'I feel like I've ambushed you with my crazy American energy.'

He looks at my hand and smiles reassuringly, his green eyes on mine.

'No, please don't think that. I suspect some crazy American energy could be exactly what we needed – a kick up the proverbial backside. To some extent Georgina was right – I am indeed tripping over my own importance, as she so charmingly put it. There's no room for pride anymore, and I need to be clear-headed about it all. It's just that right now, I'm still adjusting, and my head feels far from clear.'

He places his hand over mine, and the touch of his skin on my fingers suddenly feels overwhelming. June had talked a good game on the phone, but I'm still not sure I'm ready for any more 'moments'.

He seems to sense my uncertainty, squeezes my hand, and puts a respectable distance between us. Or maybe I just imagined the whole thing...

'I know there's a lot to discuss,' he says, 'but I think I need a break from it before my head explodes. Would you join me for lunch, or a walk around the grounds? I promise not to foxtrot you through the flower beds, or anything at all inappropriate.'

There's a mischievous glint in his eyes that makes me doubt that, which I can't deny is good for the ego. I agree to a walk, because it's a beautiful day out there, and walking always helps me think.

Within a few moments he has me kitted out in Georgie's rubber wellington boots, and has a small package of blankets and a flask of hot cocoa.

'We'll go to the tower,' he tells me mysteriously, as we head out across the immaculate parkland. The snow here is untouched by anything other than birds, their tiny feet imprinted on the ground. I glance back at the house and see how splendid it looks. We need to get winter pictures, I decide, because this is a sensational view. The perfect spot for wedding pictures.

Huh, I think, as we make our way along virgin pathways, *I just managed to think about a winter wedding in nothing but a professional manner*. This is progress.

Eventually we reach our destination, and it is, quite simply, a tower. It's a strange building, with a little square room at the bottom, and nothing else but stone steps.

'What is this place?' I ask, as I follow him upwards.

'It's a folly,' he explains. 'One of my ancestors built it. It's just for show – to look pretty – but it's fun, isn't it? Like a turret that's been taken from a castle and dumped in the middle of the grounds. No use at all, but I rather like it.'

At the very top is a plain stone bench, surrounded by round porthole-style windows cut into the bricks. It gives you a bird's eye view of the whole estate, and I spend forever simply staring around in wonder. I see the whole place spread out before us, across the grand elevations of the manor, down the hill to the village.

'Wow,' I say, sitting next to him on the bench. 'That is something you don't see every day. We could get some great shots from up here.'

He covers our laps in the blankets, and pours us both a boiling hot cup of cocoa. I wrap my hands around it, and see the steam curl up in a lazy cloud against the cold air.

'I'll add it to the growing list of your great ideas. You can actually open the windows, though they might be a bit stiff. I haven't been up here for a long time. Vanessa and I used it as a den. She'd sneak cigarettes, and I'd read, and sometimes we'd play cards. It was a refuge, I suppose. I'm not trying to make out we had anything other than a deeply privileged upbringing, but that doesn't mean that everything was perfect. She, in particular, struggled. She was quite the rebel – went to her debutante ball in some punkish Vivienne Westwood creation, refused to date any of the eligible young men that were presented to her. She longed to escape, even more than I did.'

His eyes are distant, clearly lost in his memories. I don't want to break the spell, but I quietly ask: 'What happened to her? Your sister? I couldn't find any pictures of her downstairs.'

He seems to be trying to decide how to respond, so I add: 'If I'm prying, just tell me so. Nosy Yank alert.'

He smiles his killer smile, and says: 'No, it's fine. It's hardly a secret – it was all over the newspapers at the time. Like I said, she had a wild streak. She never settled down, never married, never stopped being the rebel of the family. She drank, way too much, and the only real pleasure she seemed to get from our lifestyle was the garden, and the horses. She loved to ride.'

He pauses, sips some cocoa and grimaces when he scalds his lips.

'Then one morning, she took Georgie out riding. This is about four years ago now, so Georgie was thirteen, and also loved horses. Unfortunately, we discovered later, Vanessa had already been drinking. In fact her blood test results showed she was absolutely sloshed. Her horse – obviously the biggest and wildest brute she could find – stumbled, and threw her. He was lamed, and ended up falling on top of Vanessa. She was trapped there. Crushed.'

I stare at him in horror, trying to imagine the scene – and the panic that a teenaged girl would have felt at being part of it. I picture a screaming woman, and a screaming horse, and a helpless thirteen-year-old in the middle of it all.

'Was Georgie still with her?' I ask, dreading his response.

'Well, yes. Of course there was nothing she could do. She called for help – thank goodness for mobile phones, much as I sometimes hate the damned devices – but it took a while to arrive as they were deep at the far end of the estate. Basically, she had to sit there, holding her aunt's hand, looking on while she died. It was... well, as you can imagine, it was traumatic to say the least. She's never been the same since.'

I feel tears stinging the backs of my eyes, and slip my hand into his. He is talking about this in the calm and detached way of a man who is fighting back too much emotion – a man who has always had to fight back emotion.

'Charles, I'm so sorry. For all of you. Has she had, I don't know, therapy?'

'Oh yes. Oodles of the stuff, and maybe it's helped – maybe she'd be even more messed up without it, who knows? Her mother leaving two years after didn't help matters, plus her issues at school. It's... God, it's so hard, Cassie. I loved my sister. In fact, when I was younger I idolised her, she was so full of spirit. I miss her, but I'm also still a little angry with her. It was desperately irresponsible of her to take Georgina out riding when she was intoxicated – she wasn't only risking herself, she was risking my daughter. And even though not a hair on Georgie's head was harmed, mentally it took its toll.'

'I can understand that. And then I guess you feel guilty because you're angry?'

He laces his fingers more firmly into mine, and smiles sadly.

'Exactly that. It's all a very toxic mix. Then into all of that we add Allegra's condition – and every time she saw the pictures that used to be on the wall, it would confuse her. She'd assume Vanessa was about to walk into the room. It was upsetting for everyone, so we decided to remove them for the time being. Another thing I feel guilty about – erasing my sister's memory.'

'That's not what you've done. You're just trying to deal with a very bad situation. And moving a picture doesn't erase someone. They live on in your mind, that's where you keep them alive.'

'Yes. You're right, I know. And maybe I should remember her more kindly, exactly as she was when we were young. When we used to hide in here. She'd be listening to some dreadful music and filling the place with smoke, and I'd be lost in my books. There were happy times – it's just a matter of clinging on to them.'

I can picture them so vividly, young but not carefree. Vanessa had been expected to marry well, possibly to boost the family coffers. He probably already knew his life wasn't his own. I glance out of the round window, and look at the stunning house and the breathtaking grounds.

It's not enough, I decide. It's not enough to make anyone happy, no matter how beautiful it appears on the surface. We all carry burdens and responsibilities, we all have complications in our lives, but theirs were extreme. Too much for children to bear. I suspect that's part of his current determination to change things – he doesn't want his own daughter to be left with a world of problems.

We sit in silence for a few minutes, our hands still clasped together, drinking our chocolate and thinking our own thoughts. I want to say more, I want to comfort him, but I can't quite find the right words. I see glimpses of the real him, beneath the surface image, but he is still somehow distant and untouchable – still wrapped up in what he thinks he should be. I wonder if he's even cried, for his lost sister, his lost wife, the mother he is slowly watching slip away. The damage done to his daughter.

'So,' he says, his tone deliberately lighter. 'Enough about our sad tales. Tell me yours. I suspect you have one.' I suppose I do, but after what I've just heard, my own troubles seem silly and insignificant.

'Kind of. I had my heart broken when a long term relationship ended. It's nothing tragic, nothing that doesn't happen to people every day. It's just taking me a long time to heal.'

'There are no rules about that, Cassie. The heart is a tender organ, easily bruised. What happened?'

I don't really want to talk about, but I can hardly refuse when he has opened up to me.

I shrug, and say: 'Well, I was jilted at the altar, if you must know.'

It sounds so simple when I put it like that – and I guess it is. When I spoke to Ryan about this it felt heavy, emotionally laden. It brought with it so much pain and so much suffering.

Now, I have reduced it to one sentence – maybe this is part of the process. Maybe eventually, it won't even deserve that.

He places his hands on either side of my cheeks, and turns me to face him. I am embarrassed, but he holds me steady. He looks me right in the eyes, and says: 'All I can assume is that the man must have been the world's biggest fool. Anyone would be lucky to have you.'

He drops a gentle kiss on my forehead, and I feel a tremble run through my body.

'Thank you, Charles,' I reply, not wanting the moment to end, but also scared of where it might lead. 'Maybe one day I'll actually believe that myself.'

SEVENTEEN

The meeting is arranged for the next night, and I am nervous. I barely know these people, not really, and yet I have convinced Charles that he should trust them, throw himself on their mercy. The stakes are high, and my stomach is tied in knots.

'What if it all goes wrong?' I say to Eejit, who is curled up in front of my fire. Thanks to a quick tutorial from Eileen, I am now a dab hand at it, and the cottage is warm and cosy. My canine friend appeared again last night, though thankfully at a much earlier hour. 'What if they tell Charles where he can stuff his pleas for help? What if we all end up with egg on our face?'

He looks up at me with one sleepy eye, keeping the other one closed as he drowses.

'Yeah, you're right,' I say, stroking his furry head. 'I just need to chill.'

He thumps his tail once on the carpet, and goes back to sleep. I glance at my phone for the thousandth time today, and see that it is actually now time to go. I grab my coat and bag, and waver on the doorstep for a few moments.

'Do I leave you here?' I ask. 'Or will you feel too confined?'

He answers my question by climbing to his feet, stretching

into a perfect downward dog, and trotting out of the door with me. He disappears off into the evening, and I lock up. I probably don't need to lock up, but I guess there's still too much big city in me for that to feel right.

The lights that are strung across the streets light my way, and the Christmas tree twinkles cheerfully at me as I pass. All will be well, I tell myself, as I push open the door to the pub.

I suck in a breath when I see how full it is. Literally every person I've ever seen in the village is here, along with quite a few new faces. I return hellos and waves, and find Charles sitting by the bar on one of the tall stools – in exactly the same spot we were the first night we met. I'm amazed at how I managed to get myself into this mess so quickly.

He's wearing a dark suit, no tie, the collar of his white shirt opened a few buttons at the top. I can see that he is also nervous, and am glad that Roberts is with him. I know he's asked Georgie to stay at home, allegedly to keep an eye on Allegra, but I suspect it's to protect her in case things don't go as well as he hopes. Georgie is clearly very fond of the villagers, and it would hurt her to see them refuse her family the support they're asking for.

There is no music tonight, but the place is loud with chatter – everyone must be curious to find out why they're here, and possibly they're expecting the worst. I definitely see a few dour faces at some of the tables.

Charles greets me, and I smile reassuringly. I sit next to him, and look at the crowded room. Eileen and Ryan are nearby, and Ryan gives me a terse nod of recognition. I'm hoping that this whole project doesn't get derailed by their testosterone wars, and remind myself that neither of them is a thug. Charles is a gentleman, and Ryan is, well, an artist, I now know. For all of his play-acting at being a humble handyman, there is more to him than that, and I hope that side of him wins out.

Cormac rings the bell that hangs over the bar, and everyone

goes silent. Charles thanks him, takes a sip of his water, and turns back around to face the room.

'Hello, everybody,' he says, 'thank you so much for coming. I know how busy you all are, and I very much appreciate you turning up on such short notice. I'm sure you're all wondering what's going on, so let me start by saying this – I, like my father and those who went before him, hold you all in very high esteem. We value the life and energy that you bring to Campton St George, as well as all your hard work. It wouldn't be the place it is without you.'

A round of cheers goes up, which breaks the tension somewhat. Charles manages a small smile, and ploughs on.

'As I'm sure many of you are aware, my father wasn't the most natural of businessmen, and financial management wasn't his forte. Add to that his illness during later years, as well as some very poor investments, and... well, to cut a long story short, the family accounts are not what they were.'

'Are you wanting a loan, Charlie boy?' some clown in the corner pipes up. 'I've got a fiver for you, pass the hat around!'

'Very kind, Martin, but I'm afraid a fiver isn't enough. I'm going to be very honest with you all, because you deserve it – if things continue the way they are, within the next four years the Bancroft estate may have to be sold. Even before that, I might have to consider increasing your rents, which believe me I have no desire to do. I know times are tough for everyone, and the last thing I want to do is make them any tougher.'

'Why don't you sell your Jag, then, fella?' the same man yells, earning some applause but also some glares of disapproval.

'You be shutting your gob now, Martin Byrne,' Eileen shouts at him sternly. 'If hot air was money, we all know you'd be a millionaire – let the man speak, will you?'

There's a smattering of laughter at this, and Martin looks suitably chastened. I'm guessing Eileen is not somebody you want to mess with.

'Thank you, Mrs Devlin – and Martin, believe me I have looked at selling my Jag. But in case you hadn't noticed, it's over fifteen years old, so no quick fixes there I'm afraid. I do, though, hopefully have a solution – I want to make the most of the manor, and more importantly make money from it.

'Money that will pay for its upkeep, pay to keep the village in good condition, continue to provide you all with fair wages. Plus – I'm as selfish as the next man – ensure Georgina's future, and allow her to be independent. Nobody wishes there was a magical pot of family cash that I could endlessly dip into more than I do – but there isn't. You know how we live up there – it's not all Champagne and caviar, it's also closed off rooms and enormous fuel bills.'

'That's the truth of it,' responds Mary Catherine. 'Your man there's not lying – I fair freeze to death when I'm doing the cleaning!'

More laughter follows, and I start to unclench a little.

'What would happen to us,' Cormac asks from behind the bar, 'if you sold the estate?'

'Frankly I don't know,' replies Charles. 'Obviously, if it comes to that, I'll do my best to secure a buyer who will treat you all fairly – but at the end of the day, it won't be up to me anymore.'

'So it's better the devil you know, is that what you're saying?'

That question comes from Ryan, who is sitting with his arms crossed, staring at us intently. Uh-oh, I think, this could be where it all goes horribly wrong. If Charles rises to the bait, or reacts the way he usually does to Ryan, then we could be in trouble.

'Fair point, Ryan,' Charles says, his tone even and neutral. I can see it's taking some effort, but he's not stupid – he knows he has to handle this the right way. 'And I suppose yes is the answer. I hope that none of you see me as the devil. We've come a long way since your families first started coming here, and I certainly don't see us as master and servant. But if I am the devil, then I'm one who has tried his very best to do things correctly.'

The two men make eye contact, and you could hear a pin drop in here. I'm kind of wishing that Martin 'Hot Air' Byrne might chime in to break the tension.

Ryan seems to turn over his answer, and nods abruptly.

'Okay, Your Lordship,' he says after a few tense seconds. 'Good enough. There are far worse devils out there, we all know that. So, why are we all here? What are you expecting us to do about it, if you're not telling us the rents are going up?'

'Well, first of all, let me say that this was all Cassie's idea – so you can blame her!'

I hold my hands up in acknowledgement, and hope he's not going to ask me to make a speech. I don't mind chipping in, but I hate being in the spotlight. There's a ripple of laughter around the room, so at least I'm good for something.

'I met with some potential investors in London recently,' he continues, 'in an attempt to get some backing for my plans. Those plans at the time were quite vague – making the house available for weddings, parties, that kind of thing. Cassie, as you might know, is actually a professional events planner back home in New York, and she had several other very excellent suggestions.'

'Lap dancing bar?' shouts Martin again, and somebody lobs a full packet of Taytos at his head to shut him up. He shrugs, opens the pack, and starts eating them.

'Most definitely not, though I'm sure you'd be first in the queue, Martin! No, some of her ideas included wellness retreats – yoga, massages, that kind of thing – art classes, cookery classes, corporate events. She pointed out how versatile the place could be, and how many options we could offer.'

'That's a good idea, sure,' says Sarah, who runs the tea

rooms. 'Me and my sister were at one of those wellness thingies last year. We spent most of it drinking the Champagne, like, but the place wasn't any better than yours, Charles. And Eileen could do your baking classes! Nobody better in the land!'

Everyone agrees with this, and before long people are shouting out their own ideas. Someone suggests fishing weekends, another offers up bird-spotting, and Mary Catherine throws in 'murder mystery dinners in full Agatha Christie costume', which is actually an excellent concept. Martin, who I am fast learning is the village clown, kindly offers to be a nude life model for the art classes.

'They'd pay you good money to keep your clothes on there, Martin!' he gets told, and pretends to look offended. As he's in his seventies and has a magnificent beer belly, I suspect that's true.

Charles lets them have their head for a while longer, then regains their attention by raising one arm in the air.

'These are all wonderful ideas!' he says. 'I'm glad you can all see the potential. But before we make any of these things happen, there's work to be done, and investment to be found. We need to decorate, and buy new furniture, and look into things like a massage suite or small spa. We need to refurbish some of the rooms so they're suitable for guests, and look at boring issues like insurance, and suppliers, and marketing. And before we can do any of that, we have to find the money.'

'There's an awful lot of "we" being used there, Charles,' Eileen points out. 'And while we all accept that you not selling is for the good of all of us – that we need you and you need us – I'm still not hearing you get to the point. What are you after?'

Charles nods, and replies: 'Basically I need your help to make Bancroft Manor look like all of the things we just discussed. Cassie believes, and I trust her on this, that to attract the financial backing, we have to show what we're made of. Her idea is to stage all of this, just for one day, so we can take photos and video, and really show the place off. We need people to play the roles of guests. We need help setting up a big dinner. We need someone to pretend to lead classes. We need all kinds of things – and we need them quickly, because I'm due to go back to the investment company in January.'

There's a momentary silence, and then everybody seems to want to talk at once. Charles holds up his hand again, and says: 'Cassie, anything to add before we discuss things further?'

I take a deep breath, and look around the room. I see all the familiar faces, and note that Ryan is giving me one of his lopsided grins, raising his eyebrows as though daring me to speak. I can do this, I tell myself – I am among friends.

'Look,' I begin, 'I haven't been here long, but I don't think I've ever met a bunch of people with so many different skills, and so much energy. I think that's also what we need – it's not just someone to set up tables or whatever, it's everything that you bring with you. This is a big ask, but I think it's doable – with your help. Plus, it occurred to me while Charles was speaking that this isn't just about saving the estate. It could be a really fantastic opportunity for all of you too.'

I pause, wondering if I'm out of order, but Charles gives me an encouraging nod and I go on.

'He mentioned suppliers – well, I think he has them sitting right here in this room. There are farms all around us as well. If this takes off, it wouldn't just make money to keep Bancroft afloat – it would mean more business for you all. More jobs. More scope for entrepreneurship. More everything.'

'That's true!' Charles replies, looking enthused. 'Why would I look elsewhere for someone to create a wedding cake when I have Eileen, or source wine when I have Cormac? Why would I employ a beautician when Orla is here?'

'Why would you look for a comedian when you have Martin?' someone shouts, to much amusement.

'Even that,' he says. 'Who knows? But definitely I'll need

musicians, and people to run classes, and drivers, and waiters...
we might even end up with too much work! But to start with,
we need to ask you this favour – will you help us? I know there's
a lot to think about, and a lot to discuss, and I know Cassie has
already started filling a notepad with her wish list. We won't
move forward until we know your views. I think that's enough
for now – I'm going to linger a while longer and have a much-
needed drink. Feel free to come and chat.'

I gaze around the room and see people nodding, considering. Charles and Roberts move away from the bar to sit at a
table, and I see the older man pat Charles on the shoulder in
congratulations. I think he did as well as he could – now we just
have to wait and see.

I leave them to it, and join Ryan and Eileen. I realise my
hands are shaking, and I'm pathetically grateful when Eileen
reaches out to steady them in hers.

'You did fine, darlin',' she says, squeezing my trembling
fingers. 'And I for one think it's a grand idea. None of us are
afraid of a bit of hard work, and maybe it's time for a change in
the way things are done around here.'

I nod, and she goes off to buy me a drink. I'm left alone with
Ryan, who is looking at me seriously. I'm desperate to hear what
he thinks, but he seems to be making me work for it.

'So?' I ask. 'What are your views? We were really hoping
that you'd get involved – I'm told you're not too bad with a
camera...'

He snorts out a laugh, and slowly relents. I didn't realise
how worried I'd been until he smiles.

'I have been known to take a few snaps in my time, yeah.
And okay, I'm in – it does sound like a good idea. As long as His
Lordship keeps his distance, I'll be your photographer. I don't
like being bossed around by anyone, but especially not him.'

'What about if I boss you around instead?'

He raises one eyebrow, and I want to kick myself for giving him the opening.

'Whatever floats your boat, Cassie – not my usual style, but I'll try anything once.'

'You're an eejit, did you know that?'

'I have been told, once or twice.'

EIGHTEEN

The rest of the evening fills out nicely, with a balance of the usual sociable atmosphere, and a buzz about Charles's plans. He is very much the centre of attention, and his table is rarely without a visitor. Several people come and chat to me as well, and I'm glad I brought a notebook – the suggestions are coming thick and fast.

We assign some tasks, we make some plans, and I take copious notes, running between my table and Charles's. Everyone seems up for it, and the mood is upbeat.

'This is great,' I say to Ryan, as I sketch out a rough outline of how many tables we might need to hire in. 'Everyone's so enthusiastic!'

'Yeah. They're always up for shenanigans.'

I laugh at the word – another of Nora's favourites, often applied to me and June. 'You two look guilty – have there been shenanigans?' There usually had, to be fair. I actually thought she'd made it up until I came across a pub with the same name in New York.

'I'll need to hire some lighting gear, while you're making

your lists,' he adds, looking thoughtful. 'I still have my camera, but it's been a long time since I did anything like this.'

I look up from my notepad and give him my full attention.

'The pictures on the walls in here are beautiful. You're clearly very talented. Why did you give it up?'

'I couldn't resist the allure of unblocking toilets and clearing out guttering.'

'Really? That's all I'm going to get?'

He tilts his head to one side, and seems to be weighing me up.

'I needed a change,' he says, shrugging. 'Life back in Ireland got complicated, and I took some knocks. The kind that it's hard to get back up from. Moving away seemed like the best option.'

'I get it,' I reply. 'Fresh start. The chance to recreate yourself – I flew thousands of miles to do the same. But it seems a shame, to have given up something you're so good at...'

'Ah now, don't you be worrying about me. I'm good at many things.'

And just like that, he's back in flirtation mode, eyebrows raised and a twinkle in his eye. I can't deny that I enjoy Ryan's casual charm, but I also know that there are layers he keeps hidden. In his own way, he's more buttoned-up than Charles, even though it's trickier to spot at first.

I shake my head in exasperation, and say: 'I'm sure you are, Ryan. Practice makes perfect after all.'

'Any time you fancy a hands-on demonstration, Cassie, you just let me know...'

I have no desire to become another notch on this man's tool belt, but I can't deny that a little thrill runs through me as he says those words. The dreaded blush starts to creep over my skin, delighting him so much that he laughs out loud.

I'm saved from having to respond by Charles waving me over, and I grab my notebook and run. He wants to ask me about flowers, as Mary Catherine has suggested we contact the florist in Marshington Grange to order table decorations. I'm standing at his side discussing it when a very uncharacteristic hush falls over the pub. I've never seen anything that shuts this lot up before, and I look up to see what's happening.

A strikingly beautiful woman has walked into the room, all lustrous dark hair and eyes that flash like diamonds. She's dressed casually in skinny jeans and a red cashmere sweater, but everything about her – from the top of her glossy head to the tips of her skinny-heeled boots – screams class and elegance.

Running around her feet is a puppy – a Spaniel, I think – black and white, all adorable gangly legs and floppy ears. Everyone stares at her for a second, then the noise levels return to normal. I glance at Charles, see his nostrils flare and his body tense.

Ignoring everything around her, she strolls towards the bar. Cormac nods, and simply says: 'The usual, Lenny?'

'Yes please, darling.'

He takes a bottle of whiskey from the top shelf, and pours her a double on the rocks. She looks around, sipping, her eyes taking in everyone present and finally deigning to settle on Charles. There's no way she didn't know he was here but she feigns surprise, and trots towards us.

'Charles!' she says, widening her eyes and actually batting her lashes. 'How splendid to see you – slumming it tonight, are we?'

Her laser-like gaze falls on me at his side, and I feel like a butterfly pinned to a collector's board.

'Leonora,' he replies simply, his tone dripping ice. 'What are you doing here?'

'Can't a wife pop in to see her hubbie and child when she has a spare moment?'

'Ex-wife. And no, she can't.'

'Oopsy, silly me then. Well, as I'm off to spend Christmas in

Cape Town with Simon, I wanted to pay a quick visit to Georgie. I bought her a gift.'

She gestures down at the puppy, who very promptly squats and pees on Charles's brogues.

'Did you train him to do that?' he asks, shaking it off.

'No, but it was rather funny! Look, there's no need to go all prickly on me – I genuinely just want to see her. I know you all miss Jasper, so when I saw this little fellow, I couldn't resist. Obviously you can change his name, but I've been calling him Jasper as well. Thought it might be easier for Allegra.'

This seems like a thoughtful thing to do, but nothing about Charles suggests that he is relaxing. I glance over towards Ryan and Eileen, and see them both sitting with faces like thunder. Wow. Lenny really isn't popular here. She must know that, it's impossible to ignore the atmosphere, but she doesn't seem to care – that, or she's a spectacular actress.

'I didn't expect you to be here,' she adds. 'Just called in for a little Dutch courage. I'll only stay for the night, be out of your hair tomorrow, I promise. I haven't seen her for so long, darling.'

She sounds genuinely sad about this, and there is a pleading quality to her voice. I have no idea what kind of custody arrangements they have in place, but I remember Ryan saying she moved to the South of France. The impression I've always got is that she simply left, walked out on all of them, including her daughter. Families are complicated, and I'm not one to judge.

'Fine,' he says, relenting. 'But please don't turn up unannounced again. Mother is confused enough. And thank you – for the dog. He's rather lovely.'

He crouches down and rubs the dog's face between his hands, and Jasper the Second wriggles in delight.

While he's otherwise engaged, Leonora stares at me, and if looks could kill I'd be six feet under. I'm taller than her, even with her high heels, but somehow she still seems to be looking down on me. Her eyes take in my loose hair, my chunky sweater, my jeans and sneakers. Take them in, then spit them out. I feel like a dirty-faced street urchin next to her – especially because she smells of Chanel, and I smell of stray dog.

'Charles,' she says, as he stands straight, 'have you finally given in to temptation and found yourself a lovely village colleen to keep you company?'

'No, he hasn't!' I snap back. I am not by nature an aggressive person, but this woman is just plain rude.

She laughs, and says: 'Oh, a colonial! Well, that's different.'

'You say both those things as though they're an insult,' I reply, wondering if she'd look so smug if I punched her on the nose or threw her whiskey in her face. 'But I'm happy to be both a colleen and a colonial. At least we have manners.'

'That's the spirit!' she answers, infuriatingly unruffled.

Charles steps between us, and it immediately calms me down. This isn't the right place for a catfight – in fact, nowhere is the right place for a catfight. I was raised better than that, even if she wasn't. For all her obvious social standing, she's clearly a mean girl, and I've had my fill of those.

'Leonora, do shut up. This is Cassie. She's a friend, and we're working together. Work is a thing that normal people do to earn money – you wouldn't know about that. You simply sleep with people to get it.'

Her eyes flare, but she still looks calm as she says: 'Well, that didn't exactly go as planned with you, my love, did it?'

Roberts joins us, and I've never seen such coldness in his eyes. He glares at her, silently, and that's what seems to finally have an effect.

She knocks back her drink, calls Jasper, and walks towards the door. I see her pause near Ryan's table, and his face is deadly. Cheering breaks out in the pub as she leaves, and Martin the comedian cries: 'Ding dong, the witch is dead!'

Charles looks tired and shaken as he says: 'I'm sorry about

that. She's a handful at the best of times, and even worse when she's here and has to face up to things she'd rather forget. Look, can we reconvene tomorrow? I must get home – ideally before she does!'

I assure him that everything is fine, and go to the bar to get a drink. Orla already has a glass of Merlot poured for me, and grimaces in sympathy as I grab hold of it.

'Is that woman a professional bitch,' I ask, 'or just a talented amateur?'

'Oh, very much the professional – in a league of her own, that one! Pay no mind. She's like one of those storms that blows all the trees down – here and gone in a day, leaving the wreckage behind her.'

I nod, sip my drink, and take some deep breaths before rejoining Ryan and Eileen. She pats my hand, and whispers: 'She's all fur coat and no knickers, sure!'

It makes me laugh, which is exactly what I need. Ryan's expression is grim, and he runs his hands through his hair.

'I'll help with the pictures,' he says seriously, 'but I won't step foot in that house until she's gone.'

NINETEEN

Orla drops me off at Bancroft Manor the next day, along with Eejit, who simply hopped into the back of her car and curled up in a ball.

'It's fierce weather we're having,' Orla says, glancing at him. 'I'm glad someone's finally won his heart, poor thing. I always hated the thought of him out in the cold.'

I'm glad, too – but beneath that I am also worried about what will happen to him when I leave. When I go home, will he stray again? Or will he latch on to someone else? I really hope so, because he's a great dog. I wonder about taking him back with me, and lose a few minutes imagining all the technicalities involved. Pet passports, long haul flights – it all seems a bit daunting, but I'll look into it.

I wave goodbye to Orla, and hope I've left it late enough to avoid Leonora. No such luck, I soon realise. I can hear her dulcet tones from outside.

The front door is open, and Jasper the Second is running around the grass. He has one of the Christmas tree decorations in his mouth, and is delighted with himself. Eejit prowls over to him, standing perfectly still as the giddy puppy licks him and jumps all over him. He lets out a low yip, which clearly translates as 'back off, buddy', and Jasper immediately rolls onto his back with his legs in the air. I rub his furry belly, grab the now-discarded robin-on-a-string, and make my way inside.

The raised voices are coming from the Blue Room, and I consider simply skipping off to another part of the house. The dogs have other ideas, though, and I have to follow them through.

Georgie is sitting on the couch, legs tucked tightly beneath her, chewing on her nails. Jasper jumps up next to her, and she cuddles him close. Allegra is waving a fireplace poker in the air, and Roberts has a restraining hand on her shoulder. At the centre of it all is Leonora, which I suspect is exactly where she wants to be. Some women just aren't happy unless they're causing drama.

'You okay?' I say to Georgie, walking to sit beside her.

'I will be,' she whispers, giving me a forced smile. 'When the crazy ladies shut up. It's been going on for a while now. It'd be quite an amusing performance if not for the fact that I'm genetically related to them.'

'Where's your father?'

'Doing something horribly grown up like talking to his accountant. I hope he's in a soundproofed room.'

I meet Roberts's eyes and raise my brows in a question. He shakes his head, and I stay where I am. This has nothing to do with me, and any intervention I make will probably only add fuel to the fire.

I'm not sure what the last sentence was, it was being yelled as I arrived, but Leonora's response is an angry: 'Why should I care what you think? You didn't even know who I was when I turned up last night!'

'I may be losing my marbles,' Allegra shouts back, waving her poker, 'but I still know a tramp when I see one!'

'Better a tramp than a stuck-up old cow like you!'

'Get out of my house before I skewer you, you whore!'

My eyes widen at the language coming from their mouths. These are both very aristocratic ladies who probably went to the best schools in the land, but they sound like a pair of angry fishwives.

Allegra breaks free from Roberts and actually makes a run at her nemesis, brandishing her weapon. Leonora screams, and has the good sense to flee. Eejit chases her out of the room, eager to join in the game, and Jasper follows. I hear her running up the stairs, both dogs barking, and don't know whether to laugh or cry.

Allegra turns her angry violet eyes on me, and I see her confusion. She's already held me at gunpoint, so I don't take the threat lightly.

'Who are you?' she asks, obviously not ready to give up her fury. 'Why are you here?'

'I'm Cassie,' I say calmly. 'I'm visiting from the United States.'

Her eyelids flutter, and I see her processing what I've said. It takes a few moments, but she nods. 'Ah yes. Your accent. I remember you now. Sorry. I promise not to poke you. That dreadful woman just gets my back up.'

Roberts gently prises the poker from her hands, puts his arm around her shoulders and gives her a comforting hug. I'm sure that she has never been a violent person, but I know from seeing some of Nanna Nora's friends decline that Alzheimer's is a tricky disease. She's scared and confused, and that makes her angry. Now, though, she simply looks distressed, especially when she notices Georgie on the couch.

'I'm sorry, sweetheart,' she says quietly. 'I shouldn't have lost my rag like that. Please forgive me.'

'Nothing to forgive, Granny,' Georgie says, jumping up to give her a quick cuddle. 'She started it. She's my mum and I love her, but I'm not an idiot – I know she causes trouble. But this time, at least she brought us a dog!'

Jasper is back in the room, and she scoops him up into her arms and holds him towards her grandmother. She accepts the lively bundle of fur, and buries her face in his ears.

'Yes. He's adorable. I love the smell of wet dog – they should make a perfume from it!'

I'm not totally sure that would be a big seller, but having Jasper near to her seems to cast a magic spell. She suddenly looks happy, more in control. Leonora might be a nightmare, but she's got one thing right. Two, actually, I think, looking at Georgie. What a family – they make mine look like the Waltons.

Charles walks into the room, looking stressed, and says: 'What happened?'

'Nothing to worry about,' Roberts assures him. 'The ladies were just blowing off a bit of steam. Now we're all going to take Jasper and Eejit for a walk in the grounds – would you care to join us?'

Charles glances over in my direction, and says: 'I suspect that I am destined to be Cassie's slave for the day. There are, of course, far worse fates. Where would you like to start?'

We make our farewells to the others, and walk through the house to the ballroom. I've borrowed a laser measurer from Ryan, and tell Charles that it's a good first step to get all the different room dimensions noted down. From that, I can work on the rest.

As we move around the room, me enjoying playing with my new toy and Charles making notes, I ask him: 'Will Leonora actually leave today, like she said? Because, no offence, but she seems a little unstable.'

'No offence taken – she's totally bonkers. But she will leave today, yes, because she feels guilty when she's here. Guilty about the way she treated me, and guilty about the fact that she didn't take Georgina with her.'

'Why didn't she? It's unusual, for a mom to do that.'

'Well, she is quite an unusual woman...'

He pauses in his note-taking, looks a little wistful, and adds: 'The thing about Leonora is that she was raised by wolves. Yes, they had money, they had titles, they had the house and the cars. But what they didn't have was a single ounce of compassion or empathy. Truly awful people, cold as ice, even towards their own children, both of whom were farmed out to nannies and boarding schools as soon as possible. I suspect Leonora simply learned early on that the only way she could get their attention was to behave badly, and unfortunately it's a habit that stuck. In my calmer moments, I almost feel sorry for her.'

'You sound like you still have feelings for her, Charles?'

'Oh, I do – none of them positive! We were a poor match from the start, and I could never give her the constant attention she needed. Nobody could. She can do terrible things, and she's an expert at pushing all of our buttons, but... well, she's Georgie's mother, so I must at least thank her for that blessing. As for why she didn't take her, well, that's what we agreed – even Leonora could see there was no way she could provide a stable environment for a child. She can't even provide one for herself.'

Everything he says makes sense, but I can't help pondering how all of that made Georgie feel, especially on top of her aunt's accident. No wonder the poor girl has issues.

'I'm so sorry, Charles, it all sounds like a nightmare.'

'That about sums it up, I'm afraid. But there's no use obsessing about the past, I need to focus on the future. I thought it went very well last night, and I woke up this morning feeling quite excited about everything – until I heard the screaming match downstairs. Anyway. Cassie, tell me, once we have all of the pictures and the video and the like, how do you suggest I use it?'

'Okay, well, that's up to you – but once we have everything, I'd suggest you get a brochure written, designed and printed. I know everything is digital these days, but people still like to have something to hold in their hands. That's one of the places you shouldn't scrimp – find a good creative, and pay for high-quality paper and finishes. You don't need to print many initially, if it's just to give out to investors, but you could adapt it to send out to potential clients later on.'

'Excellent suggestion. I'll start looking into it today. Anything else?'

'Well, you need to re-do your presentation. Combine the financial projections with the history and all of our various ideas, and intersperse it with the hopefully breathtaking visuals that will prove to them that they should give you their money. Get copies of the presentation for them to take with them as well – if you really want to be fancy, get a Bancroft Manor logo designed, because you'll need one at some point. You could get it printed onto thumb drives loaded with the presentation, so they don't forget you.'

'You really are a fountain of wisdom, aren't you?'

'Far from it – I'm just recycling tricks that have worked on me! I'm a sucker for a logo on a thumb drive, I have a whole bowl full of them back home! But you could also get some destination cards printed up. So, they're like postcards, with a picture of the place on one side, and the specifications on the back. Like, a gorgeous shot of this ballroom, along with information on how many it seats, how many can stand, and what event facilities you offer.'

'At the moment, that's a teenager playing jazz piano, and a Spaniel puppy that pees in the house!'

'Well,' I say, laughing at the image, 'those are both good things in their own way, but I'd suggest you embellish the truth for now. Say you can provide a DJ, live bands, full catering, luxury overnight suites.'

'Luxury suites!' he says, snorting in amusement. 'We'd better get rid of the mice first, I suppose!'

'Yeah, that might be a good idea. Wouldn't get your Tripadvisor rating off to a good start!'

We carry on companionably, focusing mainly on the task at hand, but eventually my nosy side kicks in again.

'What about you, though, Charles?' I say, as we emerge back into the lobby. I notice that several Christmas decorations have been dislodged from the lower branches, and lie mauled and moist on the carpet. The joys of a puppy, right there.

'What about me?' he says, picking them up and smiling.

'Leonora has a new boyfriend, I gather from what she said. You're still young, you're eligible, haven't you considered getting back out there, meeting someone?'

He considers this, then gestures around him.

'There's a lot to deal with already,' he answers. 'The estate, Georgie, my mother, the impending financial doom. I'm not sure how eligible any of that makes me – my life is really rather messy. Plus, after Leonora, I don't know if I'd have the energy – she ruined me for other women!'

He looks at me for a beat, his green eyes on mine, and adds: 'At least, I used to think she had...'

I have no idea if he means what I think he means, and I'm scared to ask. Is this going to result in him offering me more dance classes, or am I imagining that this moment feels kind of significant? And if I'm not imagining it, how do I feel about it?

Before I get a chance to stutter out a reply, a whirlwind of women arrives, streaming through the front door. They're led by Mary Catherine, who has recruited a small squadron of women from the village. There are around ten of them, all wearing Christmas sweaters, all bearing feather dusters, cloths and cleaning products.

Charles grins at me, looking slightly wicked as he does so, and says: 'To be continued?' before he goes to greet them.

'Thought we'd start off proceedings with a good old-fashioned spring clean, even though it is winter!' Mary Catherine announces as they all troop through and admire the Christmas tree. 'Come on now, girls, up and at 'em! Let's get this place sparkling!'

TWO WEEKS UNTIL CHRISTMAS

'May your heart be filled with gratitude for the blessings of the past and the promise of the future'
Irish blessing

TWENTY

BANCROFT MANOR

I'm amazed at the speed with which things start to happen once the whole village is on board. We decide to create one 'luxury guest suite', and cannibalise the best furniture and fittings from the rest of the rooms to make it look swish. When it's done, the fire roaring, the four-poster bed draped in sumptuous fabrics, it looks fantastic.

The rest of the rooms are coming along nicely as well, with strategic use of what we already have, and everything else hired from local businesses. Mary Catherine and her team use a huge machine called a 'buffer' to polish up the parquet in the ballroom, and every one of the many windows and glass doors is shining.

One of the villagers' daughters, Emily, is home from college where she's studying fashion, and she is an absolute godsend. She buys in cheap fabric and transforms it into beautiful netting that we hang strategically – with the right gust of wind, it billows perfectly and will look amazing in the pictures. She's also found swathes of extra material in storage – old drapes that she remakes for the other rooms. In return, she's been given her choice of outfits from the Dressing Room. Georgie took her up there and apparently she almost swooned.

A few of the items we've hired are already here – easels, whiteboards, real business-style chairs. The rest will be coming soon, and in the meantime, the place has been a hive of activity – echoing to the sounds of drilling, hammering, and people singing as they work.

Charles is delighted with the response, and Allegra has definitely been enjoying herself. She doesn't remember people's names, and is sometimes confused by all the activity, but the lively atmosphere and the company have lifted her spirits. Maybe it's a reminder of different times, when the house was at the centre of the social whirl.

The people of the village have been generous with their time and skills, fitting it all in around their normal jobs and responsibilities. It's been a truly inspiring experience, seeing the whole community come together like this, and I feel quietly confident about the upcoming photoshoot.

Today, everyone is having a well-deserved afternoon off. As a thank you to the villagers, a gorgeous Christmas grotto has been arranged for all the local children to enjoy. It was Allegra's idea, and she and Georgie bought all the gifts and wrapped them.

The grotto has been set up in the secret garden I discovered on my first night here, and it looks magical. The winding path has been dotted with little displays of elves and fairies; the trees and shrubs are decorated with dangling baubles and tinsel. The snow is still thick and dazzlingly white, and as the children and parents make their way in, the place is filled with laughter and high spirits.

At the end of the path, installed on a bench beneath one of the huge pine trees, is Martin from the village, putting his beer belly to good use. He's dressed in full Santa gear, complete with a bushy fake beard and shiny black boots. He really does look the part, and who's to say that Santa isn't Irish?

Eileen is next to him, a table laid out with freshly baked treats – mince pies, I'm told they're called – and big urns full of drinking chocolate. Each child sits on Martin's lap, tells him what they want for Christmas, and is given a rummage in the gift sack. Then they move on to Eileen, who lets them loose with the squirty cream and marshmallows.

Someone has put carols on their phone, and an impromptu choir has sprung up, currently bellowing out 'Oh Come All Ye Faithful' with great gusto. Ryan is here, chasing a bunch of already hyped-up kids around the monkey puzzle tree with a plastic sword, all of them screaming when he catches them and inflicts a thorough tickling.

I spot Mary Catherine's grandchildren making their way to the front of the line for Santa, and hear the boys both ask for bikes. I hold my breath as Molly, their ring-leader, takes her turn. She refuses to sit on his lap, and glares at him with narrowed eyes. She clearly knows it's Martin, as do all of the older children, but wants her chance at a dip in the present bag.

'What's your name, little one?' Martin asks as she glowers at him.

'It's Molly, as you well know, Martin. And I'm not little, I'm ten!'

'Fair play. So, have you an idea what you want for Christmas, then, Molly?'

She stares him down, hands on skinny hips, and announces: 'World peace!'

Everyone in the vicinity bites back laughter, and Martin replies: 'Sure, Molly, I'm only Santa Claus – not God almighty!'

She takes her gift and moves on, leaving me with a sense of relief. I'd thought for sure he'd at least lose his fake beard in that little exchange. Possibly his life.

'This is great, isn't it?' asks Charles, sidling up to me. He's wearing an especially nice pale grey cashmere scarf, and the subtle scent of his cologne is as delicious as ever.

'It really is. So much energy!'

'I know. I'm going to do more stuff like this. We've been linked with these people for generations, but it's always felt like there was a divide, you know? Village down the hill, big house on top. We go into the pub and socialise, but there's never been anything this communal. They're as much part of the history of the place now as the Bancrofts are, and I'm determined to break down those barriers. I'm going to make sure that we invite everyone up on a regular basis, maybe hold summer garden parties, events for the children, that kind of thing.'

'That's a wonderful idea,' I say, smiling up at him. 'Better be careful though – you might end up drinking Guinness and saying "top of the mornin' to you"!'

'None of them actually do say that, I've noticed, unless they're playing up for an audience. We had a coach load of Canadian tourists in over the summer, and they practically all turned into leprechauns for the day! Even the ones who were born here suddenly spoke like they'd kissed the Blarney stone.'

I laugh, because I can imagine it – a harmless bit of fun, acting the comedy Irish, and something that probably delighted the visitors.

We catch up on a few things, and we both eat a mince pie – strange but delicious – as we watch the children trooping through the grotto. I see Sarah with Connor in his papoose, a Santa hat on his little head, and resist the urge to run over and slobber all over him. Jasper appears with one of the decorative elves in his mouth, which Charles leans down to retrieve. The dog looks momentarily crestfallen, then cheers himself up by bounding over to Martin and peeing on Santa's boots.

We're still laughing when Ryan joins us. He's wearing a navy blue beanie hat, his wild dark hair peeking out in curling strands, and the plastic sword is casually slung over his shoulder.

'You look like a pirate!' I say.

'Shiver me timbers, lassie – just be careful I don't make you walk the plank!'

He aims his sword at me, and I hold up my hands in surrender. Charles remains silent, pointedly looking everywhere apart from at Ryan.

'Cassie, I was wondering if you'd show me this folly you've been talking about,' Ryan says. 'The one with the bird's eye view? It's a fine clear day, and I've brought my camera bag with me. Thought maybe I'd make a start. If that's all right with you, Your Lordship?'

Charles nods. 'Fine by me. Cassie, would you like me to accompany you?'

'Worried I'm going to ravish her and sweep her away to a life of crime on the high seas?'

I feel annoyed with both of them, quite suddenly. I'm not a maiden who needs to be protected – and Ryan is not a slavering monster. Just an irritating one.

'We'll be absolutely fine, Charles,' I say firmly. It's always uncomfortable being around them when they're together, and I don't want the fun of the day to be spoiled. 'It's a good idea to get some shots while the sun is shining and the snow looks so pretty. And don't worry, I remember the way.'

He nods, and I follow Ryan away from the crowds. He hoists a big bag onto his shoulder, handing his toy sword to a passing boy, and I lead him off in the direction of the tower.

I wasn't being entirely truthful when I said I remembered the way, but after a few false starts I see it in the distance, its stone turret piercing the horizon. It's a beautiful walk, and Ryan takes pictures as we go. We pause when we see a sweet little robin redbreast perched on a tree branch, its shining eyes darting around and its head swivelling.

I smile as I look at it, the red of its feathers vivid against the snow, and hear the quiet clicking sound of Ryan's camera at work. Eventually, it flutters off into the distance.

When we arrive at the folly, Ryan takes some shots from the outside, and says: 'Why have I never seen this before? I didn't even know it was here!'

'Wait 'til you get up the stairs,' I reply, leading him inside.

Up at the top, the air is freezing cold, but the little stone bench is free of snow. I sit and watch as Ryan circles the small space, taking in the stunning view and the different angles. He opens one of the windows, leans out so far I have the urge to grab his feet, and clicks away. He repeats the process at each little porthole.

While he works, he tells me that as well as each frame working by itself, he could also use them to make a moving panorama. That, I know, will look spectacular – and it's exactly the kind of extra special trick that works so well for marketing.

'Gosh,' I say, as he checks the little screen on his camera. 'It's almost like you're a professional or something!'

He makes an amused snort, and carries on with what he's doing, lost in the process.

'Hey, it's just occurred to me,' I say, getting my phone from my pocket, 'that I could google you now! Before, you were just Ryan Connolly. Now you're Ryan Connolly, famous Cork-born photographer – maybe I'll find some embarrassing pictures of you!'

He sees what I'm doing, and lunges towards me, letting the camera swing from his neck by the strap. He grabs hold of my hand, not hurting me but definitely using some strength. I look up at him in shock, see him shaking his head at me, his face solemn, his blue eyes bruised.

'Don't,' he says simply, slowly releasing his grip. 'Don't do that.'

'Why not?' I say quietly, knowing that he's deadly serious

but not understanding why. He sighs, and sits down next to me. He takes a deep breath, then says: 'I'm sorry I grabbed you. Did I hurt you?'

'No, I'm fine – but you're clearly not. What's going on?'

He rubs his face in the palms of his hands like he's washing it clean. 'If you google me, you'll find stuff. And if you find stuff, you'll see me differently – and I don't want you to see me differently.'

'Okay, I won't, I promise.'

He seems to sag a little, leaning back against the cold stone wall, his long legs stretched out before him. I've never known him to be silent for more than a few seconds, and I'm worried. He opens his mouth a few times as though to talk, but each time whatever he wants to say remains unspoken.

'Last time I was up here,' I say, keeping my tone soft, 'Charles told me about Vanessa, and what happened with her.'

'Yeah? That's unusual. He doesn't like to talk about it, which I completely understand. It was awful.'

'It sounded it. But I think maybe he felt a bit better afterwards – for getting it off his chest, you know?'

Ryan gives me a lopsided smile, and looks around the strange little tower.

'Not winning any subtlety points there, Cassie... but I can see this place does have a touch of the confessionals about it, doesn't it? You're not a priest, mind, and I don't have any sins to confess.'

'I can't imagine that's true – you must have lots! But look – all I'm saying is that you want to talk, I'm here. Whatever it is, I won't see you any differently.'

'And how do you see me now, Cassie?'

'As an eejit. As a friend. As a man who seems to be in pain right now.'

I do see him as all of those things, but as I sit close to him, our bodies touching and our clouded breath mingling in the frosted air, I wonder if I'm being entirely honest with myself – I wonder whether I see him as something more.

He nods and replies: 'Well, the eejit bit's true, for sure. Look, it's a long, sad tale, so I'll give you the shortened version. I used to be married. I had a four-year-old daughter called Mia. Then six years ago, they both died in a car accident. That's that. As they say in those press conferences, I won't be taking questions, all right? Now you can google me. And feel sorry for me, of course – let's not forget that. Ryan Connolly, saddest man in the world.'

He sounds understandably bitter, and although I want to reach out and hold his hand, or pull him into a comforting hug, I sense that he will not welcome it. My heart breaks a little at both what he's told me, and the way he is reacting – I can see him shutting down, retreating, losing himself in his shell of grief and anger and self-loathing.

'I won't google you,' I say firmly. 'Your life is your own. I can't promise not to feel sorry for you, Ryan – of course I do, that's a terrible thing to happen to anyone. But I can promise not to pity you. There is a difference, isn't there?'

He nods, and stares out of the little porthole window. I suspect he's seeing something entirely different.

'There is, yeah. Thank you. Now come on, I'm freezing my arse off here.'

TWENTY-ONE

Ryan keeps his distance for the next few days, and I let him. I think he needs it, and I don't want to push him away by trying to get too close, which makes no sense at all but somehow feels right.

I'm flat-out busy, all the time, with a million and one details skittering around my mind – things to do, things to order, things to check. But when I'm still and quiet, and lying with Eejit in my green bedroom beneath the arch of flowers that Ryan painted for me, my thoughts inevitably go to him.

I have stayed true to my word, and not googled him, but in my head I have visualised his wife and his daughter. The wife was, I'd bet good money, a stunner, and Mia – well, Mia would have been perfect. She'd have his dark hair and sparkling blue eyes, and even though she was only four, she'd already have been able to charm the birds from the sky. She almost feels real to me, this ghost-child of Ryan's, and I can only imagine the inconsolable pain that he carries around with him.

Suddenly everything becomes far more clear: why he abandoned his career, why he moved here, why he is determined to

live his simple life as a full-time handyman and part-time feckless playboy.

The night before the photo shoot, I am still thinking about
it. Still drenched in second-hand sadness. I'm up late, and Eejit
keeps looking at me balefully as I toss and turn, unable to drift
off to sleep. I guess it's a combination of Ryan's story and the
busy day ahead.

Eventually, I sit up straight, and grab my phone from the
bedside cabinet. We talked to Nanna Nora about a lot of things
in those video interviews, and one of the conversations was
about loss – because at her age, she'd experienced a fair deal
of it.

I find the clip, and remember the morning it was taken. It
was a beautiful spring day, and she was sitting outside in her
beloved garden, surrounded by her flowers and her pots of
tomatoes.

'Loss is part of life, Cassie,' she says, her crinkled face
looking right at the camera. 'Nothing is permanent, all of it is on
borrowed time. Everything passes, everything changes – love
and pain and people. It's just the way of the world, and nothing
we do can prevent that. But some losses... well, some losses are
terrible hard. Some losses steal a part of your soul, so, and you
never feel the same again. You go on, and you find happiness,
and you do your best with life. But a piece is always missing,
and you never quite heal...'

She drifts off a little, staring into the distance, a glaze of
tears on her blue eyes. She's clearly in another place entirely.

'Is that how it was for you after Granddad died?' I ask, off
camera. I don't really remember him – I was only four when he
passed.

She looks back at me, almost seeming shocked to see me
there. She gives me a sweet smile, and says: 'Of course, yes. Your
granddad.'

I close down the phone, and lie back in the darkness. That

must be how Ryan feels – like there is a piece missing from his soul. Like he'll never heal.

I sigh, and roll over yet again. I slip into sleep gradually, my dreams wild and random, full of people from my past who I haven't even thought about in years. A girl called Courtney who was my lab partner at high school; Ted's cousin from Boston; Mrs Gregory, who lived next door to us when I was a kid. They all pop up, weirdly vivid, as though simply saying hello and reminding me that they once existed in my life. Maybe it was because of what Nanna Nora said – that everything is change.

It's not the most restful night's sleep I've had since I arrived here, and I abandon my newly adopted ritual of tea in the morning for good old-fashioned coffee. It's going to be a caffeine kind of day, I think, glancing out of the window.

It isn't snowing, although more is forecast for later, and the skies are clear and blue. Having been in England during their rainy season – in other words most of the year – I'm delighted. Everything will be much easier without rain and mud, and look so much better as well.

I decide to walk up the hill to Bancroft Manor, which takes a good twenty minutes or so. Everything's set up and ready to go, and I need the time to clear my head, sip my go-cup of coffee, and be alone. I need the thinking time, rather than making conversation in a car while my head is spinning.

By the time I get there, I feel calmer. I've had a message from June, along the lines of 'You go, girl', and I've also had one from my dad asking me to bring some of Eileen's soda bread home with me. Life goes on back in New York, I know, but these days it all feels very distant.

The house is a hive of activity by the time I get there, and I suspect that Eejit was wise to stay behind. Too much chaos for him – but Jasper will undoubtedly relish it.

Outside on the driveway, I see a selection of cars parked in front of the grand façade of the manor. They include Charles's green Jag, but also a red Porsche, a silver Aston Martin straight from a James Bond movie and an old-fashioned Rolls-Royce complete with its famous hood mascot, the shining Spirit of Ecstasy. It looks like a classic car rally out here, which is exactly what we'd been aiming for. Charles called in a few favours from his friends and family, and I see that pictures are already being taken.

Sarah – willowy and gorgeous despite having had four kids – is dressed to kill in a sleek black gown that must have come from the Dressing Room. Her hair is done in an exquisite up-do, and she's wearing a necklace that is dripping with what may or may not be diamonds. She's leaning against the Rolls-Royce, pretending to sip a glass of Champagne, looking every inch the elegant lady as Ryan works around her, giving her direction and snapping away.

As soon as he says he has what he needs, she exclaims: 'Thank the baby Jesus for that! These shoes are fecking killing me!'

She gulps down the whole glass of Champagne in one go, then belches. Class comes in many forms.

I'd recommended filling the glasses with fizzy apple juice, but that seems to have been predictably ignored – I suspect everyone will be drunk as skunks by the end of the day.

'Look sharp,' someone shouts. 'The boss is here!'

It takes me a few moments to realise they're talking about me, and I give a cheery wave.

Ryan notices me walking towards him, and calls me over to look at his shots.

'They're perfect,' I say, as he scoots through them. 'Who knew that Sarah was actually a supermodel?'

'You did, apparently. You should see her fella, Paddy, now – dressed up in his penguin suit, handsome as you like, no clue from the outside that he's a mechanic and usually in greasy overalls!'

'Well, that's the idea, I guess. How are you? I haven't seen much of you.'

He nods, and gives me one of his feral grins. The ones that go straight to my guts.

'I know. That'll be because I've been avoiding you.'

'Ah. I see. And now you're not?'

'Don't think it'll be possible today, and besides, I decided it was time to catch myself on. I have a present for you, also.'

'Oooh. I like presents!'

He gives me a pitying look, and adds: 'Don't get too excited, there. It's not a pony.'

He roots around in his camera bag, and pulls out a print. It's a picture – of me. I'm staring intently at something, a look of delight on my face, my hair bright red against the snowy landscape. Like most women, I don't always love pictures of myself – but this, I have to say, is beautiful. I just look so happy.

'The robin,' he says simply, 'you're looking at that robin we saw, on our way to the tower.'

I nod, and smile at the memory.

'Thank you!' I say sincerely. 'I'll treasure it. I didn't even know you'd taken one of me.'

'I'm sneaky like that. Right, I'm done out here – didn't want to get going inside until you were here to stage manage.'

We head inside, and I see the Christmas tree has had a mini makeover. The cherry has been replaced with a more traditional star, and the hand-made ornaments have been shifted to the back. It looks a lot more glossy, and Ryan tells me he's already taken some great shots – including one where they actually managed to make Jasper sit still for a minute. Christmas trees and Spaniel puppies, I think, making my way through to the library – a sure-fire hit.

Charles is in there, his favourite room, laughing at something that Jack Mullaney – the wizard man-cum-poet – has just said to him. Jack has been dressed in a tweed suit that Georgie found upstairs, and Orla is combing out his beard, tutting at every tangle. Several of the villagers are lurking around, dressed as I've asked in smart casual clothes.

'Sorry I'm late,' I say, making my way over to Charles.

'You're not. It's just that everyone else turned up early. I think they're all pretty excited about their moment in the spotlight.'

I look around at the eager faces, and realise he's right – there's a real air of jollity in the room.

Once Jack is camera-ready, objecting fiercely to the little brush of powder Orla insists on applying, I arrange everyone in their seats. They're given notebooks and pens, and jugs of water are scattered around. Jack has a little podium, and stands before reading from a book of his own poems. Georgie is here, taking video on her phone – Ryan inspected it and declared it fit for purpose, saying it would produce footage that was plenty good enough for the little snippets we need. She looks thrilled, buzzing with energy.

Leonora did indeed leave the day after she arrived, sneaking off at the crack of dawn without even telling anybody. If any of this has had a negative impact on her daughter, she definitely isn't showing it now.

Ryan checks the lighting, and after a few false starts where people giggle or crack jokes, we get going. The end result is perfect – they look for all the world like a group of eager litera-ture fans, come to hear a masterclass in the glorious surrounds of the Bancroft library.

I leave them all cheering, and head into the kitchen. This too has been transformed – Ryan and some of the other men-folk fixed the dents in the fridge, patched up the neglected plas-terwork, and painted the walls with a fresh coat of white. The Aga has been cleaned, and new, shiny copper pots and pans are hanging from the hooks on the ceiling, along with braided bunches of garlic and herbs. The windowsill is full of fresh flowers, and the big old pine table is covered in bowls, mixers and ingredients.

I move some of it around – taking away branded packets that look a little tacky, adding a big bowl of fresh fruit, pouring the milk into a pottery jug rather than leaving it in its plastic container. The eggs are stored in a container in the shape of a hen, and a big wooden chopping board is coated with flour. It couldn't look more wholesome if it tried.

Eileen bustles into the room, bearing a magnificent layer cake that is topped with fresh berries and meringue. She places it carefully on the table, curtsies, and says: 'Here's one I made earlier!'

'It looks like heaven in a cake, Eileen.'

She nods, and wipes her hands on her blue-and-white striped apron, telling me she's 'ready for her close-up'.

Once Ryan's set up his lights, we let her have free rein – I ask for a few specifics, like a shot of her plunging her hands into a big bowl of flour, white clouds wisping into the air. We have her cracking eggs and whisking, and ones of her opening and closing the Aga. After we've got the first few, I bring in a small group of villagers, and we get pictures of them watching her while holding their own bowls, as though they're at a cookery lesson. At the end, we take snaps of Eileen slicing the beautiful cake, and everyone eating a piece. The expressions of ecstasy are not faked, and I grab myself a little slice – it's going to be a long day.

We move from room to room doing similar things – the fake business meeting, the art class, the luxury suite upstairs. For that one we have Sarah again, sitting at the dresser in front of the mirror. She's wearing a white robe, and we repeatedly get her to take her diamond earrings on and off while she looks at her reflection. We also do some of her in the four-poster bed, very demurely lying in the arms of her real-life husband, Paddy, both of them gazing across at the roaring fire.

In between takes, she swears like a trooper, swats Paddy across the head for 'groping me arse under the covers, dirty thing', and swigs more Champagne.

Orla has borrowed massage tables from one of her hair and beauty friends, and we've set them up in one of the better rooms. There are scented candles and incense burning, some kind of weird new-age music is playing, and Emily the fashion student and one of her friends are lying face down with stones on their backs. There is, of course, no spa at Bancroft Manor – but if Charles gets the investment he's looking for, who knows?

This is all about showing the potential – and it is exhausting, especially for Ryan, who is involved in every single set-up. By the time we break for a late lunch, he looks tired, sitting on the steps of the terrace despite the cold weather, eating a plate of sandwiches.

'You okay?' I ask, popping my head around the door to check on him.

'Sure. I'd just forgotten that this is actually hard work. Suppose I've got used to a life of manual labour, which is tougher on the body but way easier on the mind.'

'Well, tell me if you need a break later, all right? You're the most important person here and I can't have you passing out on us. Let me know if it's too much, Ryan?'

He shrugs, and says: 'I will, yeah,' in a tone that implies the absolute opposite. I roll my eyes and leave him to it. We're building up to what will be the biggest shoot of the day – the ballroom.

We start while it's still light, with a table set up to host a bride, groom and their family. It's cheap plywood beneath, but the crisp white linens cover that up, and the whole length of it is draped in exquisite flowers – a centrepiece of roses and hydrangeas in pretty shades of pink and lilac, and scattered smaller arrangements in the same colours. There was plenty of high-class tableware and silverware in storage in the house, and

Eileen and Roberts have been busy preparing the wedding meal.

I bustle along the table, making a few adjustments that help it all look more real – as though the shots were taken in the middle of an actual wedding celebration. I move glasses, half fill some and top up others, scatter the surface with a few handfuls of confetti.

The food on the plates looks great – slices of roast beef, roast potatoes, fresh vegetables – but is stone cold by now. Luckily nobody has to actually eat it, just pretend.

A young couple from the village volunteered to be our happy newlyweds, and Emily added to her actual dress with a few lace panels and a stunning train. It all looks good, and when Ryan comes back in, we get what we need – oh-so-spontaneous shots of the perfect wedding dinner.

It's all moving quickly now, and everyone seems to have got the hang of what's needed. Charles gets stuck in with everything, shifting tables, moving furniture, shepherding villagers, fixing a plug when Orla's precious hair curlers blow a fuse.

The hardest work is changing the scenes in the ballroom, trying to show its versatility. We do a full dinner scene, with all the round hired tables set, happy diners sipping their wine and chatting as Roberts, in a full traditional butler's outfit, makes his way around the room carrying drinks on a silver tray. Once that's done, we fold all the tables down, and set it up as a party – the guests standing and chatting, spilling out onto the terrace.

The final shots take the most work – but are also the most fun. We're staging an actual ball in the ballroom. The people taking part are all outfitted in either costumes from upstairs, or formal wear we hired in just in case. It's kind of weird, seeing all these now-familiar people gussied up like extras in a glossy period drama.

The chandeliers have been cleaned and the bust bulbs replaced, and I've gone around the room adding large silver candelabras, now all flickering beautifully away. Night has fallen outside, and we leave the French doors open – the starlight and the silvery glow of the moon are shining through the now-falling snowflakes, and the contrast between that and the warm radiance of the ballroom is strikingly beautiful.

Allegra and Roberts are joining in for this one, and I smile as I see them together – definitely of the generation who learned how to dance, looking every inch the part as they stand in hold. Charles has donned a dinner suit and he wears it well – in fact he looks incredibly handsome as he walks towards the dancefloor.

'Now, everyone,' I shout, getting their attention, 'look at Roberts and Allegra! See how they're standing? Aim for something like that! It doesn't need to be perfect, nobody is going to be marking you at the end! Don't move too quickly, and please don't worry – just try and enjoy yourselves!'

There's a lot of shuffling while people figure out what hands go where, and Charles strolls around helping out where he needs to. He meets my eyes as he passes, holds out his arms and says: 'Can I tempt you, Cassie?'

Yep, I think, in all kinds of ways. But now is not the time for shenanigans. Now is the time for action. I glance over to Ryan and check if he's ready. When he gives me the thumbs-up, I wave over to Georgie.

She's on the piano, joined by the musicians from the village, who are pretending to be a string quartet. She nods, and the music starts – a kind of stripped back version of a piece I recognise as the waltz from Swan Lake. It's not a full orchestra, and the guy playing the cello has never really used one before so he's only pretending to bow, but somehow it works.

I can't help laughing as everyone starts to dance – truthfully, it's a scene that has all the jerky elegance of a zombie apocalypse. Ryan is whirring around the room taking multiple shots from different perspectives, and I can only hope that he'll manage to get something we can use. If not, I tell myself, it isn't a disaster – we have enough. Everyone has been so willing and worked so hard that I don't have the heart to direct them any differently.

After maybe half an hour, Ryan finally signals to me that he's got what he needs – or, I suspect, his shrug means he's got as much as he's likely to get. I walk over to Georgie and the musicians and tell them to wind things up, as Charles joins me by the piano.

'Everybody, hello!' he shouts, waiting for a few of the more enthusiastic feet to notice the music has stopped.

'I'm told we have everything we need, ladies and gentlemen – that it's a wrap! I can't thank you all enough for your help today. It's been humbling, it's been hard work, but most of all it's been an absolute hoot – so again, thank you! Now, Cormac tells me that against all odds, there is still some Champagne left, so please, feel free to stay for a while and simply enjoy yourselves! If I had a glass to hand, I'd raise it, and make a toast to us – to the Bancroft Estate, to the residents of Campton St George, and to a long and prosperous partnership!'

A round of cheers goes up as he finishes, and the musicians immediately switch tempos to something much livelier and more appropriate for a jig. The waltz holds are abandoned, along with all pretence at formality.

I breathe out with relief as I watch them, seeing Ryan jump right in, Georgie shrieking with delight as she joins him. Within minutes everybody else floods into the room, and pretty soon it's booming to the sound of both the music and the dancing. Some people are dressed in ballgowns, some in jeans, but everyone looks happy.

I sag a little inside as I realise it's done. It's really done – we put together this whole amazing thing in a week. I can't quite believe it, and I feel exhilarated by what we've managed.

I also feel suddenly very, very tired – I had a rough night, and today has been hard work, and now the relief of it all being over and done is finishing me off. It's as though now I know I can stop, I've run out of all energy at once.

I slip outside into the night, welcoming the chill of the cold air against my cheeks – it was roasting in there by the end.

I walk down the terrace steps, and stand at the edge of the long, landscaped grounds. I gaze around – snow, stars, and serenity in one direction, madness in the other. I look up at the ballroom, now full of light and life, and smile. We did it. We really did it.

In the big scheme of things, it's not much – it's taking some pretty pictures to convince millionaires to part with money – but it still feels like a win, not just for me, but for everyone. I can't remember the last time I felt like I had a win, and I know that it's not just Bancroft Manor that's been brought back to life – it's me as well.

TWENTY-TWO

The next day, Ryan and I return to the estate to do a final walk through. The snow stopped last night and the forecast says we're now heading into the land of rain, so he wants to get a few more pictures of it white and untouched.

We call into the house, and find Roberts busy at work in the kitchen, frying up bacon and brewing tea.

'Good morning!' he says brightly, apparently completely untouched by the night before. 'Help yourselves – I just need to take a mug through to Martin Byrne. He seems to have spent the night sleeping beneath the piano, and he tells me he's got a bad case of "the fear", whatever that might be.'

Ryan laughs. 'It means he has a terrible hangover, with a side helping of remorse! I'd add a slug of whiskey to that, Roberts, then start making loud noises – he'll soon clear off.'

'I see. Perhaps I'll play the piano to encourage his recovery then. Charles is upstairs in his office if you need him, and Georgie is... missing in action. I suspect she's trying to avoid the clean-up, and as Jasper is gone as well, she'll be on the grounds somewhere. If you see her, please remind her she has an appointment in an hour's time.'

We promise that we will, and head on out to enjoy what might be the last crisp, clear day we have for a while. The sun is sparkling on the snow, and the sky is so blue it looks like it's been painted on. Birds are chirruping and fluttering, and everything feels peaceful as we stroll.

Ryan takes pictures, and I snap some shots of my own on my phone to send to June and the folks back home, and we chat about our upcoming trip to Cork City.

He's flying back in a few days, and I'm going with him. I've booked a hotel despite the offer of staying at his sister's place, because I want to have my independence. Eileen's cousin Moira has come up with some information about Nanna Nora's life before she moved to the US, and I'm excited to see the place she came from. My dad is even more excited.

'So, does everyone go back to Ireland at this time of year?' I ask as we walk.

'Not everyone. Cormac and Orla stay because of the pub. Mary Catherine and her tribe all decamp back to Wexford, and Eileen goes to Dublin – but not until Christmas Day itself, because she's finishing off all her orders until then.'

'Wow. I didn't even know there'd be flights.'

'Not many, but it's a lot of fun – the Christmas Day flights are always a good craic. What will you do, Cassie, on the day?'

'I'm not sure. Charles has invited me up to the house, which is nice. But I think I might be just as happy in Whimsy, with Eejit.'

It strikes me as I say this how far I've come, and how good this whole trip has been for me. There are some obvious advantages – no sneering Suzie, no sitting around missing Nanna Nora. No more watching of the dreaded wedding video, which I have decided to delete for good. No more feeling sorry for myself, basically.

'He's taken a shine to you, he has. Eejit. Never known him get so close to anyone.'

'Are you jealous?' I ask, nudging him. 'You were the alpha dog before I arrived!'

He pretends to be offended, waves his fists in the air, and says: 'I'm still the alpha dog, and don't you forget it, woman!'

The effect is spoiled by the fact that he's so busy showing off he accidentally knocks against a tree branch, and the dislodged snow tumbles down all over him.

'Alpha snowman more like,' I say, laughing as he freezes, his head covered in the stuff.

He's busy swiping it off when my phone rings. It's Charles.

'Hi – are you out on the estate?' he asks.

'Yes, we are. Everything okay?'

'I'm sure it is, but we seem to have a bit of a situation with Georgie. Her therapist is here, but she is not.'

I glance at the time, surprised to see that we've been out for so long. Charles sounds worried, and I say: 'Could she just be, I don't know, avoiding her? I know she said she was hoping to get her to resign before Christmas!'

'That could well be it – but she's not answering her phone either. This isn't unusual, she does like to take off and roam, but she seemed tired this morning after all the excitement.'

Ryan raises his eyebrows at me, obviously picking up on the change in mood, and I say: 'Okay. We'll go and look for her. Do you have a tracker on her phone, one of those friends and family things?'

'No, which now seems like a foolish choice. I'm going to send the therapist away, and ring round some of her friends just in case.'

'I'd try a kid called Ollie Kerr, lives on a farm near Marshington Grange. Sounded like she had little bit of a crush on him.'

'How do you know that and I don't? Am I the world's worst father?'

'Don't be stupid – no teenage girl is going to talk to her dad about stuff like that! Look, let us know if you hear anything, okay?'

I fill Ryan in, and he stands with his hands on his hips studying the landscape. I know he's very fond of Georgie, and can see how concerned he is.

'Shall we try the tower?' he suggests. 'She might be in there, having a ciggie and hiding? And if not, we'll get a good view around the place.'

It's a good idea, and we strike out across the snowy paths, reaching the folly about twenty minutes later. I shout her name as we go inside, running up the stone steps and hoping to see a puff of smoke in the air. I sag in disappointment when I find the place empty, but join Ryan at one of the windows. Together we move from one to another, him using his camera zoom and me using my eyes, trying to spot any sign of her.

'Nothing,' he says, shaking his head. 'Has he checked if her car's gone?'

I quickly message to ask, and receive a reply telling me her car is still in the garage, and that Ollie Kerr was a bust. I try to cast my mind back to the first day I met her, and the little tour she gave me of her favourite places on the estate.

'Where's the pond?' I ask Ryan, staring out at the grounds.

'I think there's a few. Which one?'

'It had steep sides, and reed beds, and she said she used to like hanging out there.'

He nods and goes back to his survey, looking out in a westerly direction.

'I think I know the one you mean. Come on, it's worth a try.'

It takes us another twenty minutes to reach the pond, and we shout Georgie's name as we go, me keeping an eye on my phone. I'm hoping for a message saying she's been found, but when nothing lands, I start to feel increasingly worried. Georgie has seemed in good spirits recently, but I know she has issues that lurk beneath the surface.

The rising sense of panic is of no use to me, so I try to breathe through it as we climb over snowdrifts and check beneath every dense tree and hedge we pass.

As we get nearer to the pond, I hear a faint cry. I stop, hold Ryan back and gesture for him to be quiet. We stand still, and I shout: 'Georgie! Are you here?'

'Yes! I'm in the pond! Please, please help me!'

Ryan takes off, his big boots eating up the distance, scurrying through the long, frosted grass and coming to a stop at the top of the steeply sloping side. I catch up, and stare on in horror at what we see.

Georgie is in the middle of the pond, which is coated in thin shards of shattered ice. She's keeping her head above the water, and has Jasper held high in her arms, trying to keep him clear of it. The puppy is whining and wriggling, pawing at her face in distress.

'My foot is caught!' she yells. 'I can't move at all, and I'm f-f-f-freezing!'

Ryan doesn't hesitate – he strips off his fleece jacket, unties his boots, and gallops down the steep bank of the pond, kicking his way through the snow and the vegetation. He leaps right in, and I hear him gasp as it soaks through his clothes.

'It's okay, Georgie, I'm coming!' he cries, splashing through the frigid water, pushing aside chunks of ice to get to her.

I can see that her lips are blue, and her skin is pure white. Her hair is a drenched trail spread out behind her, and every part of her is shaking.

Ryan takes a deep breath and dives down beneath the surface. I hold my breath with him, tense until he emerges again.

'Cassie!' he shouts up towards me. 'She's proper trapped, one of her feet is basically tied up by the weeds. Look in my jacket pocket, there, find my Swiss Army knife!'

I'm not sure what that is, and my fingers fumble uselessly in his pocket. Eventually I just tip everything out – car keys, a wallet, and finally a little portable tool that seems to combine a knife, screwdriver and corkscrew. This must be it, I think, and I turn back to Ryan.

He's standing shivering in the water, talking soothingly to Georgie, then taking Jasper from her grasp. Her arms immediately slump down, splashing onto the broken ice. He clutches the fretting puppy close to his chest, and strides to the side, water splattering around him. As soon as he puts the dog down on solid ground, Jasper starts running around in a circle, shaking his coat, and barking. The poor thing is terrified, but still doesn't want to leave Georgie.

Ryan holds up his hands, and gestures for me to throw the knife. I'm worried I'll mess up, that I will miss, that it will sink to the murky bed of the pond and never be seen again. He lurches nimbly to one side and catches it in both hands, heading straight back to Georgie.

Another deep breath, and down he goes again. More heartbeats, more worry, more fear – for both of them. The pond is not deep enough for them to drown in, but the cold could kill them, I know.

Eventually he comes back up, spluttering and sucking in air, telling Georgie to try and move her foot now.

'I don't th-th-think I can!' she stammers. 'My whole body is dead. I can't feel anything at all!'

I can hear the terror in her voice, and Ryan acts immediately. He puts his arms around her, and physically hoists her towards his body. She's a tall girl, but he manages to scoop her up, the effort obvious on his face as he grimaces and starts to take slow, waterlogged steps back towards the edge of the pond.

'Call Charles!' he shouts up to me. 'Tell him to get as close as he can in the car, and to bring blankets and hot drinks!'

I do as I am told, cutting Charles off when he tries to keep me on the phone, because Ryan and Georgie need me. She can barely move, and the steep climb back up is beyond her. Ryan shoves her upwards, and I lie down on my belly and reach out for her. When I finally grasp her hands, her fingers are blue from frost, dangling lifelessly in my grip. I pull and Ryan pushes, and eventually, inch by agonising inch, we have her out. Jasper races up towards us, trembling and licking at her face. It's covered in scratches where he panicked and clawed her.

I start to rub her hands, pull off my own jacket and slip it around her shoulders. She gazes up at me, eyes bleary, and says: 'I'm so s-s-sorry...'

'No need to be sorry. Just stay with us now, okay? Your dad's on his way, everything's going to be fine.'

She nods as the dog nuzzles her, and Ryan lays his fleece on top of her. He's soaked through and his teeth are chattering, and he really needs to warm up – but I know there's no point in telling him this. I know he won't listen, and neither would I.

I hear the sound of car doors slamming, and sigh in relief as the cavalry arrives. Charles runs towards us, followed at a slower pace by Roberts, and both men are carrying bundles of blankets. Charles pushes us aside, kneels in the snow by his daughter, and immediately starts to wrap her up. Roberts passes him a flask, and she manages a few sips of whatever is inside.

'It's okay, darling, you'll be okay... we're here now. What happened?'

He sits her up and wraps his arms around her, sharing his body warmth, her wet hair plastered across his chest.

She looks up at him with slightly more alert eyes, and says: 'I fell in the bloody pond!'

'You fell? You weren't trying to... hurt yourself, were you?'

'No, Dad, no – I promise! I know the ice isn't thick enough to walk on, but the stupid dog didn't! He just r-r-ran off, straight onto it, and he was right in the middle when I heard it cracking! He can't swim yet, and I couldn't leave him, could I? I couldn't just stand by and watch him die...'

I realise that I'm crying, the tears freezing on my eyelashes as they escape. She had to stand by and watch Vanessa die, and was obviously determined not to let that happen again. The agony on Charles's face is clear as he clasps her to him, kisses her face, tells her again that everything will be fine, that he loves her, that he's got her. That she's safe.

Ryan meets my eyes, and we share a sad look. He knows her history as well, and it's heartbreaking.

Roberts puts his hand on Charles's shoulder, and says: 'We should get her to the hospital, Charles. It looks like she's on the mend, but we need to make sure she's okay.'

'Yes... of course, we should do that,' Charles replies, clambering to his feet, his daughter still in his arms. He's cradling her like a baby, and I wonder if he will ever let her go.

He seems to remember that we're there, and looks directly at both of us.

'I can't thank you enough. I'm going to drive her to the hospital – it'll be quicker than calling an ambulance. Will you be all right?'

'Off you go,' Ryan says firmly. 'We'll be grand. I need to dry off, and we'll see you there, yeah?'

Charles nods, clearly in shock, and starts to stumble away towards the car. Roberts lingers for a moment, taking in our bedraggled appearance and Ryan's shivers.

'Get back to the house, you two,' he says. 'Get showered and warm, and help yourself to anything you need. If you could take Jasper that would be helpful. Allegra is there somewhere, but we haven't told her about any of this, so tread carefully until we know Georgina is well. Thank you, again. I shall be rooting out medals to present to you both later – I'm sure we have some knocking around.'

The walk back to the manor is excruciating. It's bad enough for me, damp and without a jacket, and for Ryan it must be even worse – his clothes are clinging to him, and when I hold his hand, I'm worried that he should be going to the hospital too. We take turns carrying Jasper, who is very loudly heartbroken at being parted from Georgie and keeps trying to run away to find her.

We make our way minute by slow minute, moving at a steady jog, and I feel a huge sense of relief when I see the terrace come into view. We run faster once we see it, and soon we are inside. I find a bowl of water and some food for Jasper, and give him a rub down with the kitchen towel. He seems fine, mainly because Georgie kept him out of the water I guess.

I pour us both a big glass of whiskey from the decanters in the Blue Room, then lead Ryan up the stairs to the suite that used to be mine.

'Get your clothes off,' I say, 'and get in the shower. I'll start the fire.'

He manages a suggestive smile, and says: 'I've waited a long time for you to ask me to get my kit off, Cassie...'

'Yeah. Well, your lips are turning blue, and that's not the sexiest of looks – go on, away with ye!'

I lay on the Irish with the last part, and shoo him towards the en-suite. I soon have the fire roaring in the grate, and wrap myself up in the comforter for extra warmth. I hear the water flowing in the bathroom, and after a few minutes I start to regain feeling in my numbed face. I sit on the edge of the bed, and my heart is racing so fast I can almost hear it.

That was so close, I think, to being a disaster. I don't know how long Georgie had been stuck there, but I do know that if we hadn't turned up, it could all have been a lot worse. I will be fine, and so will Ryan – we just have to hope that she is as well. As the adrenaline starts to flood through my system at the thought of what might have been, I rub my hands together, tell myself that she is okay. That the worst did not happen.

I sit like that for a while, letting myself settle, focusing on the crackling of the fire and the sensation of blood running into my chilled extremities. I need a shower too, but it can wait. Everything can wait.

The sound of the shower stops, and after a few moments Ryan emerges in a cloud of steam. His hair is wet against his neck, and he is wearing nothing but a white towel knotted around his waist. I stare at him, transfixed by the shining skin, the curve of muscle on his torso. The trail of hair that runs from his chest to his waist. He stares back at me, standing proud and unashamed, and raises an eyebrow.

I'm preparing myself for some flirtatious comment when the door to the room flies open. Allegra strides in, still wearing a Japanese-style robe, her feet encased in plaid slippers that don't match it at all.

She stands still, and her eyes go from Ryan to me and back again. *Oh Lord*, I think, *please let her remember who we are – I'm not up to a sword fight right now.*

'My goodness,' she says eventually, smiling as she eats up the sight of Ryan in his towel. 'I haven't seen anything like that in quite a while!'

TWENTY-THREE

Within the hour we receive a message from Charles telling us that Georgie has had her initial examination, and she's doing well. We explain the situation, very carefully, to Allegra, starting with the fact that everything is okay.

She grasps it quickly, goes off to get dressed, and we all drive to the hospital in Ryan's truck. He's had to scavenge for dry clothes, and Charles's don't really fit him. Charles is taller and leaner, so everything Ryan currently has on looks like it's about to burst at the seams as if he's the Incredible Hulk.

Charles meets us on the ward, where Georgie has her own side room, and he hugs his mother reassuringly before Roberts leads her away to see her granddaughter. I see him take in Ryan's outfit and fight back a snigger.

'All right, all right, Your Lordship,' Ryan says, 'we didn't come here to be judged by the fashion police. How's your girl doing?'

'Well. They've got her in some special blankets that are bringing her temperature back up gradually, and some kind of drip as well. They're keeping her in overnight just to make sure, but they're positive she'll recover and be able to come home tomorrow.'

His face is pale and drawn, his green eyes dark with worry. His usually groomed hair is tousled, and he looks so stressed out that I give him a hug – he looks like he needs one more than Allegra did. He sinks into me, his arms going around my waist, and I feel him sigh into my hair.

After a few moments he pulls away and straightens, looking mildly embarrassed by the display of emotion. Heaven forbid he should reveal weakness in any form.

He looks from me to Ryan, and says: 'She'd been in there for a long time. Her phone was in her pocket and soaked, so she couldn't use it, and she didn't want to risk dropping the dog anyway. The doctors have told me that if she'd been stranded much longer in those conditions then she might not have made it. She said you just jumped right in and rescued her, Ryan.'

'I did, yeah – why wouldn't I?'

'Well, the two of you might have literally saved her life. I don't think I'll ever be able to find a way to thank you.'

'Roberts promised us a medal,' I reply, grinning in an attempt to lighten the mood.

'And I'll have a bottle of that thirty-year-old Bushmills whiskey I know you keep. I've a terrible thirst after all my heroics.'

'It's a deal – medals and outrageously expensive whiskey all round! Seriously, thank you both, so much. I don't have the words to tell you how much I appreciate what you did.'

I look from one man to the other, and come to a decision that is probably rash, probably foolish, and definitely inappropriate. Somehow, though, I just don't care. It's been a day.

'I've got a few words,' I say, standing between them. 'And I'm going to say them while we're here, with all these nice doctors and nurses to make sure you're on your best behaviour. Charles, Ryan never slept with Leonora.'

They're both silent, their expressions comically shocked. Ryan recovers first, and retorts with an edge of anger: 'What did you go and say that for, now, Cassie? It's none of your business!'

'That's true,' I reply, holding my ground and glaring back at him, 'it is none of my business. But it's just stupid, and it's gone on too long. Didn't yesterday teach us anything? Didn't today? Don't you both realise that we're always stronger when we work together? You two need to start acting your age, not like a pair of... fecking eejits!'

It's actually my voice that is the first to rise, and I feel questioning eyes on us. *Oops.* I give a little wave of apology and make a zipping motion on my lips.

Ryan tries to stay angry, but I can see that he's losing out to laughter. In fact, both of them are, which is a little bit annoying – but better than them fighting, I guess.

'Yeah, yeah, laugh it up, boys – but I'm only telling it like it is!'

'Ah, Cassie,' says Ryan, once he's stopped laughing. 'I knew you had the spirit of the redhead somewhere inside you!'

'Yes,' adds Charles, trying to look serious and failing, 'you were quite terrifying for a moment there, Cassie.'

'Plenty more where that came from – so, make friends, play nice, and stop behaving like little kids, okay?'

Charles nods thoughtfully, then turns to look at Ryan.

'If you didn't sleep with my wife, Ryan, why on earth didn't you tell me so before?'

'Well, you never asked, Your Lordship – you just assumed the worst of me straight away, now, didn't you?'

'I suppose I did at that. Even though Leonora had given me no reason to trust her word, I accepted it. I think perhaps it was easier... having someone else to blame.'

Every word that comes from his mouth sounds like agony, and even though I started this, I'm desperate for it to end.

Ryan nods, looks awkward, and answers: 'She's good at pushing the buttons, sure.'

Charles holds out his hand, his nostrils flaring slightly from the tension, and says: 'Ryan, will you accept my most sincere apologies?'

There's a moment when I'm not sure which way it's going to go. I'm proud of Charles, for the way he has reacted. For not trying to make excuses. He's simply taken it on the chin, and seems to want to make amends. Ryan, though, still doesn't look convinced. He rubs his fingers over his face, and seems to be weighing it up. *Oh God*, I think, *please shake his hand – don't leave him hanging like this, you big fool.*

Eventually, he says: 'Make it two bottles of the Bushmills, and you've got yourself a deal.'

Charles laughs, tells him that is not a problem, and they finally shake. It's a weird shake – one of those where they clasp each other's hands at the same time.

'You should hug it out,' I add helpfully, earning horrified stares from both of them.

'For feck's sake, Cassie,' Charles says, in a perfect Irish brogue, 'what do you think we are, American?'

ONE WEEK UNTIL CHRISTMAS

'May love and laughter light your days and warm your heart
and home.
May good and faithful friends be yours wherever you may
roam.'
Irish blessing

Georgie is indeed home the next day, slightly bruised but none the worse for wear. Jasper goes incandescent with joy when he sees her, and I suspect there's a bond been made for life right there.

When I ask her how she is, she replies: 'I'm fine! I'm kind of hoping one of these scratches on my face might leave a scar, then I can make up stories about a shark attack...'

I laugh. Yeah, I think, she is definitely feeling fine.

On the less dramatic work front, Charles has found a copy-writer and designer, and I've curated Ryan's shots. They're magnificent, and if I didn't know any better, I'd swear that Bancroft Manor was already fully operational.

I'm heading for Cork the day after tomorrow, and have had exciting news. Sadly, the street that Nora grew up on has been demolished, but Moira has found a relative still living in the city, a distant cousin, on a DNA ancestry site. She's called Deirdre, and we've arranged to meet up during my visit. Dad is fizzing at the news – it's made his Christmas. After our chat he was heading straight off to set up an account himself, ordering testing kits and getting lost in his enthusiasm.

Today, though, I am being treated to a day out by Charles. Georgie is safely at home with Allegra and Roberts, and he says it's only fair that he shows me some sights, because he's monopolised my time with work since I've been here. He's right – I've been so busy with Bancroft that I've not had time to do anything else.

We started with a drive-past of the famous Stonehenge, but we don't stop there. Charles wants to take me to see a different stone circle, and tells me that Wiltshire is 'jam-packed with Neolithic treasures'. He looked so excited when he announced this that I couldn't help but be infected by his enthusiasm.

Even the gloomy, grey day couldn't spoil it – in fact, as we strolled from rugged stone to rugged stone at Avebury, the black clouds only added to the mood. Charles gave me some background, clearly filled with a sense of joy, his hands stroking the scarred pillars as though he was somehow trying to connect with the men who erected them thousands of years ago.

He showed me the curved profile of Silbury Hill, and we walked up through snow-logged fields to a place called West Kennet Long Barrow. It's an ancient burial chamber that you can go inside, cavernous and eerie in the falling light. Charles looked around in wonder, and I caught a glimpse of the other Charles – the one that became an archaeologist in a parallel universe.

'You're good at this,' I said as we drive towards Oxford. 'Explaining it all. It's a shame you had to give it up.'

'Well, I'm not going to bleat about it – my life is hardly awful, is it? Besides, I do have a cunning plan. If things pan out the way we hope and we can put Bancroft back on a solid footing, I'm considering a little archaeological dig of my own.'

'Really? Where?'

'On the estate itself. There have always been stories, folk rumours – a spot tucked away near the woodlands that is supposed to be magical. The kind of place villagers used to go when they wanted a baby, that sort of thing. Sometimes these tales, passed down the generations, have some substance – I think it might be worth exploring. It would make me very happy to actually find out.'

I love this side of him – boyish, charming, full of energy. He never seems to feel the need to hold himself in check when he's talking about these things, and the formal edge slips away in front of my eyes.

By the time we arrive in Oxford, the bleakness of the skies is being overtaken by darkness, and we walk around the city beneath the light of the emerging stars. It is absolutely stunning, the sense of history dripping from every cobbled alleyway, every ivy-covered college, every dreaming spire.

He shows me his college, St John's, which is vast and beautiful, laid out in quadrangles and exquisite gardens. It's quiet, most of the students now at home for Christmas, but there are still earnest academic types shuffling around the snow-covered lawns, still golden light shining from libraries and rooms, still the sound of chatter and laughter and music escaping into the evening.

We grab some dinner at a pub called the Eagle and Child – or the 'Bird and Baby', as he tells me it's known by students – and make our way back to the car. He takes me via a place called Radcliffe Square, which is a little slice of perfection.

The square is lined by old college buildings and the Bodleian Library, and in the centre is a grand circular structure called the Radcliffe Camera. I stand and look up, as I'm told to, and the landscape piercing the starlit sky is breath-taking – crenulations that make the colleges look like castles, gargoyles and ornate water spouts, the magnificent round dome of the Camera, the slender spire of St Mary's church soaring pale and proud into the air.

As I gaze around me, it starts to rain – but I find that I simply don't care. In fact, I welcome every drop that spatters against my upturned face. Everything about this place is miraculous, and I feel so alive I'm convinced I could almost flap my arms and fly up into the constellations.

Charles laughs at me as I do a little jig of happiness, but it is not a mocking laugh – it is one that says he understands. He gets it.

When I finally slow down, dizzy and full of joy, I say: 'I can't believe this is real. I can't believe I'm here.'

I pause, and feel an emotional shadow creep over me.

'I can't believe I have to leave.'

Charles reaches out, takes my hands in his. He pulls me close, his handsome face slick with rain, blond hair shining in the moonlight, and says: 'Do you, though? Cassie, why don't you just... stay? You could keep Whimsy. Or move in to the manor. Whatever you like – but you don't have to leave. I don't want you to leave. I can't imagine Bancroft or the village without you in it.'

I look up into his eyes, feeling the tug of our physical closeness.

'Are you offering me a job, Charles?'

'I'm offering you a lot more than that, Cassie, and I think you know it. Yes, you've been an asset in a professional sense, of course you have – but it's more than that, isn't it? These kinds of declarations don't come easily to me, but I haven't felt this way for a very long time. There's something here, between us – a spark. The kind that I'd almost forgotten existed. The kind that I think could lead somewhere very special. It's something I'd very much like to explore. Or am I just a deluded fool? Am I imagining it?'

His hands run up my arms, come to rest on my shoulders. He gently pushes a strand of wet hair away from my face, and I am suddenly a teenager, full of ideas she's absorbed from romance novels. I am standing with this man, this beautiful man, in this beautiful place, and he is looking at me with such intensity that I can barely think.

I could stay here. I could stay in England. If I let it, this fantasy could run and run – I could explore that spark with Charles. I could even marry Charles. I could be the lady of the manor. I could live there, in that life, in a totally different world to my own.

I could work, I could play, I could love. I could be anything I want to be – but I'm still not exactly sure what that is.

'No,' I reply shakily, 'you're not imagining it, Charles. The spark is real. But I don't think I'm there yet. I don't think I'm anything but a work in progress.'

He nods, sighs, and says: 'You're not ready for the tango?'

'Absolutely not!' I respond, laughing. 'The tango is way too hot – the kind of dance that takes a spark and turns it into a raging inferno!'

He pulls away, but takes one of my hands in his. He opens my fingers, and lifts my palm to his mouth. It's just one delicate touch, the soft skim of his lips against my sensitive skin, but it is enough to make me realise how close to ignition I already am.

'Right,' he says, smiling at my trembling response. 'Well. I'm a patient man, and I don't give up easily, I warn you. Now come on – you're soaked through, and we have a long drive ahead of us.'

TWENTY-FIVE

I'm home for maybe fifteen minutes before Eejit scratches on the door, and I sit with him on the rug in front of the now-roaring fire as I call June.

When she answers, I see that she is sitting on a bench in Central Park, and feel a pang of homesickness. She says hello, and moves the phone around so I can see the familiar landscape.

'It snowed!' she says, sounding excited. She's wearing pink ear muffs, and looks about ten years old.

'I see that!'

'I picked up a veggie gyro—'

'With extra hot sauce?'

'Of course with extra hot sauce! Just thought it'd be nice to sit here and enjoy it all while it's still pretty. Before it turns to urban slush. I'm meeting Neil for drinks in the East Village – it's all feeling real Christmassy right now. How about you? Any news? I loved the pictures you sent! I can't believe you went to the other side of the world just to work...'

'I know. But it's been good for me. Today, I went to see some stone circles.'

'Oooh! Were you caught up in their pagan magic? Are you now pregnant with druid triplets?'

'I hope not! And then I went to Oxford. It was even better than you can imagine.'

'Oh my God! Was it just like *Oxford Blues*? Did you see Rob Lowe?'

I laugh at her excitement. We used to love that movie, even if it was old. She had it on an ancient VHS cassette in her basement, and we used to watch it and do terrible English accents. Now I come to think of it, it's probably as much Rob's fault as Hugh's that I got so obsessed with coming here. Colin Firth doesn't come out of it blameless either.

'No, I didn't see Rob Lowe – but gosh, June, it was so beautiful! Charles took me.'

She finishes a quick bite of gyro, and her eyes narrow.

'Did I detect a little sigh there, Cassie? Something about the way you said *Charles*, like you were out of breath... has something happened? Has he kissed you punishingly in the stables?'

'No, because he's not actually the hero of a Regency romance novel. But... yeah, I guess something happened. He told me he has feelings for me – though he didn't specify exactly what, because, you know, English. There was talk of a spark.'

'A-ha!' she says, like she's Sherlock Holmes figuring out a mystery. 'Spark is surely code for wanting to ravage you? What else did he say?'

I scratch Eejit's furry ears, and feel the warmth of both the fire and the memory.

'He said he wanted me to stay. That I could have Whimsy Cottage, or live at the manor. That he couldn't imagine life here without me now.'

Even as I rehash the conversation, I am poking and picking at it – looking for ways I might have misinterpreted it.

'I'm not really sure what he meant though. I might have got it wrong.'

June laughs, and wraps up the remains of her gyro.

'Cassie, only you could do this.'

'Do what?'

'Take what sounds like an actual real-life declaration of intent, of goddamn *spark*, and try to convince yourself you made it up. Why wouldn't he feel like that about you?'

I think about what she's said, and reply: 'Yeah. You're right. I really need to stop doing that. But it was kind of a surprise, and now I'm wondering if I was just swept away in some kind of Oxford-inspired hallucination. Or if he was just caught up in the moment, and right now he's lying in bed thinking, shit, what did I just do…'

'Right, yeah. Can I ask you something?'

'No.'

'Tough. Is Charles a rash man? Is he impulsive? Does he strike you as reckless?'

'Ummm… well, no. Totally the opposite in fact.'

'Well then, Captain Jackass, stop questioning it all – accept the fact that he's *into* you! Did he kiss you?'

'No. Not really. He, ah, he kissed the palm of my hand, very, very softly.'

I feel a blush developing as I tell her, as my body remembers the way his lips felt against my skin.

Her eyes go wide, and she sighs out loud.

'My God,' she says dreamily. 'That's even better. That's so… sneakily hot!'

I nod, and she continues: 'So, what are you feeling about all of this? Is it something you're interested in – staying there?'

'I don't know, June! I'm all over the place. I hate the thought of leaving, and Charles is… well, he's sparky, what can I say? But I'm also aware that this is just a vacation. That my real life is back home. Just seeing you sitting there in the park makes me want to get the next flight to JFK.'

'Yeah, I can imagine. And I'd be devastated if you didn't

come back, you know that – I've felt like my right arm's been chopped off ever since you left! But honey, maybe this is something you need to consider – maybe it's something you owe yourself?'

'You think I should stay?'

'I'm not saying that, no. I'm just saying think about it. Let it settle. Maybe see where things lead. You've got another week, right?'

'Right.'

'And you've got your trip to Ireland as well. I know you won't admit this, but I have a sneaky feeling your hunky handyman might still be in the mix as well.'

'No, no, Ryan is just a friend...'

Even as I say it, spluttering the words out with such fervour that Eejit raises his eyebrows at me, I know I might be protesting too much.

'Yeah, you just keep telling yourself that! Look, there's a lot going on. Just don't reject anything out of hand, okay? And bear in mind that if you do end up as Lady Bancroft, I'll be expecting tiaras and ballgowns even when you're in McDonald's!'

TWENTY-SIX

The city of Cork is blazing with Christmas lights. Everywhere I look, they cast a multi-coloured glow over the bustling streets. The energy of the place is palpable, crammed with people shopping, chatting and laughing, while street performers fill the late afternoon with music and song. Groups are spilling out of pubs, and the cafes and restaurants have steamed-up windows. The atmosphere is one of fun and potential, and even better, everyone talks like Nanna Nora. I've had to get used to yet another currency – the euro – but nothing's perfect.

We arrived late last night, and Ryan and I parted ways at the airport. He saw me safely into a taxi, and within minutes I was checked in to my hotel. The city is shaped by its history and its geography, by the River Lee that runs through it in two separate channels, enclosing part of the town inside its meandering curve.

My hotel room overlooks one of the impressive bridges that span the water, and I spend forever staring out at it before I finally get to sleep. The bridges are old, and they would have been here even when Nanna Nora was a child. It's strange and comforting to imagine her here, breathing this same air, walking these same streets.

Today, Ryan has been showing me the sights. We've visited churches and cathedrals, beautiful parks dressed in their coats of snow, and the grounds of the university. We've seen amazing graffiti art on the sides of buildings, and even been to the Butter Museum, which was a lot more interesting than it sounds. It's been busy, which is exactly what I needed to distract myself from thoughts of Charles, and the decisions I need to make.

After a late lunch, we had a ride on an enormous Ferris wheel, and I video called my dad from the very top. I showed him the sights, and introduced him to Ryan. Dad had stared at him sternly, and said: 'Ryan, is it? Well don't be getting any ideas, son – don't be stealing her away from me now, you hear?'

'I can't promise, Mr O'Hara,' he'd replied, grinning. 'But I'll do my very best.'

After that, as dusk started to descend, we went up to the northern part of the river. We crossed one of the stone bridges, the water roaring mightily beneath us.

Ryan is obviously proud of his city, and gets a kick out of showing it to me. His accent becomes even heavier once he is home, and as we walk he tells me stories about his sisters and his nieces and nephews. One of them – an eight-year-old called Sean – has apparently asked Santa for a cow this year.

'And will he get one?' I ask, as we stroll along the riverside.

'He just might. Spoiled rotten – only boy in a family of girls.'

'Yeah, that kind of family dynamic sets him up to be pampered, doesn't it?'

'That it does, as I can well testify. It's been gas to see all the kiddies again.'

We chat and we walk, bundled up against the savagely cold weather, and Ryan points out important landmarks – some more personal than others.

'See that alleyway, across the road there?' he says, pointing. 'That's where I had my first ever kiss. I was thirteen, and her name was Lucy Gallagher. We wore each other's faces off, and I was in love.'

'I'm amazed there isn't a plaque, possibly a statue?'

'I know, yeah. Maybe I'll start a petition. And look down there, Pope's Quay? Well, that used to be the busiest part of the docks, going back a few hundred years. More importantly, it's also where I fell off my skateboard and broke my wrist when I was fifteen.'

'Again, why is this not more widely known? I didn't read that on any of the tour guides!'

'Shocking. Ah now, I know one that might actually be of interest...'

We go further up into the sides of the city, the streets getting steeper, and he points out a fairly ordinary looking small house. This one actually does have a plaque, and I smile as I read it. This humble little building is the former home of a woman called Annie Moore, who travelled to New York as an emigrant. On January 1, 1892, she became the first person to officially pass through Ellis Island, starting a new life in a new world.

It makes me smile, this tangible connection between us all, and I quickly snap some pictures for my dad. I wonder what became of Annie, and hope that life in the US treated her kindly.

We wander on, passing packed bars with live music spilling out in bubbles of pipes and fiddles. Eventually we reach the bottom of a road that stretches almost vertically off into the distance, cars parked perilously at ridiculous angles, a big blue building visible at the very top of the slope.

'This is St Patrick's Hill,' he says, gesturing up it. 'Feel like a climb? The views from up there are savage.'

I nod, tell myself I need to channel my inner mountain goat, and we head on up. There are steps cut into the sidewalks but it is still tough. The snow is heavy and thick, and we trudge up and up and up, past houses of all shapes and sizes. Some are huge, multi-storey mansions, others more humble. Ryan tells me it was constructed in the 18th century, and it shows – the steepness of the hill makes all the gorgeous buildings feel a little higgledy-piggledy, crushed against each other as they rise higher and higher.

We reach the top, and as promised, the views are amazing. The city is glimmering beneath us, the river shining in the moonlight, the Christmas Ferris wheel and lights dazzling pinpoints of colour in the distance.

'It's beautiful,' I say, gazing down at the sights before me.

'It is. We used to sledge down here on days like this. I've even known people to ski!'

'Really? That sounds dangerous.'

He looks a little serious as he stares down the hill, his hands shoved firmly into his pockets and no trace of his normal smile. Not so long ago he was full of his usual charm and gabby energy, but it seems to have disappeared bit by bit as we climbed the hill.

'You okay?' I ask. 'You seem a bit... off.'

He looks at me for a few moments, as though trying to make his mind up, and then replies: 'I want to show you something.'

A statement like that would normally be my cue to raise my eyebrows, but his tone is not, for once, at all flirtatious. I nod, and he leads me to a little plateau off the main hill. I see a sign that tells me this is Audley Place, and wonder why we're here.

After a few minutes he stops in front of a townhouse. It looks Georgian, like the others, and is three storeys high, set in the middle of a terrace. It's painted white, and has grand windows taking in the views. The drapes are drawn, but light escapes from inside, casting a glow on the pretty courtyard garden.

Ryan stands and stares at it, lost in thought, eyes shining. His silence is heavy, and as I follow his gaze and study the house, I start to figure out where we are. What he wanted to show me. This isn't the scene of his first kiss or a skateboarding accident – this is the scene of something much more special, much more heartbreaking.

I slide my fingers into his, and he glances down as I stand at his side.

'Is this where you lived?' I ask quietly. 'With your wife, and Mia?'

He smiles sadly, and nods.

'It was on the rough side when we bought it,' he says. 'Alice was pregnant, and I thought we should look at somewhere ready to go. But she fell in love with this place, and that was that, my fate was sealed. I lived up ladders, had paintbrushes for hands, a head full of plaster... but we did it. We brought it back to life, and it was a happy time for us.'

'I'm sure it was. It's a beautiful home.'

He seems content to stand silently for a few more minutes, undoubtedly remembering those times. Picturing his daughter in the garden, his wife at her side. The life they led together here. His mind must be swimming with memories of all that he had, and all that he lost.

Eventually, he squeezes my fingers and says: 'Sure, I don't know why I brought you here. Bit of a buzz-kill.'

'Don't be silly,' I reply. 'Not a buzz-kill at all. I feel honoured that you did. You don't need to be "on" all the time with me, Ryan.'

He studies my face, and drops a quick kiss on the top of my head.

'I know. Thank you. And if you have the inclination, we could make one more stop?'

'Guinness?'

'For the soul,' he answers, keeping hold of my hand and

leading me away. I glance back over my shoulder, taking one more look at the building that is so much more than a building. It is the place where Ryan's heart lived, where part of it always will.

We walk together through the cold evening air until we reach a church. It's small, tucked away, built of red brick and topped with a soaring tower. This is not what I expected, and I say to him: 'Church? I didn't think you were the type to go to Mass, Ryan.'

'You'd be right. I had a bit of a falling out with the big fella after Alice and Mia died. I'm still angry, truthfully. But being angry with God means you believe in him, doesn't it? So every now and then, I feel the tug. You can stay outside if you like, I won't be long.'

'No way. You can't shake me that easily.'

He laughs, and we make our way inside. I was raised as a Catholic, albeit one who only goes to church on holy days now. Still, as we enter the church, the familiar smells of incense and candle wax are comforting, and I find myself automatically dipping my fingers into the water of the font and making the sign of the cross.

There isn't a service taking place, but the church is still busy. Women are cleaning and polishing the pews, and a few scattered individuals are sitting or kneeling, heads bent in prayer. It is quiet, and peaceful, and perfect.

Ryan walks towards a row of small candles on their metal stand, takes one that is already burning, and uses the flame to light another. He bows his head, and I see his lips move in silent prayer. It is an incredibly touching sight, seeing this big man so humbled by his emotions, and I feel the sting of tears.

I light a candle of my own, close my eyes, and add my prayers to his – for Alice, for Mia, for Nanna Nora. For all of us.

TWENTY-SEVEN

'Do you think Eejit is all right?' I suddenly ask Ryan, coming to a stop in front of a stall selling cheese.

It's the next day, and he has joined me in town ahead of my meeting with Deirdre. We're in a place called the English Market, which is a magnificent building packed with different traders. Fresh seafood, butchers, bakers, wine merchants, fruit – it's all here, spread out around us in glorious Technicolor.

'Sure, why wouldn't he be?' he says, pulling me to one side so we don't interrupt the busy flow of human traffic. 'Eileen's keeping an eye out for him, and he was fine before you came, you know.'

'I know that,' I reply, firmly. 'I just hate the thought of him scratching at the door to Whimsy and being all confused and sad because I'm not there to let him in. What if he thinks I've abandoned him?'

He shakes his head and looks amused, before saying: 'He's a dog, Cassie. A tough dog at that – he's a survivor, that one. He's definitely tougher than you, you big softie!'

I stick my tongue out at him, and walk away. He's right, I

know he is. I suspect I'm feeling nervous about meeting a new relative, and I'm feeling anxious about the future, and all of it is focusing in on my adopted stray instead. I'm not sure that being worried about Eejit is a good enough reason to relocate to England, but sometimes it seems like it might be.

I've bought a few gifts for the folks back home, mainly from a shop so Irish it almost felt like a parody, and I've picked up some small items for Charles and the others as well. The retail therapy hasn't cheered me up much, but it has passed a couple of hours.

Now, I realise as I glance at my phone, it's nearly time to head upstairs to the Farmgate Cafe.

Ryan sees me look, and says: 'You have a while yet.'

'I know, but I prefer to be early – it'll give me time to start acting like a normal human being instead of someone she wants to disown.'

He sees how flustered I am, and I hate that my nerves are getting the better of me. I've been in a little bubble since I arrived in Campton St George – after a bumpy start, everyone now feels reassuringly familiar. I feel safe with them, and step-ping outside that bubble is a little harder than I expected.

'Do you want me to come with you?' Ryan asks, tilting his head to one side. 'You seem a bit on the skittish side today.'

I bite my lip, and know I should say no – that I will be fine. Except I kind of do want him to come with me, and maybe this is all part of my changing outlook on life – not being afraid to ask for what I want.

'Erm... maybe, if you can? I mean, I don't want to take away from your family time.'

'I'm here until New Year, Cassie. I'll be altogether desperate to get away from them before then. Look, it's no bother or I wouldn't offer. All right?'

'All right. Thank you. I don't know why I feel jittery about it, but I do.'

'You're allowed. We all have our moments.'

We head up the wooden stairs, and I stare around for a few minutes as we wait for a spot to be cleared for us. It's a beautiful space, tables and chairs laid out in a galleried level that overlooks the rest of the market. Sweeping wooden beams soar above us, pale light flooding in from windows in the roof. The décor is classy and the atmosphere bustling, the aromas reminding me that I barely ate at breakfast. I hope my stomach doesn't start rumbling in the middle of our conversation.

The waitress settles us at a table, and we stare at the menus. It takes Ryan all of thirty seconds to decide, but I'm coming to the conclusion that coffee might be all I need after all.

'Will you have some toast at least?' Ryan pushes, as we order. I agree that might be a good idea, and I go back to checking the time on my phone.

'She's late,' I announce, frowning.

'By three minutes. She's coming in from Glounthaune, did you say?'

I nod. I have no idea where that is, but she'd assured me by text message that it would be a lot more fun for her to come into the city, where she could 'make a day of it'.

'I'll just message her,' I decide. 'I sent her a picture so she'd know who to look out for, but she'll be expecting me to be on my own.'

'You needn't worry. I'd say this is her now, coming right at us.'

I look up from my screen, and see that he is most definitely right. She doesn't have my height, but there is a definite family resemblance. She's in her forties, with an identical shade of red hair to me and Suzie, and a surprised look on her face that says she's thinking exactly the same as me. I stand up to greet her, my chair scraping across the floor.

'Will you look at that!' she exclaims as she reaches us, looking me up and down. 'It's like somebody stretched me!

Sorry I'm a bit late, the trains were awful slow because of the weather. I'm Deirdre, in case you hadn't guessed.'

She looks Ryan up and down, a glint in her lively blue eyes, and says: 'And who would this be?'

He stands up and introduces himself, and she laughs when she realises he's local.

'And here's me thinking I was about to meet a dishy American! Nice to meet you both, anyway. Plus a fine excuse to get away from my kids for the day.'

'You have children?' I ask, amazed at the thought of this whole other family, linked to me by Nanna Nora.

'I have four, and they're all evil.'

The waitress comes back with our drinks, and Deirdre orders tea and toast. Once we're settled and have exchanged small talk, she says: 'I was so pleased to hear from you, Cassie. I've been pulling together the family tree for a while now as a Christmas present for my daddy, and this is the icing on the cake. I'd heard stories about your nanna, but they were just that, you know? Tales told in the family. She always seemed very mysterious, the way she disappeared.'

'Disappeared?' I repeat, frowning.

'Oh yes. Upped and left, she did, and nobody was certain what became of her. If I have the right of it, she'd have been my great-grandfather's youngest sister – there were quite a few years between them, I'm told. So your dad and my grandmother were cousins, and you and my dad are third cousins – you share great-grandparents. I think that's what it is, anyway – it's enough to make your brain bleed, to be truthful. Anyway – you're family at least! No doubting that now I've met you.'

She chatters away merrily, and I ask: 'I'm still confused about the disappearing thing. Nanna Nora never talked much about life back here, she just said she'd come to the US for a fresh start, like thousands of others.'

'I don't know the ins and outs, it was a long time ago. But

from what's been said in the family, once she left she cut off contact with everybody back home. Sent a postcard saying she was safe and well, and that was that. My granny used to say it was on account of her broken heart.'

'Her... broken heart?' I repeat again, stirring my tea so hard it spills over the edge of the cup. 'What do you mean?'

'I'm told there was a man – isn't there always?'

She winks at Ryan as she says this, and he grins back at her, nodding his agreement.

'Bear in mind, now, that none of this was talked about very much – they were hard times, and that made for hard people, so. A lot of what went on in the past was hidden, and Ireland seems to have an endless supply of rugs to sweep things under.'

My mind immediately goes on high alert, recalling the various national scandals that my nanna commented on as they were exposed – forced adoption, the awful Magdalene Laundries, sexual abuse within the church. She sees my eyes widen, and lays a hand over mine, obviously guessing where my thoughts have led.

'It was nothing like that, Cassie. Like I said, she had a man, and they became engaged when she was maybe seventeen or eighteen – it sounds young now, but it was normal back then. But as soon as he was old enough, during the Second World War, he ran away to England and joined the army.'

Ryan leans forward, obviously interested, and says: 'I guess that didn't go down well?'

'No, it did not. From what I hear, Nora's daddy was a proud Irishman, and he wasn't pleased. Felt like Nora's fella had shamed them.'

My head is spinning, and I'm not processing this as quickly as I would like.

'Hang on, I'm confused,' I say. 'I thought the South was neutral during the war?'

'It was,' Ryan confirms. 'But it's emerged since that thousands of men went and joined up. Those that came home were often not treated well.'

'But why? Why was it such a disgrace?'

The two of them share looks, and Deirdre says: 'It's hard to explain, but the politics were complicated at the time. Ireland had basically been at war itself in the not-so-distant past, fighting for independence. There was a lot of bitterness, a lot of anger. A lot of resentment towards the British. Nora's man was far from alone in what he did, but in our family, it caused trouble. I don't even know his name – her daddy banned it from being mentioned ever again!'

'But she was single when she moved to the States,' I insist, trying to fit the pieces together. 'She got a job in a hat shop, and met my grandfather and married him. There *was* no other man.'

'That's because he never made it home. He was killed in the Normandy landings I believe. Your poor nanna must have been heartbroken, but wasn't even allowed to speak his name in the family home... apparently there was some huge disagreement, and she was told she was lucky he was dead so he couldn't drag her down with him. You can't imagine, now, can you? They were very different times. To have to live like that, hiding her pain. Terrible. Nobody could blame her for leaving.'

I stare at Deirdre, adding up dates and piecing together information. Nora arrived in the States in 1951, I think, when she was twenty-six. That means she lived at home, with a father who refused to let her grieve, for years after the war.

'Why did she stay so long?' I ask. 'Why didn't she just move out?'

'I'd be guessing that she couldn't. She'd have had no money or independence, and I know her mammy was sick and died sometime in the late forties. Maybe that's why she stayed? Or maybe she was saving for her fare? We'll probably never know. I was hoping that you could maybe fill in some of the blanks for us.'

I shake my head, trying to dredge up any memory of Nanna Nora mentioning any of this, or my dad knowing about it – but I come up blank.

'No, I'm sorry. It was like her life started when she arrived in New York. It's... God, it's so sad! She was such a wonderful woman, Deirdre, she really was. She never seemed miserable or heartbroken, she was always full of life. She only died earlier this year, just before her 100th birthday, and right up until the end she was singing and drinking her Guinness and cracking jokes...'

'That sounds like one of us, sure,' Deirdre replies, smiling at me. 'I'm sorry I've upset you, darling – it's a sad tale. But tell me about her life after the sadness – tell me what happened to her! I've always been fascinated, I truly have.'

I nod, and swipe away tears. What happened to Nora was awful, but it doesn't negate the rest of her life, does it? She did go on to marry, have a child, build a whole new future for herself.

'She had a good life,' I say, fighting back the emotion. 'She settled in New York, and married my granddad, Brendan O'Hara. They had one son, my dad, and he had me and my sister, Suzie. She lost my granddad when she was in her sixties, but she never seemed to let anything defeat her. She liked her gardening, and she took art classes at the community college, and she had a wide circle of friends. She was a wonderful cook – I grew up eating her soda bread and colcannon and apple cake. She was kind and caring, and so damn funny – she cracked me up, she really did! I still can't believe she's gone... now I have all these questions to ask her, and no way to do it!'

Ryan looks me in the eyes, and says: 'You already know everything you need to know about her, Cassie. Everything that matters. She sounds like an incredible lady.'

'She was. She really was. And I know all of this will settle in my mind eventually – I just wish I'd known earlier.'

'Ah, sure look it,' announces Deirdre, 'she clearly wanted to leave the past where it was, and who can blame her? She lived life to the full, it seems.'

'I think so, yeah. I often thought that about her – she always seemed so full of spirit. Ready to take on the world even in her nineties.'

'That's what she learned, I suppose,' Deirdre says. 'To enjoy the moment. We should all be so wise!'

We chat for a while longer, Deirdre giving me a potted history of the family and showing me pictures of her parents and children. Ryan takes some pictures of the two of us together, and Deirdre records a little video message for my dad, inviting him to come and stay.

'You might regret that,' I say. 'He retired last year and he's been bored silly ever since. He'll probably be on the next flight!'

'And he will be very welcome, as will you, Cassie. Not so sure about you, Ryan – reckon my fella would get a fit of the green-eyed monster if I brought you home!'

'As he should, Deirdre,' Ryan replies easily. 'You're a fine-looking woman.'

She blushes slightly, and I laugh. He is unstoppable, he really is.

After an hour and several more pots of tea, Deirdre tells us she has to get moving. We hug each other firmly, and she departs after a flurry of mutual promises to stay in touch. I watch her disappear off down the wooden stairs, swallowed up into the bustle of the market, and feel strangely sad to see her go. I barely know her, but she is part of me – part of Nanna Nora.

I sit back down, deflated, and Ryan pushes a plate of thick toast towards me.

'I'm not hungry,' I say.

'That's not the point. You need to eat, line your stomach.'

'Why?'

'Well, obviously, because I'm taking you on the world's best pub crawl. You look like you need it, and we can raise a glass to Nanna Nora in every bar we visit. How does that sound?'

It sounds, I think, like the perfect plan. I raise my mug of tea, and say: '*Slainte!*'

TWENTY-EIGHT

I soon realise that Cork pubs are not quite like other pubs. There's a whole heritage trail based on them – there's even a map.

This, though, is Ryan's trail – and we start at a place called the Hi-B Bar, which is located up a steep flight of stairs and is basically a bit like sitting in a very lively living room with a bunch of friends you haven't met yet. We raise our glasses to Nanna Nora, and down a pint of Guinness each – me quite a bit more slowly than Ryan. After that, we move on to a place called The Long Valley.

There, we snag a little table at the back of the pub, where we enjoy people-watching a group of office workers on their Christmas night out. Everyone is dressed as an elf, which is a feast for the eyes.

After our toast, Ryan says: 'Have you any pictures of her, the famous Nora? If I'm going to be celebrating her until my brains dribble out of my ears, I'd at least like to see her.'

'I can do better than that,' I say, grabbing my phone and heading to the videos. I pick one at random, and he leans close to watch.

'That's my sister, Suzie,' I tell him, seeing that it's a video we did together, sitting on lawn chairs in the yard at my mom and dad's house.

'Does Suzie always have that face on? Like she's just eaten a rotten kipper?'

'Yeah, she does actually! She looks like me, though, doesn't she?'

'Like a version of you that's been ironed, and had all the joy sucked out.'

'She's not that bad! Well... you know what, she kind of is! But I'm her sister so I'm allowed to bad-mouth her, and you're not.'

'Fair play. Ah... just look at your nanna. She's a treat for the eyes!'

It was a sunny day, and she'd insisted on wearing a hat a friend had brought her back from Australia – like a cowboy hat but with corks dangling off it on strings. It's very, very silly – and very, very Nora. I suspect she did it just to annoy Suzie.

'What's the secret to a happy life, Nanna?' I asked, the cheesy question making Suzie's eyes roll. 'Tell us how you always manage to seem so upbeat!'

I smile as I watch, but I also feel a rush of sadness. Nanna Nora's life had been blighted by pain, by heartbreak. By the loss of both her first love, and in the end the family that rejected her for loving him. You'd never know it from the mischievous grin that creases her wrinkled face.

'There's no magic formula, girls – if there was, I'd have millions in the bank! But if you're wanting my tips, I'll give you a few. Firstly, don't worry about the things that don't matter, or what other people think of you – and I'm aiming that one at you, Boozy Suzie!'

My sister raises her wine glass at her, and Nanna thinks before she goes on.

'Go for long walks,' she says next. 'There's not much in life that can't be figured out over a good long walk. The world is a beautiful place, and it's best seen with your own eyeballs and not over a wee screen. Now, then, what else... well, laugh, as often as you can. Sing, dance, make a fool of yourself. Life is all about the craic. Enjoy every moment, because believe me, they go by faster than you'd believe – even when you've had as many as I have!'

She cackles at her own joke, and all the little corks on her hat wobble around her face. She looks up at me from between the strings, and adds: 'I'd say, above all else – always follow your heart. It might lead you into trouble, but at least you'll enjoy the ride – I know I have!'

I press pause, and she freeze-frames on the tiny screen, her eyes shining and a playful smile on her face.

Ryan leans back, raises his half-empty glass, and says: 'Well now, that deserves an extra toast – to Nanna Nora, may she rest in peace!'

'Well,' I say, clinking my glass against his, 'if she's in heaven, there won't be any peace, I'm pretty sure – she'll have everyone organised into a conga line!'

'That's all for the good – bet it can get pretty boring up there, what with all that perfection. Right. Come on. Next stop.'

Our crawl goes on, taking in live music, singers, and even a poetry reading. By the time we reach our fifth stop, the Mutton Lane Inn, I am feeling much better about life. In fact, I'm feeling great about it. We are settled into a cosy corner seat in the dimly lit pub, and I stare around at the pictures on the walls, realising that I can't quite read them clearly.

'I think the walls might be moving,' I announce solemnly. 'Could be an earthquake – should we get under a table?'

He laughs, and says: 'I think we should probably get you back to your hotel after this one. You're scuttered.'

'I am? What does that mean?'

'It means you're ossified. Blathered. Stocious. Completely battered.'

'Wow, you guys have a lot of words for "drunk", don't you?'

'We do. Part of our rich cultural heritage. Now come on, let's be on our way.'

I consider protesting, because I don't really want this to end. I haven't thought about anything bad for the whole session – and Nanna Nora would be proud of the way I've concentrated on living in the moment, I think. But I know he's right – I'm not usually a heavy drinker, and I am starting to feel the call of my bed.

We make our way back onto the street, and it's deliciously full of people in a similar state to me. I call out hellos, and make new friends, and giggle when I slip on a patch of snow. We come across a busker singing alone with a little keyboard on a stand, and I immediately decide that it's a good idea to start dancing. I jig around, catching strangers by the arms and taking them for a spin, loving every moment of it.

When Ryan finally takes hold of me, putting his arm around my shoulders and steering me away, I protest: 'Why do we have to leave? What's wrong with having a little jig?'

'Nothing at all, darlin' – it's just that the fella there was singing a ballad. "My Heart Will Go On" from *Titanic*, as it happens.'

'Oh. Yeah. That's not a very jiggy song, is it? Was he annoyed with me for spoiling his Celine moment?'

'I left him a few euro to make up for it. I'm sure his art will go on.'

I laugh way more than this joke deserves, and we make our way through the busy streets towards my hotel by the river. Once we're inside, Ryan snags some candy bars and a can of soda from the bar, and accompanies me upstairs.

He lays them on my bedside cabinet, as though he thinks I might need them in the morning. He may be right, I think, slightly dizzy. I might wake up tomorrow with a case of Martin Byrne's 'fear'. I tip the contents of my purse out on the bed, smoosh everything around, and finally find what I'm looking for – a strip of painkillers. I add them to the supplies, feeling quite pleased with myself for being such a Girl Scout.

'Excellent idea,' he says, grinning.

'Well, I'm a details person! Wow. I've had an amazing night. So much fun. I didn't think I'd ever smile again after hearing that story about Nanna Nora. Thank you, Ryan, for taking such good care of me. You're a lot nicer than you pretend to be.'

'Keep that a secret, now, won't you? I have a reputation to protect.'

'Ha! You and your reputation... you know, you can't be *that* much of a playboy. I've been here for weeks and although you've flirted, you've never once made a move on me. It's enough to give a girl a complex.'

I'm being playful, but I'm also standing close to him, looking up into that gorgeous face. Looking at that thick, dark hair, and wondering what it would be like to bury my hands in it. Admiring his muscular arms, and imagining what it might be like to be held in them. Remembering the sight of him back at Bancroft Manor, wearing only a white towel slung low on his hips.

That single image is enough to make me blush, and I suddenly feel a little out of control. Like the booze has unleashed something inside of me that has been lurking there all along.

I reach up, run my fingers along his cheekbone, entwine them in his hair. He leans into my touch, and I see the change in his eyes – the humour is gone, replaced by something darker. Something wilder.

'Be careful now, Cassie,' he says, his voice low. 'I'm only human.'

'So am I. And isn't this the most human thing in the world? Wanting somebody?'

He makes a noise that is half growl, and tugs me towards him. I fall into his body, feeling his arms go around me, his hands on the small of my back. I wind my hands around his neck, holding on tight, refusing to break the eye contact.

One of his hands runs up my body, twines into my hair. He holds me there, and I know I should pull away. I know I should end this before it begins, but I can't. I stare at his lips, and want them on mine.

When he finally leans down and kisses me, it is electric. Every cell in my body responds to him, every part of me comes alive. I mould myself into him, losing my senses as the kiss deepens, as my hands roam, as all thought disappears. My knees literally go weak in a way I've never experienced before.

I cling on to him, lost in the sensations of having him close, of the touch of his fingers and his mouth. If what I'd felt with Charles was a spark, this is a full-on forest fire, and I am happy to burn alive.

When he eventually pulls away, I can almost hear my heart thudding, and feel abandoned as he sighs and shakes his head.

I keep my grasp on his shoulders, trying to pull him closer, but he takes hold of my hands and removes them from his body.

'This isn't right,' he says, sounding as lost as I am. 'I have to go.'

'It is right! Nothing has ever felt so right. Don't leave. Stay here with me.'

My fingers are curled inside his, and the heat is still there – even a shadow of that kiss is enough to make me reckless.

He gazes into my eyes for what feels like an eternity, obviously wrestling with himself, and then says: 'No. You're drunk, Cassie. You're drunk, and you've had a hard day, and I'm sorry. I shouldn't have done that. It's your Nanna Nora on my shoulder like a devil, telling me to follow my heart.'

He gently pushes me away from him, disentangles his hands from mine. He softly touches my face, sweeps aside my hair, and gives me one more kiss – a chaste one, on my forehead, that is a pale imitation of what came before it.

'Damn,' he says, his eyes bright and shining as he drinks me in. 'Look what you've gone and done.'

'What have I done?' I reply.

'You've gone and made me break one of my hard-earned rules, that's what.'

He shoves his hands in his pockets, and I frown in confusion.

'No, I haven't! I'm not married, and I don't really live in the village – I'm only visiting!'

He laughs, and turns to leave. As he reaches the door he looks back and adds: 'I'll let you ponder that one, darlin'. Now get some sleep.'

CHRISTMAS DAY

'The magic of Christmas lingers on,
Though childhood days have passed,
Upon the common round of life,
A holy spell is cast.'
Old Celtic verse

TWENTY-NINE

BANCROFT MANOR

I wake up early, in the bedroom I used on my very first night here. It seems so long ago now, so much has happened.

To start with, I know how to make a coal fire, which I do immediately. I also seem to have acquired a dog – one who doesn't seem especially enthusiastic about getting off the bed.

'Oh Eejit,' I say, ruffling his fur. 'You've come so far, boy! When I first met you, you were a street dog – look at you now, snuggled up in four poster luxury!'

He agrees by thumping his tail once on the comforter, and keeps his eyes on me as I open the balcony doors. The snow is still here, but has been trashed by a couple of days of rain. The sky is dark grey, and even the village below looks dim. So many people have gone home for the holidays that it feels a bit like a ghost town.

I go back inside, and check my phone. It's in the early hours back in the States, but I smile when I see a message from June. Well, more a string of Christmassy emojis and some love hearts to be accurate, but it's the thought that counts.

I start to compose a message of my own – to Ryan. A simple one, wishing him a happy Christmas. One that should be easy to write. Except, of course, that it's not – because Ryan no longer just feels like a flirtatious friend who I can share casual greetings with. Ryan feels like something altogether more dangerous.

I'd woken up the morning after our kiss feeling absolutely terrible. It was a combination of a hangover, the emotional rigours of Nanna Nora's tale, and, most importantly, a big fat dollop of embarrassment. No, not just embarrassment – it was more than that. I didn't just invite him to kiss me, I practically begged him to stay. I threw myself at him, and he turned me down.

I'd rolled over in bed, my head clanging and my mouth dry, gratefully grasping the soda he'd left for me.

I felt sick, and nauseous, and deeply ashamed. But underneath all of that, I could still remember that kiss – I could still remember how he made me tremble. How much I desired him. I'm glad that he went when he did – glad that he acted honourably – but part of me still wishes that he hadn't.

I'd also been left with the mystery of his rules, and it was really hurting my brain trying to understand what he meant. His rules dictated that he wouldn't fool around with anyone married, anyone who lived in the village, or... anyone he thought he might fall in love with.

I'd slapped myself on the forehead and given myself a good telling off. I was obviously remembering it all wrong. Ryan has never given any indication that he feels that way about me. He only even kissed me because I basically forced him to, and then he left. I go over and over it, feeling worse and worse each time, and I totally get why they call it 'the fear'.

In the end I'd messaged him.

> Thanks for getting me home

> Hope I didn't behave too badly. I am paying penance with the world's worst hangover. Let me know if we're good?

Even the pinging sound of his reply landing seemed to make my sore skull vibrate, and I'd gobbled down a couple of the pills along with the soda.

> We're good, Cassie

> Always. Safe travels.

Since then, nothing. I tell myself I'm being stupid. That Ryan means nothing to me. That even if he did, he isn't doing anything wrong – I haven't exactly been communicative myself. What do I expect from the man? I'm probably being a typical woman and over-thinking everything, analysing it all from every angle while he hasn't even given it a second thought.

I take a quick snap of the dog on his throne-like bed, and send that to him with one line:

> Happy Christmas from Eejit. Woof!

There, I think, standing up and deciding to forget about it all for the rest of the day. I've done it. Now I need to get on with enjoying myself.

Charles invited me over to spend Christmas Eve night with them all, and I'd gratefully accepted. The village was so quiet, and the lack of its usual energy and liveliness was a little depressing.

I'd barely seen anything of him since our night in Oxford. As soon as I was back from Cork, he'd taken Allegra to London to see a specialist for a consultation and they'd stayed in the city to see family. I don't ask which family, just in case it's too regal for me to handle.

Last night had been wonderful, in the way I've come to expect from this family now – fish and chips from the restaurant in Marshington Grange, several spirited games of charades, and a treasure hunt around the grounds. Even in the drizzle it was fun, and Roberts had obviously spent a long time carefully composing clues and hiding them. In the end, the treasure turned out to be a mechanical duck perched in the branches of a tree. It has a remote control that makes it flap its metal wings and quack. They all insisted I should keep it as a memento, and it pretty much sums them up I guess. Totally quackers.

Charles and I haven't had any time alone to discuss my future plans, and I have to say I'm relieved by that. I still haven't come to any conclusions, and after what happened with Ryan, I also feel weirdly as though I've cheated on him. I know it's ridiculous, but I can't quite shake it. Charles is gorgeous, and kind, and he has made his feelings clear – unlike a certain Irish man I know. I do find him attractive, extremely so, and maybe under different circumstances I'd feel more inclined to give it a try.

Right now, though, I am too unsettled. Too distracted. Too confused by everything I'm feeling.

I get dressed, grab my gift bags and make my way downstairs, followed by Eejit. Jasper meets him half way, and excitedly runs around him, wagging so hard his whole little body shakes. Jasper is up, which means that Georgie is. It's only just seven, and this is insanely early for her – I guess Christmas still floats her boat.

I find all of them in the Blue Room, lounging around in their nightclothes, the fire roaring. The table is laden down with desserts of every kind – sponges, tray bakes, fruit loaves, scones, dainty little fruit tarts.

'We only eat cake for breakfast at Christmas,' Allegra shouts out. 'Family rule!'

She's been in good spirits since London, taking heart from a new doctor and a new programme of medications. Today, she is wearing a magnificent silk robe decorated with peacocks, and her hair is held on top of her head by knitting needles. Despite this, she looks elegant and relaxed.

I plate up a scone, and join them on one of the couches. Charles is opposite, looking freshly showered but still wearing a set of blue cotton PJs. Another family tradition, I guess.

'Can we do presents now?' Georgie asks excitedly. 'I think I'm on a suitable sugar high! Cassie has parcels, look!'

She pokes at my bag, and I snatch it away.

'Who's to say there's anything in there for you?' I ask.

'I bet there is! Come on, everyone, I'm bored already!'

There are groans all around, and Charles finally says: 'All right. If we must. Cassie, just to warn you, this year we decided to only give gifts that we managed to find on the estate, or in the house. It's been rather hectic since you got here, and there's been very little time for shopping.'

As this place is pretty much a museum, I can't say that I object to their logic – it beats getting battered in Macy's, anyway.

We take it in turns giving and receiving, Jasper helping with the unwrapping, Eejit going off to mooch – he knows where the dog bowls live these days. Allegra gives Charles a first edition of the poems of Tennyson that he's never even seen before, and Roberts hands out little boxes full of exquisite home-baked candies in the shape of fruit. Georgie has made everybody extravagant tie-dye T-shirts from old clothes, and I laugh as Allegra immediately puts hers on. Between the silk peacocks and the neon colours she's looking pretty amazing.

'Do I look groovy, baby?' she asks, doing a little shimmy.

I hand out my comedic Irish keepsakes – Baileys chocolates for Allegra, a Guinness hat for Roberts, a cuddly leprechaun for Georgie and a hideous green tie covered in shamrocks for Charles.

His eyes widen when he sees it – they're probably dazzled – but he quickly recovers and puts it on, managing to find a way to let it hang around his pyjama shirt.

'I love it,' he declares convincingly. 'I've never felt more chic!'

'Count yourself lucky,' I reply, laughing. 'My dad's getting a dickie bow!'

The gifts continue to flow, Georgie exclaiming that every single one of hers is exactly what she wanted, until eventually, Charles hands me a jewellery box. I have a moment of concern, worried at what I might find inside – and hoping that he hasn't done anything extravagant.

'Don't worry,' he says, a glint in his eyes telling me he has successfully read my mind, 'this is from all of us. And it did come from inside the house.'

I feel all of them watching me as I open the ribbon on the box, and gasp out loud when I see a beautiful pair of drop earrings. I take one out and hold it up to the light, admiring the way the emerald green of the stones shimmers.

'I love them!' I say, delighted. 'But... they're not real, are they?'

The gems are enormous, the setting is antique gold, and they're possibly the most beautiful things I've ever held in real life.

'Of course they are!' pronounces Allegra. 'Do I look like the kind of woman who wears paste, darling?'

I glance over at her, in her tie-dye T-shirt and peacock robe, now complemented by the careful positioning of an enormous Guinness hat on top of her head.

'Umm... right now, yes? But seriously, I can't accept these. They must be worth a fortune!'

'They're worth no more than you deserve, dear,' she says seriously. 'And that's the last I'll hear of it. I have all sorts sitting in my jewellery case, and I'm unlikely to use most of it. I might sell it all off, and go on a world cruise!'

I'm still protesting when Charles reaches out, and takes my hand.

'Stop arguing,' he says simply. 'And put them on.'

I meet his eyes, moved by the sincerity I see there, and do as I am told.

'There,' he says, leaning back and looking satisfied. 'Perfect. Now, can I read my newspaper in peace, Georgie? Or will you be a pain all the way through until lunch is served?'

'At a guess, yes, I will,' she snipes back. 'Merry Christmas!'

I sit and look on as they bicker good-humouredly, as Allegra eats her chocolates, and Roberts stokes the fire.

I love them all, I realise, feeling tears come to my eyes. I love their kindness, and their resilience, and their crazy English quirks. I love this house, and the estate, and the village. I love everything about being here, and I have been made so welcome. It would be so easy to stay. So easy to picture myself with these people forever – sharing in their triumphs and their losses, their ups and downs. So easy to relax into this life, this family.

Except, I realise, it wouldn't be right. I'd be doing it for all the wrong reasons, and I'd be living a lie. I touch the dangling earrings, and suddenly know that although I will keep them and treasure them, I cannot accept any more from them. I cannot accept what Charles has offered – I care about him, about all of them, too much to do that. Charles wants more than I can give, and it is not fair to keep him in the dark about that, even for one more day.

I'm here, with them physically, but I have to face the truth. I've been trying to hide it away, even from myself, but something about the purity of this Christmas scene makes that impossible to do for even a minute longer. I'm here, but my heart is still in Ireland. Still with Ryan.

'I'm... I'm just going to find Eejit,' I say, rising to my feet unsteadily and leaving the room. I feel overwhelmed, shaky both physically and emotionally. I sit on the bottom of the stairs and take a few deep breaths.

I don't know why this feeling has suddenly and spectacularly turned up on the scene, but I cannot fight it. All the time I was sitting there with them, I was waiting for my phone to ping. Waiting for Ryan to reply to my message. Like a besotted teenager, all I can think about is him – my handsome, charming, damaged playboy.

I can't stay here, because I cannot give Charles what another man already owns. I hate myself for it, for being such a fool, but I can't help it. Whatever Ryan feels about me, I know that I am in love with him – and that is a terrifying and powerful thing.

'Are you okay?' Charles says, appearing in front of me. He looks concerned and serious, despite his stupid tie. Life would be so much simpler if I could fall for this man instead, I think – but it wouldn't be fair to even try. He deserves better. He deserves someone who feels about him the way I feel about Ryan.

I stand up, and give him a quick hug.

'Not really. Charles, I can't stay for lunch. I think Eejit and I will walk back to the village.'

'Why? Is everything all right? Have I done something wrong?'

I smile at him, and say: 'Not a single thing, Charles. I just... I can't. The thing you asked me in Oxford? About staying here, with you? I can't do that. I'm so sorry.'

I see a flash of hurt cross his face, but as ever he reins it in with supreme control.

'Right. Well, I'm sure you have your reasons, Cassie. Is it... is it the mess? The mess of my life? Has that put you off?'

'No! No, please don't think that, Charles – I love your mess! I love every last scrap of it! You're wonderful, and I'm probably an idiot, but... well, as a wise woman once told me, I have to follow my heart, even though it might lead me into trouble.'

He stares at me for a moment, then says: 'Ah. And would your heart happen to lead you to Ireland, Cassie?'

I nod, and bite my lip. I hope that I've not hurt his pride, made him feel second-best to Ryan once again. The two of them have figured out their differences, but for a long time, he saw Ryan as a rival. This time, though, it's actually true, and I can't bear the thought of being the source of any more conflict between them.

'I see,' he says calmly. 'Well, I have to admit defeat then. I've been beaten by a—'

'Don't say better man! He's not a better man, Charles – he's not, at all. You're an amazing man.'

'True, I am. Okay then – he's not a better man. But he is a good man. Go, Cassie, if you need to – with my blessing.'

I hug him once more, not quite able to stop myself from inhaling that gorgeous cologne of his.

'Are you sure, though?' he asks, grinning as I run away up the stairs. 'I swear to God you were just sniffing me then...'

Within a few minutes I have packed up my stuff, and headed off into the rain. Eejit is collected from the kitchen, and together we slink off into the dull day. I will message the others later to say goodbye – I just couldn't face them right now. My head is too messed up. I need to be alone for a while, and decide what I'm going to do.

The walk helps – yet another thing Nanna Nora was right about – and by the time I arrive back in Campton St George I am soaked but feeling a little calmer. I amble through the almost-deserted village, the pub and the tea rooms closed, lights off in most of the homes. I intend to simply get back to Whimsy, maybe have a long bath, and think things over.

Eejit, though, has other ideas – and he heads straight down the side of the bakery, barking outside Eileen's door.

'All right, all right, what's with the racket?' she says, opening the door to let him in. 'Smell the bacon, can you?'

She stares at me lurking behind him, and shakes her head, grey curls bobbing.

'Don't just stand there, Cassie – I'm letting all the heat out!'

She shoos me inside with a dishtowel, and I head straight for the fire. It strikes me, as I sit there warming my hands and drying off, that this is exactly the position I was in the first night I got here, almost a whole month ago now. Taking refuge in Eileen's cosy living room, surrounded by her knitting and her paperbacks and her knickknacks.

There's also a small suitcase, and I remember that she is flying to Dublin today.

'I'm sorry, you're busy,' I say, making to stand and leave.

'Never too busy for you, my love. Now, what's the craic? I thought you were off away to the big house?'

'I was, yes,' I say, falling back into the chair. 'But I... well, Eileen, I had little bit of a revelation, and I guess you're as good a person as any to talk to about it.'

'Stop with the fancy compliments now!'

'Sorry – you're actually the perfect person to talk to about it. It's Ryan.'

'Ah, I see. Ryan. What's he gone and done now?'

'He kissed me, or I kissed him, I'm not so sure. We kissed, anyway. And then he told me he'd broken one of his rules, and left. I've been thinking about it ever since, what he might have meant. Do you think he meant the rule about women who live in the village?'

She throws the dish towel at me, and it flutters against my face and drops to the floor.

'Jesus, you young people – you're not half slow! Of course he didn't mean that – I'd call you an eejit, but it'd be an insult to that perfectly clever dog. You and Ryan have something, and it's more than his normal nonsense. And looking at you right now, it's clear as the nose on my face that you've fallen for him.'

'But—'

'There are no buts, Cassie. You might be able to fool yourself but you can't fool me – I've seen it coming. So, the only question now is, what are you going to do about it?'

'I don't know – get therapy? Go home? Change my identity?'

'Sure, all of those are options – but how's about this? Why don't you just tell him how you feel?'

She makes it sound so sensible, but the very idea of it paralyses me.

'What if he doesn't feel the same?' I ask. 'What if that kiss was just a fluke? What if he rejects me? I've had enough of that to last a lifetime...'

She shrugs her shoulders, and replies: 'Then you could always get therapy, or go home, or change your identity, couldn't you? I've a feeling he won't though, child. I've an inkling he feels exactly the same, but he's too stubborn to do anything about it. Or too scared, maybe. One of you is going to have to be brave. Who's it to be?'

THIRTY

I can't quite believe what I'm about to do. I can't quite believe that I've come this far without chickening out.

I am being dropped off by a chatty taxi driver in the drizzly rain, on the outskirts of Cork. There were no flights here on Christmas Day, and the one to Dublin was sold out – so in the end, Eileen gave me her seat. I'd protested, but she'd been insistent.

'This is for love, Cassie – I'm very fond of you, and that big oaf Ryan, and I know what his mammy would want me to do. He's been in the wilderness for too long, so, and you're just the girl to bring him out of it. You'll take my flight, and you'll get yourself to Cork – it'll cost you an arm and a leg in a cab today, maybe even a kidney, but... look, that man is worth it.'

I couldn't find a way to talk her out of it, and when Ryan's reply to my message landed, I didn't want to.

Lucky dog

He'd said, in response to the picture.

> Happy Christmas, Cassie. I find that I'm
> missing you, but I suppose my heart will go on.

That harmless little message carried me all the way to London, then all the way to Dublin, and then all the way to a small line of taxis outside the airport. It carried me through the shock of the hundreds of euros it cost. It carried me all the way to this spot, on a quiet road lined with big detached mini-mansions.

Now, I'm starting to think it's not enough. I mean, 'lucky dog'? That could just be his usual flirting – and he's missing me? He's probably missing Eileen as well. It means nothing!

It's getting dark despite the fact that it's only just after five, and the air is still damp from the last downpour. I am standing on a neatly landscaped street, hiding behind a bush, holding the strap of my purse so hard my fingers are white. What am I doing here? Why did I let Eileen talk me into this?

I've made a terrible mistake, and now I'm stuck here. The taxi has driven off, and I'm alone. I have no idea where I am, and I'm not sure the city is within walking distance. I get out my phone, looking at the map and wondering where the nearest hotel is. If I leave now, he'll never even know I was here.

It's cowardly, and I despise myself for it. I thought I'd moved on. I thought I had more confidence than this – but as I stare at that brightly lit house, all I can think of is Ted. He's not been on my mind for so long, I'd almost forgotten what that particular stone in my shoe feels like. But suddenly, there he is – looking down at me at the altar, in front of everyone we knew, telling me he can't go through with it.

I hate Ted, I decide. And I hate myself for letting him creep back into my thoughts. I wrestle with the urge to call June, knowing that I need to make my own decisions. Whatever I do, I need to own it.

I'm still trying to figure out what to own when I hear a

strange sound coming up the street. I freeze still, and listen. I can hear a little boy, chattering away, and a man laughing. And over all of that, I hear a cow. Yep, I think, frowning – it's an actual cow, mooing in the moonlight as it clops up the road.

It's wearing some kind of harness, and is being led along towards me. I realise in seconds who this is – it's Ryan's nephew, Sean, who wanted a cow for Christmas. Looks like he got one.

As I watch them draw closer, I see that the laughing man is Ryan, and my heart skips at the sight of him. He's wearing a chunky sweater and jeans and his big old boots, and he's got a cow on a rope. Of course.

I'm safe where I am, I think. I could easily stay here, hidden from view. I could disappear from this street, from this country, from his life. But is that what I really want? Isn't that something I will always regret, something that will leave its mark on me in the same way that Ted did?

I need to be brave, I tell myself. I need to see where the ride takes me. I step forward, and both of them jerk at the unexpected intrusion. Ryan instinctively steps in front of his nephew, presumably in case I'm a threat, and I wave at them both.

'Hi!' I say brightly, as if it's a completely normal thing for me to be here. 'It's me... um, I was just passing!'

Ryan stares at me as I walk towards them, and a slow smile starts to appear on his face.

'You were just passing? Really?'

'Yeah. In the neighbourhood, you know.'

He nods, hands Sean the rope, and closes the distance between us. He doesn't touch me, but it feels like he does – even having him near makes my pulse race. He reaches out, pushes my wet hair away from my face.

We don't have time for anything more, because the little boy starts jumping up and down and tugging his hand.

'Uncle Ryan, come on! I need a wee!'

'You go ahead now, Sean. I'll stay out here with Buttercup a minute.'

Sean gallops ahead, and disappears off down the side of the house. We're left alone – apart from Buttercup. She's a big girl, black and white, with enormous shining eyes. I swear to God she's laughing at me.

'What's the with cow?' I ask. 'Shouldn't she be, I don't know, on a farm or something?'

'She will be, later on. She's from one of those family places, you know, where people take their kiddies to feed the goats and the like? A friend of Sinead's fella owns it, and he let us have a borrow of Buttercup for the day. She's very tame, and she likes a nice walk. Did you come here to talk about the cow?'

I'm trying to formulate an answer when the front door to the house flies open, and a man and a woman come running out of it. The woman is substantial, tall and strong with curly black hair. Sinead, I'm guessing.

'Brian, have you no eyes? Ryan is busy – take the cow back to the garden now, will you?'

She strides towards us, her gaze jumping from me to Ryan and back again.

'You must be Cassie,' she says, smiling as her husband nods and takes the rope from Ryan. 'Ryan's told me all about you, so.'

'He has?' I say, surprised. 'What did he say?'

Ryan shuffles slightly uncomfortably between us, and she laughs at him.

'Enough for him to look shady, there, eh? Look, I'll need to go inside and stop the wee ones battering each other. Come in when you're ready, all right?'

'Alone at last,' he says, as she shuts the door behind her. 'So, you were about to tell me why you're here?'

'I'm here because I need to be brave,' I say, deciding that I have nothing to lose. 'Because I needed to follow my heart, even if it did lead me to a man with a cow. I'm here because I love you, Ryan. I have no idea if you feel the same, or if I'm being an eejit, or if I've just made a colossal fool of myself, but—'

I don't manage to get another single word out, because he suddenly takes hold of me, crushes me against him, and kisses me. It's a phenomenal kiss – hot and passionate and epic. The kind of kiss they should write poems about.

'You were talking too much,' he says, when we tear away from each other, both breathless. 'And I love you too, Cassie. Jesus knows I've tried hard not to, but I do – I'm a hopeless case. Now you're here I warn you, I may never let you go. You're stuck with me.'

I feel a rush of warmth through my whole body, and not just because of the kiss. Because of the look in his eyes, the love I can see there. Because I have followed my heart to exactly the right place.

I hear a cheer go up in the house, and guess that we must have had an audience. He grins and holds me in his arms, and everything feels right.

I don't care that it's raining. I don't care that people are watching. I don't care that there is a cow, mooing in the background. All I care about is this moment – this one perfect moment, here with my man.

EPILOGUE

'Always follow your heart. It might lead you into trouble, but at least you'll enjoy the ride.'
Nora O'Hara, RIP

CHRISTMAS EVE

ONE YEAR LATER

The first official wedding held at Bancroft Manor is mine and Ryan's. It's an informal affair, because the last time I had a big fancy one it didn't work out so well.

Today, it is just me, Ryan – and a village full of our closest friends. I'm wearing a beautiful, pale-green sheath dress from the room upstairs, and he is in a suit. It's the first time I've seen him in one, and I feel a familiar rush of heat at how good he looks.

My parents are here, along with Suzie and her boys. I've only seen them once in the last year, when I flew home to take care of things. When I told my mom and sister what my new life plan was, I'd expected mockery or stern advice – but they were actually delighted for me. There were even a few tears – the happy kind.

Deirdre's crowd from Cork have all flown over, and my family are planning a trip to stay with them in the new year.

The ballroom is packed with Murphys and O'Haras and the rest of my extended Irish family. June has flown over, and brought a surprise guest – a life-sized cardboard cut-out of

Hugh Grant in his *Four Weddings* era, who is standing next to her.

Charles got his investment, more than he'd even asked for, and Bancroft Manor has been transformed. Bookings for the year ahead are looking good, and I should know – I manage the place. Charles is thrilled, and has also started his archaeological dig. Today, he is accompanied by his new friend Charlotte, a consultant archaeologist he's hired to help. I suspect she's interested in more than ancient artefacts, and I can't say that I blame her – Charles is as dashing as ever in his tailored tux.

Georgie is on the piano as my dad and I walk down to the front of the ballroom, playing her version of 'It's A Wonderful World', her hair a golden sheen down her back.

I nod to everyone we pass – to Eileen in her fancy hat, to Orla and Cormac, to Mary Catherine and her tribe. To Eejit and Jasper, sitting near the front with Allegra and Roberts.

The room is full of friendship and love, and I can't help agreeing with the music – it is truly a wonderful world.

I wish that Nanna Nora was here with us, but I can't help feeling that in some way, she is. She's raising a wine glass of Guinness to us, and making a toast.

My dad and I finish our long walk, and I stand looking up at my handsome man. He is no longer the playboy, and I am no longer the girl who was dumped. We are something new now – something stronger.

Ryan gives me the grin. The feral one that always went straight to my belly. It still does, but these days, there's so much more to it. These days, there is love.

I gaze into his eyes as the service begins, and I have absolutely no doubt that I am doing the right thing. Absolutely no doubt that this is forever.

Absolutely no doubt that I followed my heart, and it led me home.

A LETTER FROM THE AUTHOR

Dear reader,

Huge thanks for reading *A Very Irish Christmas*; I hope you enjoyed Cassie's story. You can sign up to find out all about Storm books, and the great releases they have in store (including mine!) by signing up here:

www.stormpublishing.co/debbie-johnson

You can also sign up to a newsletter that I send out myself – you'll be the first to hear all my news, book gossip, and more – there will be giveaways, free samples, and short stories. It's totally free, I won't send so many your inbox hates me, and I promise it will be fun!

debbie-johnson.ck.page/32bc38fdb7

If you enjoyed this book and could spare a few moments to leave a review that would be hugely appreciated. Even a short review can make all the difference in encouraging a reader to discover my books for the first time. Thank you so much!

Thanks again for being part of this amazing journey with me and I hope you'll stay in touch – I have so many more stories and ideas to entertain you with!

Debbie Johnson

KEEP IN TOUCH WITH THE AUTHOR

ACKNOWLEDGMENTS

As ever, so many people need a big 'thank you' in this section – mainly my family and friends. Thank you for tolerating the take-aways, the missed dog walks and the cancelled social events while I race to meet my deadlines. Thank you in particular to Paddy Shennan, who invited me and a group of amazing people to go to Cork to celebrate his 60th birthday in style – even the hangovers were inspiring.

Thank you to my agent Hayley Steed and her team at Janklow & Nesbit, and to the Storm squad – in particular my editor, Kathryn Taussig.

Mainly, thank you to you – the reader who got to the end of the book! I can't tell you how much I appreciate your support.

Made in the USA
Monee, IL
20 November 2024